The Language
Of Belonging

The Language of Belonging

CRISTIANE LIMA SCOTT

Holland House

www.hhousebooks.com

Paperback ISBN 978-1-910688-02-1
Epub ISBN 978-1-910688-03-8

Cover design by Eric Gaskell
Typeset by handebooks.co.uk

Published in the USA and UK

Holland House Books
Holland House
47 Greenham Road
Newbury, Berkshire RG14 7HY
United Kingdom

www.hhousebooks.com

To my daughter Gabriella, my angel

PART 1

CHAPTER I

After darkness, there was light.

My mother's death was the worst experience of my life and it gave me the opportunity to become the woman I was born to be.

Mother was all I had: she sacrificed herself for me; she gave up her family, her friends, the only life she knew; she faced the unknown with all its risks; she became an illegal immigrant so I would not endure the life she and so many like her endured.

She was proud that I became a nurse, and it allowed us to live more easily, without survival being a constant struggle. With her gone, even my career seemed pointless.

About six months after Mother's death my supervisor at New Hampshire General Hospital told me of a family seeking a Portuguese-speaking nurse to live with and care for an elderly woman. Although I didn't want that or any job, I needed it. I applied for the position and was granted an interview.

Mrs. Woodard lived in a big house in Hampton. It was away from the road, and in the front there was a well-tended garden with a fountain. The flowers made me realize it was spring. The sunshine stirred my skin; it was so bright, I squinted. The house was elegant, like nothing I had seen before, and there was a sense of peace and happiness that was uncomfortable to me.

Mrs. Woodard asked, *"Você realmente sabe falar, escrever, e ler em português?"*

[Do you really speak, write, and read in Portuguese?]

From her accent, I knew she was Brazilian. *"Sim, senhora Woodard, eu realmente falo, escrevo, e leio em português"*

[Yes, Mrs. Woodard, I really speak, write, and read in Portuguese.]

Our conversation continued in Portuguese. She asked me about Brazil and about Brazilians I knew in America. Apparently, she had little or no contact with Brazilian immigrants and didn't know much about their problems. At the end of a two-hour interview, she hired me.

Right from the first, Mrs. Woodard asked me to call her by her first name, Elena. She said she wanted to hear someone say her name the way her mother did.

Elena's husband had died five years earlier, and she missed him very much. She never had children of her own, but her husband had a daughter and a son from a previous marriage: Grace lived in North Hampton and Michael in Florida. Elena also had three step-grandchildren: William and Abby belonged to Grace, and Claire belonged to Michael. And there was Brendon. I already knew him and was surprised to learn he was close to the family. We graduated from high school in the same year. But we never talked to each other. He was the most popular student in the school. Elena seemed to regard Brendon as a kind of grandson.

In a few months time Brendon would become an attorney and Abby would be a veterinarian. Claire was already a school teacher, and William was a business man. Together, the four seemed at the center of Elena and Grace's worlds.

Elena and I shared stories about Brazil and about life in America. She seemed interested in who I was and where I came from. I wasn't used to such attention.

"Cecilia, do you miss Brazil?" Elena asked me in one of our first conversations.

"Sometimes I do but I don't know really what I miss. There is nothing there to return to."

"Are you in touch with anyone there?"

"No," I answered, "there is no one. We were not supposed to contact anyone. And now that my mother is dead, I have no reason to contact anyone. What about you?"

"Not anymore, but I used to correspond with my mother and a couple of friends."

There was a brief silence, then I said, "Every time I think about the ones I left behind, I remember why my mother and I left Brazil. They made our lives terrible. Nobody cared about us then, so why should I care about them now?"

In a soft tone, Elena said, "Cecilia, you were so young when you left. There is more than one side to things. The ones left behind have to pick up the pieces and make sense out of them."

"It is easier to think they forgot us, because I want to forget them. Your life there must have been very different. You probably don't know what it is to be scared, and have no one to defend you, no one to protect your loved ones." By now, I was holding back some tears.

Elena responded, still in a soft tone, "You're right, I don't know what your life was like. But I believe there is more in life than what we think we know. One cannot know all about the people we left behind. We don't know what it is like for them. It's the same way between me and you: Just because you know me now doesn't mean you know everything about me."

This was Elena's way. She was soft but strong; I was hard but weak. She became my turning point. The day following that conversation, Elena asked me to get her journal from the library upstairs. The room had shelves all round, and more books than I had ever seen in a house. The journal was a very thick folder of papers next on a shelf amongst several books. One next to the folder caught my attention: on the spine it said 'Dom Casmurro'. Carefully I picked it up and opened it. It was by Machado de Assis, and had the date 1899. It was in Portuguese. It felt like something from my past, from my country. It reminded me of my mother, though I was sure she had never read such a book. *Saudade*: I hated it especially when it filled every cell of my body.

When I handed her the folder, Elena said, "I began to write this journal about forty years ago. It is time to finish it." She gave it back and asked me to read it aloud to her. It was all in Portuguese. She said she wanted me to help her translate it, to finish it. That's when I understood why she needed someone fluent in Portuguese.

From then on, we began working together on the journal. I would translate, and read aloud to her.

CHAPTER 2

I have become old and anxious. Today's light rain brings some tran-
quility. My pulse still vibrates, but not with the passion I once had.
Autumn raises memories: the good ones are pleasing, and the pain-
ful ones cannot hurt any more.

I often thought that when I left one place, my story stayed be-
hind and everything started anew elsewhere. But I was wrong. Your
past travels with you wherever you go. When I close my eyes, there
is the aroma of coffee brewing in the afternoon, the scent of fruits I
have not eaten in years and the adventures we had in getting them.
It was a simple, uncomplicated life. I see us as children playing. And
I can see Julio.

In reality, decades have passed since I last saw him. My pas-
sion for him was partly fantasy and disappeared with my innocence.
There are times when I yearn for the life with him that I did not
have; and there are times when I'm glad I did not have a life with
him. The years have helped me forgive and continue living. Today, I
can say goodbye to memories and fantasy without resenting what he
forced me to face alone.

Once, Julio and I were good friends. He was my first real con-
tact with anyone outside my family. We grew up together and used
to say the word "forever" to each other. For a while, we learned and
shared the secrets of true friendship. I wanted to trust my feelings for
him. What I did not know was that my feelings spoke for me only,
not for him. From this ignorance, I enjoyed love but also suffered
hate and disillusion.

Until I was fifteen, I lived with a family that told me many
times my real parents left me with them, promising to be back in
two days. But they never returned. In this new family, there were
five other children. It was a simple life. My main concern was hav-
ing dolls for amusement. I used to make them with the help of my
new mother.

We were a nomadic family, like many others who constantly fled the Brazilian droughts that killed the crops, the animals and the forests. Occasionally we encountered religious processions in village streets, Brazilians singing to God and praying for rain. But the cries weren't heard. Before our eyes, the plants withered, the animals turned to dust, and small dead children were buried. Along our way, we saw hundreds of child's crucifixes. Mother said they were angels in heaven; I felt sorry for them and did not want to become an angel.

We walked for so long, I had time to befriend rocks. There were little rocks, big rocks, dead rocks, and friendly rocks. Mother told us to look for gold, so we spent days looking for gold through the roads and stopped asking her for water. We never found gold. Every now and then, we would meet a traveler who would tell stories of distant parts of the world. One showed us a rock and he told us his family was living in it. He said a woman had used bruxaria/witchcraft *to send his wife and his children into that rock; he was travelling in search of that witch. But the biggest of all encounters was a few days before we reached our destination.*

At distance, we saw poeira/dust. *When you saw things out the ordinary, we were told to stop and wait for it to reach you or, with blessings, pass by you without noticing your presence. Someone told us there were horses coming. The dust told there were many horses. Now you must understand, there was only one man feared more than the Devil in that part of the world: Lampião. Some even thought he was the devil himself. We were thought to make the sign of the cross when either name were mentioned. But when asked if they had to choose to confront the devil or Lampião, the answer used to be unanimous. The first. O Cangaceiro Lampião was known for travelling around those states with his wife Maria Bonita and their* bando/group *of outlaws. Some said he could kill by just looking into someone's eyes. As we walked through those roads, we learned to watch for signs of him.*

After someone screamed, "Horses!" Someone else screamed, "Lampião!" They all ran and hid behind the rocks, the fences, the dried bushes. I could only watch the dust. I heard mother's voice but I couldn't move. They were approaching fast. I closed my eyes and wished they passed by without seeing me.

I opened my eyes again when I heard a woman's voice, "Wow girl, sleeping standing up, poor thing."/"Oxente menina, e tá dormindo em pé coitadinha" (there is no translation for 'oxente) I was overwhelmed by my vision. She came down from her horse and asked if I was alone. I didn't answer. She looked around, then asked my name. "Elena," I said. "Bonita Elena," she said. She asked if I wanted to go with her. "No," I said. She took a dumpling/pamonha (traditional food made with sweet corn and milk and wrapped in corn husks, like dumplings) from her bag, took a gourd of water that was hanging on the side of the horse and gave them to me. She had kind eyes.

"Maria," said a man. I looked at him. He was looking at her. She mounted the horse and the two of them led the group in the same pace as before.

All the people who had hidden came back. Some women were crying. Somebody took the water and the food out of my hands. Mother took me in her arms asking me why I wanted to die.

Father and the other men told the story of how our group survived Lampião and his bando. Many different stories came out of it. None told exactly what had happened. For years to come, men, women, and children would sit around the fire to listen to those stories.

Years later, there was three special days of festejos in our village from the day Mr. Valério received the news of Lampiao's death. Mr. Valério bragged about having put a man to follow the band and help the police/as volantes kill them. Maria Bonita was beheaded alive. I still remembered her eyes. Although Mr. Valério never liked to travelled, he went to see the display of their heads. Now, only the devil was left to be feared.

After months of going from farm to farm, looking for somewhere to live and work, we arrived at Santa Maria, a plantation owned by Mr. Valério, that had green leaves and clean water, like an oasis in the desert. We joined about twenty families working there. On a corner of the property was the administrator's large house, well made of brick, surrounded by many small attached houses made of clay. We were in the third house on the right. On rainy days, water passed through our roof, soaking the walls, the floors and our modest furniture. From a dry corner, I sometimes watched the water drip. But most of the time we children enjoyed the rain, jumping in the puddles, running against the wet wind and chasing frogs.

We were at the bottom of society. There were the people in the town: they were considered civilized and well-educated. Next were the people in the village: theirs was a bigger community than ours, with a school and a church, and most of the residents owned properties. Then there were people like us, the ones who lived and worked on the farms. We had no property, no education. Those in the villages and town considered us uncivilized.

Soon after we arrived at Santa Maria, we started to attend school for the first time. It was an old building with two classrooms in the nearby village. Father broke two pencils in three equal pieces each so we all had something to write with. He also gave each of us one piece of paper each day. But the three older children never had time to go to school, they were always working.

There I was, a scared seven-year old, going to school for the first time in a village where I knew no one. I became embarrassed when I realized that a single sheet of paper was not enough for even one school day! Then, a boy across the room (he was in the second grade but we shared the same room) came over and gave me two sheets from his notebook; this saved my first day at school. It was a lovely gesture. I didn't know it would begin the story of my life.

The boy who helped me that morning was Julio. He was the son of Mr. Valério. The Valérios were the richest family in the village, so of course, they had the best of everything. Julio and his two sisters had the best clothes, the best toys, pets, everything. The family was the only one in the village to have servants. Mr. Valério was a man of stern appearance. Even though his three children were afraid of him, it was the kind of family we wished were ours.

Julio was the only one who tried to get close to me. I was the poorest girl in school, shy and, I thought, very ugly. My clothes were more like rags because my mother could not afford newer ones—if she bought clothes, there would be no money for food. Mother would say she was not hungry at dinnertime, even though it was often our only meal of the day. I knew it was because there was not enough to go around. With all the difficulties, school became the source of most of my happiness, including the occasional snacks to quell my hunger. School was also where we learned about life beyond the town.

I remember being constantly busy. At seven in the morning, we were supposed to be at school. At eleven, it was time to go home. At noon, we were supposed to eat our meal. It was always beans except when Mother worked for Dona Josefa; then we could eat their leftovers. Sometimes, there was a lot of food left in the pots; other times, we ate what was left on their plates. But we did not care; what was important was that they allowed us to eat it. During the afternoon, we helped Mother by working in the bean field plantation. After work on weekdays, we children ran to the dam and washed ourselves by pouring buckets of water over our heads. Sundays, we could take longer showers and wear our cleaner clothes.

Sunday was our shopping day and it was the only trip to town we would make weekly. Sometimes, I accompanied my mother to get groceries, two bags of food that would have to last us all week. But how good it was to enjoy the walk home with our neighbors. Some of them had donkeys to carry their food, and Julio's mother, Dona Josefa, had a horse-drawn wagon that carried her, her servants and her many bags of groceries. This always attracted the eyes of the poor women who went home to their families with half as many purchases or less.

I stopped reading here and asked Elena about the grocery shopping. I remember as a child going to what we called 'feira' which was a mix of a farmers market and a town fair. They had tables for all the different products from produce, meats, fish, to clothes, shoes, toys, guns, and any household products. We also had entertainment. Local singers and musician playing the accordion were popular attractions.

I wanted to replace the words 'grocery shopping' with 'feira' as we could not find a word that fairly represented the place and activity Elena was mentioning. She refused to leave the Portuguese word there. For Elena, this was irrelevant and it would contribute nothing to the journal. She said, "I am not interested in teaching Brazilian culture. No one besides my family will want to read this and I know they would not care to know what is a 'feira'." So, she chose to use 'grocery shopping'. I wasn't sure if she did not like my suggestion, or if she just didn't want too much of my ideas in her writings.

She asked me to keep reading.

These were difficult times, yet I can say they also were happy times, times of childhood, times that do not return.

My mother was a humble woman. She had a sadness without explanation, but she was firm and never complained about life. She had never attended school, but was proud to say that her children did. She seldom spoke, but was always thinking.

When she was only two years old, her mother left her with her father. Mother's father remarried, and the stepmother often mistreated her. When Mother was thirteen, she ran away from home with a fellow she vaguely knew. He was thirty years old at the time. Over the years, she had five children with him, and then she took me in as an unofficially-adopted daughter.

Despite a life full of sacrifices, Mother was sweet and generous, a good woman. I remember accompanying her to the pond to wash clothes. She would take a basket full of clothes on her head and the youngest child in her arms, and made me walk in front of her so I wouldn't be distracted by everything around us. She knew that I could easily lose myself in my own little world. She was busy and she could not spend long hours looking for me, so she made sure she always knew where I was.

There was the time when, while she was cleaning my brother, I saw and followed a big butterfly. The biggest I ever saw. It was beautiful with its brightly colored wings, all the colors of the rainbow it seemed. I felt as if the wings were beckoning to me. I passed through the bamboos and reached the tall bushes. There were wild flowers and many more butterflies. It was like a paradise. I started to collect some flowers because I knew mother would love to have them. After I collected all the flowers I could carry, I sat down and arranged them.

The next thing I remember is mother screaming a couple of steps from me with one foot holding a snake down close to its head, smashing it against a rock. She was crying and screaming. When she was done, the snake's head was separated from the rest of it. Mother then buried the head. Mother hated and feared snakes. She was shaking, crying, and screaming at me al at the same time. She grabbed me by my hair, then by my arm, and pushed me back to the pond. There were some women who had heard coming towards us. They sat mother on a rock by the pond. And they all screamed at me saying that one day I would kill myself and my mother. They never told it to my father. He might really have killed me.

I again stopped and asked Elena how old she was then. "I don't know, maybe five, or seven. It was so long ago. You do not need to put my age there." And, she pointed to the pages.

Dona Josefa sent for my Mother whenever extra help was needed. My mother welcomed this, it meant more money. Whether working in the bean field or for Dona Josefa, Mother usually worked from six in the morning to six at night. She got up at three to prepare food for Father to take to work. Then she would have a cup of coffee before getting us ready to go to school and go to work herself. After her day at work, she went home to make supper and clean up. Be-

fore bedtime, mother and father would usually spend some time in front of our house talking to the neighbors.

My father was a hard worker. His skin was burned from the sun, and his calloused hands were proof of his labor. Every day Mr. Valério's foreman assigned portions of land to each worker. Usually, he assigned the largest portion to my father; it was more work, but it meant more pay. The foreman used to say that Father could work faster and better than much younger men. Eventually, Father became the foreman's helper. From what I heard, that was a title with no extra money. Still, it raised my father above the other workers in Mr. Valério's eyes.

There was one thing Elena kept from her northeast, the way she referred to her father and mother: "O Pai" and "a Mãe." It is a very distinct way as 'o' and 'a' are articles used for male and female. But for one to understand the message, we need possessive adjectives like meu (my), seu (your) after the article so one knows who's father or mother it is. Brazil's northeast is well known for its own ways and Elena proudly, or maybe unconsciously, kept it when she spoke. But she preferred me to use the word 'Father.'

My three older brothers worked in the sugarcane fields with Father. I did not like to see them when they returned home because they would have cuts on their hands and legs, with blood mixed with dirt all over them. And there was such pain in their faces. I just wanted to have the power to heal and take away their suffering. They would scream when Mother doused their wounds with special herb mixtures. Father used to take me away until it was all over. When they were old enough, the two younger boys joined Father and the others in the field.

Growing up, we were taught to obey Father and Mother regardless. Father was the executor of punishment whenever we misbehaved, and Mother was the one who would stay up all night with us after we got punished. She would tell us how we hurt Father more than he hurt us.

Father always carried a long, almost thin, flexible, but strong stick.

She was getting annoyed with me. She wanted to put the word stick. But I told her it was a 'tabica.'

"At this speed, I will be dead before we reach half of this journal," she said.

It was the dreadful torture instrument called 'tabica.' I think all fathers had one. When he lashed at our backs and legs, the tabica made the sound of a kiss. We jerked uncontrollably like jumping beans. Each time he struck me, it felt like a sharp knife cutting through my skin. My brothers seemed to be able to always brave it.

I only experienced it twice.

The first time, I was ten years old. I had gone to the woods with Julio and we had played there for a while. We started for home before dark, then he left me in front of our backyard fence and went home. By that time, my family was already looking for me. Father was really mad, and used the stick, but I felt he was also glad to see me alive. My brothers said that Father was easy on me because I was his favorite child.

I was not so lucky the second time, and I need to tell what led up to it.

When I was about nine, Mr. Valério let us live in a small house he owned in the village; it became available when one of his servants moved away. Then, my mother worked more often for Dona Josefa, usually doing the laundry. Living in the village, we were closer to school. It was easier to play with the other children and attend church. Once a month, the priest came to celebrate mass, a service that was attended mostly by the village women and children.

Julio and I were together whenever possible. As children, we were like brother and sister. Other children who wanted his atten-

tion became jealous. I think Julio liked me because, while ugly, I was pretty smart. Compared to the other children, I did the best. In fact, midway through my second year in school, I was promoted into his grade.

With Julio, I learned to play, swim, climb trees, chase and get chased by the chickens in his backyard. As teenagers, we found we did not love each other as brother and sister. The first kiss changed how we felt about each other. We discovered that we were not children anymore. With Julio, I became a woman.

I was in love and I believed it was love for the rest of our lives. It was my fairytale come true. I believed his simple sweet words were full of love and truth. I only needed him in order to be happy, not just for a moment, but forever.

In June we commemorated São João and São Pedro: Festas Juninas. My favorite time of the year. We had fogueira, sanfoneiro, canjica, pamonha, and fresh corn. All in front of the Valérios house. They used to build a big tent with wood, sticks, and palms from coconut trees. Mother and other women helped Dona Josefa and they cooked for days. Julio and I danced all night. He held so tight I could hear his heart and my heart beating as one at the rhythm of the baião. Other girls were so jealous. Then, we would secretly sneak in his back yard.

To my surprise, I did not have to argue to keep Portuguese words in section. Elena did that on her own. For a moment, her eyes sparkled remembering her old days.

Julio and my mother were the best things in my life. My heart could not ask for more. I believed every word he told me, every gesture, and every demonstration of affection.

I was so young and innocent.

Back then however, giving oneself up to love was wrong, unacceptable, and unworthy of a daughter, even of the poorest family. Ah, but I was so happy that none of that mattered. I was over-

whelmed by my feelings for Julio, and I was willing to take whatever risks were necessary to have him and for him to have me.

It seemed everything was perfect for us. But I was a nobody from a nobody family. I was not meant to find pleasure or happiness. Worse, Julio's parents had already planned his future: He would study, have a prestigious job and, of course, marry a woman who was "worthy" of him.

People in the village had begun to talk about our relationship. Mother happened to be working in the main house the day that Mr. Valério came home enraged after learning Julio and I were more than just friends. He demanded Julio explain. Julio said we were in love and wanted to get married.

Mr. Valério then threatened to banish Julio from the family forever. "You decide," he said. "Either break up with that girl immediately or you are no longer a Valério. If you choose her, go after her right now and take her away with you. Hurry up!"

But Julio did not answer. He just stood there. Mr. Valério said, "I am going to talk to her father." Then he left to find him.

Julio and his father did not realize Mother had overheard everything. And they probably never gave a thought that I would learn about Mr. Valério's ultimatum.

My poor mother! She ran out of the house to tell me. Just as she was ending the story with, "You must run and hide in the woods," my father stormed into the house and grabbed me, and then the stick. He was madder than I ever saw him, and it seemed his eyes were full of hate.

Father dragged me by my hair to the village square where he beat me until I was almost unconscious. It was a public humiliation; people came to watch me get beaten. My mother cried helplessly. I could see she was desperate but she could not prevent my punishment. My brothers hollered at my father to whip me harder. I never forgot their voices saying, "Now she learns."

No one intervened. First, the crowd wanted my pain and humiliation to be an example for other girls. Second, it was a kind of entertainment not seen very often. They wanted to see the beating and the bloodshed and to hear me scream.

While my father was beating me, he yelled how ungrateful I was, and how much he had helped raise me. "Your real parents are glad they abandoned you! You are a root that should be cut off forever!" For a brief moment, I could see him and how humiliated he was. Somehow, he was trying to transfer his disappointment and desolation in life to me.

But more than the pain from the blows and my father's words, what hurt me the most was Julio's weakness. I would give my life to save Julio, but he gave me to the lions. I didn't see him in the village square, but I felt his presence. Oh, the pain was great.

To this day, I remember that terrible episode. When my father got tired of beating me, he ordered me to leave the village and, in words that still ring in my ears, "AND DO NOT COME BACK – EVER!" he turned and walked away as if there was nothing else left to do.

I dishonored my family. That was the last time I saw them. And just like that, dirty, bloody, and hardly able to move, I was totally abandoned by my family and the people in the village. I was about fifteen years old at the time.

Somehow, through the rest of the day and during the night I walked to the next town, about eight miles. I do not know why. I think I just wanted to die, but something made me go on. To this day, I do not understand why I continued. Many times, I stopped walking just to cry myself out. I had blood all over me but the real pain was in my heart. I stumbled onward, completely lost and scared. Outside my village, I knew no one.

Night came quickly, but the moon lit my way. The sounds of birds and animals in the trees were eerie company. There were night shadows and a cool light wind in the sugarcane leaves. These could cause fear in the most rational person. It was the longest of nights. I did not expect to survive, nor did I want to.

Finally, in the distance, I saw the lights of the town. I kept walking. There was a small square in front of the big church. There, while trying to reach a bench, I lost consciousness. As if in a dream,

I heard church bells but was unable to move. I was racked with pain and had strong cramps. My whole body throbbed.

People came and took me to the hospital. There, the nurses cared for me. My physical injuries were extensive. As I had nowhere to go and no one to care for me, I was hospitalized for several weeks; although I do not really know for how long. At one point, a nurse told me I "lost" the baby that I did not even know was inside me.

When I was ready to leave the hospital a nurse gave me some clean clothes and a little money. She had been an angel to me. Many others also helped without asking for anything in return. I never knew their names, but I can still see them in my mind.

Again on my own, I did not know what to do or where to go. So I just started walking down the main road. A few hours later, a woman in a carroça, a simple horse-drawn wagon with wooden sides, stopped and asked where I was going. We talked briefly, then she offered me some work. I did not ask what it was, but went along with her. We traveled an hour or so until arriving at a building just outside another town.

It did not take long to discover the work she had in mind. It was a bordel, a brothel-like place where liquor is sold and men pay for sexual favors. I was scared, but again I had no place to go. The owner was the woman who brought me there.

I went on to the last fight of that section. The word for the place Elena was referring to is 'cabaré' and it was the lowest of all prostitution places. Elena's description is beautified by her shame. She refused to place that word in her journal. We settled for 'bordel.'

First, she put me to work washing dishes, cleaning floors, and doing other household chores. Then she made me serve drinks. She told me it was temporary until I got used to the situation. But I never really got used to it.

There were so many men. The whole place smelled rancid. The first time I had to give myself to one of those men, I was terribly scared. I never thought I would be with someone else in that way. I thought it would always be only Julio in my life.

I wanted to run, but the owner told me, "If you don't do your job tonight, there is no place for you here. You will leave this very night." Outside, the world seemed so big and unpredictable; I couldn't dare leave. But I loathed that night.

The customers just used us for their narrow satisfaction. We were just things to them. I wanted someone to save me from the horror of it. Then, I felt nothing. I was hopeless, empty. Nothing made sense to me.

I lived my worst fears in the bordel. I was too young and not ready to deal with what went on there—actually, all the women were in constant fear of their customers, of the customers' wives, and even of the other women working there. The men considered us their property and the owner let them do whatever they wanted with us. In front of everyone, they would slap the women's faces, burn them with cigars, humiliate them.

We did not leave the bordel very often because townspeople screamed at us and called us names. One day, a man in a carroça [a simple horse-drawn carriage with wooden sides] dropped a woman by the front door. She was nearly unconscious and was covered with blood. Her face seemed smashed and her hair was cut off. We learned some town wives saw her walking; they attacked her and used the opportunity to send us a bloody message.

Also, there were fights among customers who competed for certain women. This sometimes got very brutal. They would tear at each other, cut each other's clothes, and slash at their bodies with knives.

At the same time, each woman had her own story and her own reason for being there. Some had become pregnant before going to the bordel, eventually giving their babies away. Others were actually born into bordel life.

The owner, Miss Marcia, grew up in a bordel. It was the only life she knew. But by the time she brought me there, she did not work the customers anymore, she only managed the business. She was a beautiful, powerful, and mysterious woman who knew the most influential men in the region and seemed to know their secrets, too. Even though she was the owner, townspeople respected her. Or maybe they were afraid of her, just like we were, because she knew so much.

When the incident with the town wives occurred, she went to town and talked to the mayor. Later, she told us that something like that would not happen again. And it didn't, at least while I was there. Most of the time, Miss Marcia stayed in the bordel. But when she traveled, she dressed elegantly, presenting herself as a distinctive figure.

Miss Marcia became protective of me and let the other women know I was to be left alone. I'm not sure why, maybe because I was much younger and therefore more appealing to many men; or perhaps I reminded her of herself. At any rate, she kept me for "special" customers. The other women said I was very beautiful but I would not believe them. I felt uglier than ever. Still, I guess I was the luckiest one in the bordel.

Some men wanted me to go with them when they left the house, but I never did, though some of the women did leave with men. Some came back and some did not. Of the latter, we never heard what happened to them. I knew of a couple of women who married their customers.

Nevertheless, the other women were often jealous because I seemed to get the most valuable customers. They threatened me more than once, especially one in particular. I began carrying a small knife in my handbag, but I managed to avoid confrontations.

One man came frequently to see me and sometimes brought me gifts. But I couldn't like him. I hated all the customers. I hated everything. The only good thing was when they gave me extra money that I was able to hide away. But I never took it from their hands. They usually left it somewhere in the room, on a chair, on the table, on the bed.

The bordel had customers from many different towns,

classes and backgrounds. There were customers who were there weekly, some even daily, and some who only came once. There were married men alone, and fathers bringing sons for their "first time." There were groups of friends. There were men looking for a friend. We never knew what to expect. We just did our jobs. I did not think about what was happening; it was easier that way. I never tried to satisfy anybody. I was a body without a soul.

To get away from all of that, I would go for walks in the woods during the day where no humans could remind me of my life and my disgrace. I just wanted the nights to be shorter…

By the end of this section, Elena was crying softly. When I started reading to her, I had wondered if it was all fiction. But I could see in her eyes it was true. I had so many questions, but neither of us could look at each other anymore.

How did Elena endure two years in a cabaré? I remembered hearing stories of women like that when I was a child. I remembered a situation when a wife threw hot water at a *rapariga* (a cabaré woman) that was passing by her house in the village. These women were in the bottom of society. Anyone could do anything to them without consequences.

I wanted to go away and not face Elena again. Instead, I prepared lunch. We ate together, but we did not talk about her journal for the rest of the day.

CHAPTER 3

While my life was expanding, Elena's was contracting. Slowly at first, she began emptying her house of furnishings. Buyers came and went, carrying away treasures in their vans. But certain keepsake items had special memories, so she gave them to an appreciative few family members and close neighbors. During Grace's visits, for instance, she and Elena spent hours together looking over the albums and mementos that filled the shelves and closets. Every item evoked an exclamation or a nod of approval. There was a colorful story for every picture on the wall, every child's handicraft from school, and every holiday gift that arrived over many seasons.

Occasionally, Grace and Elena would just look at something and then absorb it without speaking. One day, Grace stayed longer than usual, expecting a phone call from her daughter, Abby, to Elena. While they waited, Grace and Elena held a photo album. "Mom, do you remember how much Brendon loved to come here just to look at these pictures? He would look at every album and he listen to you tell the same story again and again as if it was the first time." Elena did not reply, and Grace continued. "You know, Abby called you twice yesterday, and the day before, too, but no one answered."

"Cecilia and I have been busy with our little trips," Elena replied.

"I'm glad you two are enjoying each other. We are lucky to have found her," Grace said with a smile in my direction.

"She has been very good to me."

"I wish I could spend more time with you," Grace said.

"My girl, you are the best daughter a mother could ever hope for and I know you spend as much time as you can with me."

Grace's cell phone rang. She looked at the screen, pushed a button and said, "It's Abby! Hi, honey. We were waiting for you to call. I'm at Grandma's. She is doing very well. I know you want to talk with her. Hold on a moment." Grace passed her phone to Elena.

"Hello, Sweetie. I am well. How are you? Is Brendon with you? Sure, sure, and how's school? That's good. Wonderful. Good. Have you talked to Claire and William lately? Good. Of course. Yes. You both plan to come? Oh, we miss you for sure. I understand, Honey. Okay. Yes… Okay. I love you, too, Honey." Elena passed the phone back. "Here, Grace, she wants to talk to you."

Grace walked out of the room while talking to her daughter. The mention of Brendon suddenly made me uncomfortable to be alone with Elena. To avoid conversation, I asked, "Elena, would you like a cup of tea?"

"A cup of hot tea would be nice, thank you," she answered. I think she knew how I was feeling.

"I'll be right back."

"Thank you."

I put some water on to boil and looked for a tray, teacups, spoons, tea bags, and pot. The kitchen was still strange to me. It was extremely large and filled with wooden cabinets, porcelain dishes, and metal utensils. I intended to stay in the kitchen until Grace and Elena had settled back into the room. But they were too happy with the news and wanted to share it with me right away.

As I arranged the tray, Grace called out to me, "Cecilia, Brendon is coming to spend a week with us the end of May!"

The message was like a blast of cold air and I was not dressed well enough to protect myself.

"We are so happy!" she continued. "We haven't seen him for almost two years. We miss him so much. Unfortunately, Abby will not be able to come with him but she will spend few days here later this summer." It seemed she was trying to make excuses for her daughter, and she would not stop talking.

I wondered if it would be more natural to ask Grace when

23

exactly Brendon would arrive, or else what kind of tea she'd like. Even though I was not listening to her anymore, I wanted to act according to her expectations. When she stopped, I just said, "Tea is ready."

She said, "Okay, but I have to leave soon." The rest of the afternoon went quietly; Elena and I did not mention Brendon again.

After awhile, she asked me to read from her journal again. I was surprised because I thought she did not want to bring back any more memories for a while and I felt she did not quite like my interference in the journal. But that was more than a task for Elena, it was as if she was having a second chance to see it all happening again. So I took down the folder and started to work on it again.

I had been working in the bordel about two years. One night, while bringing a customer a drink, I saw someone who looked like Julio entering the bar. I said to myself, "It is not him, it cannot be him." I looked again. Then, with a shaking heart, I realized it was Julio. A fellow was with him. They were laughing.

I felt so futile, so worthless. I did not want to see him, but more than anything, I did not want him to see me. What could we have to say? But I could not stop looking at him. That was the man I loved. He was everything to me. I could not let him see me.

Two of the women approached them. I glanced around for Miss Marcia, to tell her I had to leave. But it was too late.

Julio saw me. Our eyes met. The shock on his face was like the shock I had felt a minute before. But his lasted only a second or two, then he acted as if we were strangers. For a second time, he denied me. And yet, I still wanted to believe that what we once had was important and meaningful.

I did not know what to do. I wanted to leave the room, the bordel, and run away; but at the same time, I wanted to stay close by and seize that moment. My mind said he was sorry and wanted to make things right. But it did not look that way. I thought a thou-

sand things.

I ran to the bathroom, washed my face, and stayed there for about ten minutes. I missed him and wanted his love again. How could that be wrong? I could only remember our good times. I had so many good memories. I wanted to return to the safety I had felt with him.

There was a knock at the door. Miss Marcia called to me. "Is everything okay?" I replied, "Yes, fine." She said that she needed to talk to me. I composed myself as best I could, then ducked out, and hurried to her room. Fortunately, I did not see Julio.

Miss Marcia was waiting. She said a customer would pay well to spend the night with me, and I knew she meant Julio. She talked about the advantages I could have. She talked on, but I wasn't listening. I was paralyzed. Was everything that already happened two years ago not enough? My pain was so great my heart was tight, and I could hardly breathe; I could not feel my body, just my chest pounding. This was the lowest point of my life. Nobody believed me worthy of anything.

That very moment, I lost the fear of life, the fear of what could happen to me.

And I was angry. I told her I would meet the young man in my room, but to give me some time to prepare.

I went to my room, packed my few clothes and money in a small bag, and waited about fifteen minutes alone. I felt hatred. I hated the man I loved. I hated the bedroom because I would have to share its air with someone I now despised.

A knock on the door, the knob turned. The time had come. Julio entered and closed the door behind him. We were in a long silence that seemed eternal. Then I began, "How are you, Julio?"

"I thought I would never see you again. I miss you so much..."

He tried to hug me.

"No," I said.

"How did you get here?"

"Why do you care now? It doesn't matter how I got here. I am here because of you. You allowed your father to decide our lives.

You are such a weak man!" I continued, "Instead of anger, I should feel sorry for you, you were the one who was humiliated that afternoon in that village. Does your father know you are here? Or it is another one of your secrets? See, you are a prisoner and jailer of your own life. But, above all, it hurt me you didn't care about what would happen to me."

My outburst surprised him. "You know I love you and don't want to live without you. We can continue to love each other and no one need to know. We can live in peace, away from everyone."

"No one needs to know!" I shouted. "Shut up! Don't say another word! Each word is one more reason for me to hate you. You do not know how I feel about you—"

"Of course I know what you feel," he said. "Why would you be here with me if you do not love me? Please, forget the past. We can start over."

"Start over?"

"You don't understand me," he said, as he reached a hand to me.

I was enraged. "Do not touch me! I understand you all too well. I know you. I do not care what you think. I do not care about—"

"Why did you accept my proposal for tonight?" he insisted.

"I did not accept your proposal. I wanted to answer it personally. I don't want your money. I don't want you. And believe me, you are the last man in the world I would submit to. Actually, you are not even on the list of men. Every other man in Brazil might have me tonight, but never you and never again. From the day I left that village, I put you out of my life. Now, do the same for me. Forget you ever knew me." My throat hurt, I was sweating and chilled at the same time. I was clutching the small traveling bag with clothes and money, ready to leave in an instant.

Calmly, he said, "You don't understand, Elena. I want you to come with me. I want to take you away from here. I have a friend with a house in town where you can stay until I find a place for us." I said nothing, and Julio hesitated. "But, there is something." He paused again. "I'm married, and she is pregnant. I respect her but I cannot love her. I can only love you."

"Liar! You never loved me. You just want a mistress. Go home to your wife and learn to be a man before you talk to me again!" I caught my breath and continued. "I know you were in the square that afternoon. I know you saw what happened. It was you who really whipped, tortured and almost killed me." Then I approached him very closely and lowered my voice, "And let me tell you, that day you killed our child."

With the small bag, I left the room and slammed the door behind me. In an instant, I left my dreams, my past, and my love, all that I once was. I left the bordel without saying a word.

Even as I hated him, I still loved what we once had.

I closed her journal. I asked Elena, "Why did you still care about that man? He was selfish and a coward. He did not seem to really care about you."

It disappointed me. Instead of hatred, Elena loved him, I knew it. Why would such a woman be so weak? She let me talk to release my evident frustration. We were alone in the large room, with the old photographs on the walls, the Brazilian mementos on the shelves, and what was left of her opulent furniture.

After a brief silence, Elena said firmly, "For me, love was never a sign of weakness; it was a sign of freedom. Only a free heart can love unconditionally," and continued. "Julio and I were just too young."

I wondered if I was ever free. I was afraid of love and thought my mother's experiences were enough lessons for both of us.

Many days, I felt like Elena and I changed places. She carefully listened to me, called up and nurtured my memories, and sat silently beside me when I just wanted cry. With Elena, pains that I didn't know existed began to heal. They were below my day-to-day surface, blocked by a desire to pretend their sources never existed.

CHAPTER 4

Reading Elena's journal brought back my own years in Brazil, although our lives were quite different. My earliest memory is of my mother and me walking to and from school together, a short distance through the woods. Often on our way home, we enjoyed the wonders of the trees, the flowing of the stream, songs of the birds, and all the aromas of nature. It was magical to me.

Many times we arrived home late and Mother got in trouble with my father. One afternoon, we got close to the house and saw Father in the doorway, drinking. Mother also saw something else that I didn't. She stopped, looked at me, and said, "Stay here. Do not go home. Soon I will come and get you." I stayed in the bushes. I could see them but they could not see me.

When my father saw Mother, he started to scold her. "Why are you coming home so late? Who do you think you are? I am hungry and there is no food ready!" He was screaming. I couldn't hear what she replied, but I saw his response. He clutched the almost empty glass bottle and then threw it against the wall. Glass splintered everywhere. He grabbed my mother by her hair and threw her into the house. I was horrified. The sounds were indescribable, a mix of screaming and glass breaking, the sounds of agony and destruction.

"Please, don't do this, please! God!" Mother screamed.

Leaving my hiding place, I rushed into the house. Mother was in a corner, crumpled on the floor, bleeding, and holding her arm awkwardly. It was broken. I ran to her. In a high wail, she screamed, "Run, Cecilia! Get out of here." Instead, I hugged her. Father had a large, sharp knife in his hands.

"No! No! Please, no. Don't do it!" I pleaded. For a second, he looked at me, then turned around and threw the knife on the table. When he heard our neighbors stirring—they always came when Mother and Father fought—he stormed out of the house and did not come back that night. I was about six years old at the time.

But I also remember how much I liked my school and the friends I played with, Maria and Paulo.

I remember playing soccer with other children. The two teams always had a mix of boys and girls on each. The soccer ball was an old one that the manager of the local team gave to his son. In the afternoons, we'd go to the field, and the two usual goalkeepers would choose up sides. I didn't know if I was good, but I was often the first girl picked. Father did not like me playing soccer; he'd say it was for boys. But Mother would take me to play when Father was working.

My mother taught elementary school in the village, although she never went to college. Back then, in most Brazilian villages and small towns, teachers weren't required to have higher education. So they let her work and make some money.

At the time, it was not common for a woman to work outside of her home. But it was very common for them to be mistreated by their fathers and husbands. Unfortunately, the boys learned this behavior and repeated it from generation to generation. Because of it, Brazilian communities accepted the practice. Many wives suffered from it and sacrificed themselves for the sake of their children.

Father was abusive and an alcoholic, and like most men in my village, never finished elementary school. They had to work. Boys as young as six or seven years old were sent to the fields. "What good is school if you don't have money to buy food?" Working kids would say to kids walking to school. Father was often ill because of his drinking. When he was drunk, he would beat my mother. Mother was a good woman and a hard worker who fell in love with a man who did not care about life or about the people around him. She could not defend herself for fear of being killed and leaving me alone with him.

The authorities did nothing to protect us, the same as they did nothing to protect our neighbors who looked for help and ended up facing greater violence and humiliation from the fists and wrath of their husbands. I remember a neighbor crying on her doorstep because her husband did not allow her to see her children. That was her punishment for going to the police after a beating. I remember her going back into the house but I never saw her again.

One woman killed her drunken husband, shot him in the head with his own gun. She said she was defending her life but the judge sentenced her to thirty years' prison and put her three children into an orphanage. The story passed through villages and towns everywhere. Some said she got what she deserved. Others thought she did what she had to do. In the end, she just went from one kind of prison to another.

Another time, a husband killed his wife by stabbing her seventeen times; he said she was cheating on him. For a few months, he hid from the police, leaving the children with his parents. Then he returned and married another woman. That ended one story and began the next.

My mother wanted neither that kind of ending nor that kind of life. Above all, she did not want me to face the same future.

Mother heard stories of Brazilians who entered America from Mexico without papers. She decided to do it, to take me and leave everything else behind. When she went to teacher meetings, she heard about *"coyotes,"* people you'd pay to take you across the border. Finding one, she negotiated to pay one part before leaving and the remainder when she found work in the U.S. She knew there would be dire consequences if she did not pay the balance. Grandma helped us. She sold one piece of land her husband left her. Even so, it took Mother more than a year and a half to raise the first payment. She forged my father's signature on our Brazilian exit papers: while she could leave alone without them, his written permission was required for her to take me away.

When the time came to leave, she told Father we had to go to Grandma's because she was very sick. He was drinking when we left. It was the last time we were all together. He was angry, telling my mother she better be back in a couple of days or else he would come after us.

We went to Grandma's to say goodbye. I remember her last words to Mother, "For yourself and for your daughter do not come back. God bless you both."

They hugged and kissed each other. Then Grandma kissed me and we left. They were crying.

I was eight years old when we went to Mexico and illegally crossed into the U.S. Mother held my hand almost every minute we were moving, from the time we left Grandma's until we arrived in America. I know the trip was very difficult, much of it I don't recall. But I remember there were a lot people with us. We walked for days and were thrown into crowded vehicles every now and then. I almost drowned crossing a river. I also remember my mother crying.

In later years, she never wanted to talk about that trip. It gave me the impression something happened to her while crossing the border. Whenever I asked, she would change the subject. I once asked if she would do it again.

Nervously, she said, "If I knew what would happen at the border, we would have stayed in Brazil. I knew it was bad when I lived with your father and I thought I knew what life was about. But no, I would not do it again. I am glad we are here now but I would not do it again. I would rather have stayed and dealt with your father." She kept repeating, "No, I would never do it again."

I never brought it up again, but I thought I knew what happened.

When Mother and I arrived in America, we seemed to be inside a tornado that carried us across the country. It was beyond our control.

First we lived in Florida with a group of Brazilians who were the *coyote's* friends. They taught Mother to drive, gave her false identification, found her some work, and sent me to school. Altogether, seven of us lived in a two-bedroom apartment. I was the only child. Everyone worked and saved money. Some of it went back to families in Brazil, and the rest to the *coyotes*. Mother worked perhaps seventy to eighty hours a week. I was alone much of the time, but the others in the apartment were good to me. There were many other immigrants crowded into our building, but the only ones who spoke Portuguese were in our apartment.

We became friends with a Mexican family across the hall. Miss Lupe had two children by her first husband—Manuel was about nineteen years old and worked for a construction company, and Mara was seventeen and worked in a beauty salon. Juan was ten and was born in the United States; Miss Lupe had him by her second husband who was in jail for drug offences.

Miss Lupe was much older than Mother and worked as a janitor in a nearby school. She was very protective of her children and of others she cared about. At home, her oven was always on and the aroma of her cooking filled the building. Miss Lupe was loud and talkative. At times when she was just talking to her children, it sounded like she was arguing with them. She was always asking questions and her conversations were always very animated.

In the beginning, it was difficult for my mother to understand what Miss Lupe said. But soon they both got comfortable with the differences between Spanish and Portuguese and could carry on with each other non-stop.

While Mother and Miss Lupe were cooking or doing housework, Juan and I would play together, often sharing the delicious food that came out of his mother's kitchen. Juan was my first friend in America. He knew English and I felt safe when I was with him. We shared a love of soccer, and I was a regular on Juan's team. He and I also went to school together.

At first, school was very difficult. I rarely spoke because I did not know what to say or how to say it. I was a strange child in a strange world. For several months, school was the place of pain and humiliation. I missed my little school back in Brazil and my old friends. Other kids would come to me, tell me a bunch of words that I didn't understand, and run away laughing.

I didn't do much there. The little work I did was with the Spanish teacher because the language was easier than English. Mother tried to help me but it was difficult for her, too. Eventually, Juan started to help me, and English began to come as easily as Spanish.

I guess the tornado was losing its power over us. I became my mother's translator even at school when Miss Lupe was not there. Mother would go to speak with the teacher and I would interpret for them. I also interpreted at the hospital, the banks, and the stores, both for Mother and for the others we lived with.

About a year after we arrived in Florida, Miss Lupe and her children rented a house in a nicer neighborhood, and she invited us to go live with them. We agreed. It was a big house. Mother and I shared a large bedroom, bigger than anything we had ever occupied.

Soon, I noticed that Mother and Miss Lupe had become confidants, not just friends. When Juan and I were underfoot or interrupting them, they'd send us outside or on errands, or to bed. Many times, when they thought I was asleep, I was actually by the door listening to their conversation. They talked about other people, about our fathers and sometimes about themselves.

One night, I had gone to sleep but for some reason something woke me up. Mother was not in the bedroom so I got up and went to my hiding place behind the door. Mother and Miss Lupe were talking about a man who was interested in Mother.

Miss Lupe said, "You are still young. You cannot stay alone forever. He's a good man, has a good job, and comes from a decent family. He just wants to know you better."

"Lupe, I know he seems to be good, and if things were different I might be interested. But I am still married to someone in Brazil and that will never change. Besides, I don't want anyone in my life. I can't be with a man anymore."

Miss Lupe reached out and touched her. "How can you say that?" she said. "You are a woman and every woman needs a man by her side."

Mother argued, "What for? To be beaten and raped?"

"No, to be protected and loved."

"No man ever loved or protected me. Why would one do it now? He doesn't even know me."

"But he likes you, he wants to know you, and he might be different. You can give him a chance. He told me it doesn't matter where you came from or what you did. I think he just wants to love and protect you and he'll care for Cecilia as if she were his own daughter."

There was a silence.

"At least think about it," said Miss Lupe.

Then another silence.

"Has he ever made you uncomfortable?"

"No," said Mother, "he has been polite. And I do like him. But I will not take chances anymore," she said, already crying.

"Please, what happened? It will help to talk. You can trust me."

"I know. It just hurts to even think about it."

By then mother was sniffling and trying to talk at the same time. "When I left home," she said, "I thought I was leaving my problems behind. I thought my husband was the worst kind of man and that by running away from him, I would save my life and my daughter's."

"Tell me, what happened at the border?"

Mother continued, "The night before we crossed over, one of the *coyotes* came to take me to their leader. Cecilia was sleeping; she was worn out from walking. I asked if we could go in the morning instead, but he refused. His leader would not stay overnight. I didn't want to leave Cecilia but I didn't want to take her with me either. So I left her with the others and went with him. The men were drinking in the back of the truck. They were noisy but went quiet when we approached.

"One of the men stood up and said to me, 'Tonight we need a woman, and you and your daughter are the only ones without a man with you.' I turned and tried to run back to Cecilia. They grabbed me and said that they already had Cecilia somewhere else. So I had to choose if it would be her or me."

"Oh my God, oh God."

"I pleaded, 'Please, don't hurt my daughter, she is just a child.' They told me that it was up to me. I said, 'Do what you want with me, but leave my daughter alone, please.' They said that if I did all they asked, then Cecilia would be safe and I could see her afterwards. Then, they made me remove my clothes in front of them. They started drinking and yelling again, screaming like animals. And one after the other, they raped and beat me."

"Oh, my God," Miss Lupe kept saying.

"There was nothing I could do," my mother wept, "all I could think of was Cecilia. It went for hours, all night." Mother was sobbing. "I thought I would die there and Cecilia would be alone, and it was all my fault."

I peered in at them now as Miss Lupe put her arm around Mother who was trying to talk between her sobs. "When they finished, they sent me to Cecilia. I hurried but could barely walk. She was sleeping the same way I left her. Even though I was bleeding and broken, the sight of her relieved me."

It was too much for me to listen. I ran back into bed and pulled the blankets over me. Now I was crying. At the time, I didn't know exactly what "rape" meant, but I knew it was bad. Mother saved my life.

At the time, the conversation and the crying deeply affected me. It was several years before I realized how devastating it was, that night and crossing the border. The more I understood, the more guilt I felt. I still do.

Next morning, I was afraid to face Mother. I did not know

what to say. I spied on her and I shouldn't have. When I entered the kitchen, though, Mother and Miss Lupe were talking as if nothing happened the night before. They were having a lively talk about Miss Lupe's brother and his family in Massachusetts. From what Miss Lupe said, only good things happened in Massachusetts. People had money, they were better educated, and their children had better schools. She said people were safe there. It was the perfect place to live. The only reason Miss Lupe hadn't moved yet was because her older children did not want to leave Florida and she would not leave them.

About two years later Mother finally paid the *coyote* the rest of the money. Then she wanted us to move away from anyone who knew us from Brazil. During those years, she worried about the Brazilian authorities finding us. She could go to jail for forging my father's signature and taking me out of the country. In fact, she was afraid my father would come after us.

Meanwhile, things changed for Miss Lupe. First, her daughter Mara rented an apartment with her boyfriend, and then her son, Manuel, prepared to return to Mexico to marry his fiancé and bring her to America. That helped Miss Lupe and Mother decide it was time to move. They would take us - me and Juan - to Massachusetts. It was to be a secret; no one should know where we were going. Later, it seemed to me that anyone looking for us would likely first go to Miss Lupe's brother in Massachusetts.

Within a month, we were ready to go. Miss Lupe and Mother sold or gave away their possessions, bought a truck and then we drove all the way from Florida to Massachusetts. We spent three days getting there, sleeping two nights in the back of the truck before reaching our destination.

First, we stayed two weeks with Miss Lupe's brother, Don Fernando, who lived in Newburyport, a seacoast city north of Boston. Then we moved north across the river a few miles to a three-bedroom, third-floor tenement in Salisbury. It was a block away from the ocean.

For work, Mother and Miss Lupe had jobs in a restaurant where Don Fernando's friend cooked. Mother washed dishes and Miss Lupe prepared food, but they often helped each other. Mother also got part-time night work cleaning hospitals and offices. And she would keep house for the wife of one of the restaurant owners. The wife liked how well Mother cleaned their house.

Between jobs, Mother managed to go to school and learn English. She was always busy but we were satisfied with our life.

Massachusetts to me was very different from Florida, especially the weather. Massachusetts had the coldest weather I ever knew. But I loved the snow and winter became my favorite season. Juan and I waited excitedly for those huge snowstorms. We watched from the windows as the snow accumulated, anxious to go outside and play.

I was doing well in school, and put all my time and effort into learning. I wanted Mother to be proud of me. My English reading and writing made her happy, but she also insisted I learn how to translate everything to Portuguese. With her help, I did it. At home, when we were alone, we always spoke Portuguese. But otherwise, we lived as though the life before America never existed. We never talked about the years in Brazil.

We met other Brazilians and we made friends with people from other countries, too. But for the most part, our life in Massachusetts centered on just the four of us: Mother, me, Miss Lupe and Juan.

Because Miss Lupe was "legal," everything important among us was in her name: the cars, the auto insurance, the rent. At the same time, the term "illegal" was part of us. Mother and I were not Brazilian, nor American, nor human. To the government, we were "illegal" and to the neighbors, we were "aliens." Those were the only terms to describe us and people like us. It did not matter if we were young or old, rich or poor, or that we had fled for our lives rather than simply emigrated from Brazil. Our past did not matter. Our feelings did not matter. We were illegal and that was all. We were in constant fear of every encounter and involvement.

For example, one of the cooks would pick on Mother; he called her names and gave her more dishes to wash than necessary; he screamed at her and said obscene things to her when others weren't listening. One day Miss Lupe heard him and loudly scolded him. The waitresses and other workers rushed to the kitchen. Fortunately, the restaurant owner realized the truth and transferred the cook to another shift. Later, he was fired. When I asked my mother why she didn't protest the cook's harassment, she said, "I am illegal. I'm afraid that the same laws that would protect me would also punish me."

Juan's father discovered us about a year and a half after we arrived in Massachusetts. An American court had ordered him to leave the country, and he wanted to take Miss Lupe and Juan back to Mexico with him. But Miss Lupe refused. He went back alone but telephoned often. It had an effect. Every time Miss Lupe got off the phone with him, she would have a new list of reasons why Mexico was better than America, and why Mexicans were happier. This went on for six months until she decided to return to Mexico with Juan. She left the car and the apartment for Mother, except that both were still in Miss Lupe's name.

Eventually, the auto registration expired and the insurance could not be renewed. And because there was no one to share the rent, that also became too expensive.

On top of everything, one afternoon after grocery shopping, a police car followed us, its lights flashing, signaling us to stop. Mother acted really nervous. At first, it seemed she did not want to stop. She started to pray aloud, then slowed and stopped. I was scared. The officer walked over and asked for the registration and driver's license. I knew the license was a fake one given to her by a Brazilian while we lived in Florida. I was afraid she'd go to jail. This already happened to two immigrant neighbors.

Sure enough, he said her papers were not right. He told her she could go to jail if caught driving again without proper documents. This time, he gave her a ticket and had her car towed away. We never saw the car again. It was a long walk home with all the groceries, but, at least, he let us go.

After that, Mother decided to move from Salisbury, this time a short distance over the state line to Seabrook, New Hampshire. Although it was just a few miles up the coast, rent for a two-bedroom apartment was much cheaper. Also, car insurance was not required, and some New Hampshire towns allowed illegals to register their cars without documentation. The only requirement was proof of residency.

The move to New Hampshire meant another change in schools for me. That was hard, and I didn't want to go through it again, but I had to be strong for Mother. I thought she had her own troubles, so why should I add to them? She had done so much for me. I continued feeling guilty that Mother had to leave Brazil because of me. And now we were both illegal in America.

During high school, my illegal status weighed heavily. Most of the students were dreaming about their futures while, for me, it did not matter how much I dreamed. Although I was a good student, it would never be good enough unless our status in America became "legal."

To compensate, I played soccer. It was girls-only games. I played tough and strong and often got yellow penalty cards for rough play. I had to learn to keep my feet on the ball and my body from colliding with other girls. I might as well have been playing with the boys.

Not many people showed up for games, mostly just a few parents. However, after the third or fourth game, attendance grew, including more students. One day, I noticed Brendon with several other boys, and over the season they returned for the rest of our home games. For some reason, his presence pushed me to prove myself. Sometimes I'd imagine Brendon or one of the other boys was there just to watch me. I admit it was a bit distracting and I had to concentrate a lot more to play my best.

Soon, soccer became an escape from worries and frustration, but it couldn't substitute for my need to belong somewhere. I wondered: "What if we had stayed in Brazil? What if times have changed, and husbands don't beat their wives anymore?" I put my thoughts away because I felt I was betraying my mother with those kinds of dreams.

In high school, I did not belong to any group nor was I welcomed. I tried to cope by concentrating on my studies and playing soccer, as if they could attract the attention I wanted. But I still felt unnoticed.

Besides being an illegal immigrant, we lived in the poorest town in the school district, and some of the kids from wealthier towns always seemed to be picking on someone or something. Within their exclusive circle, for example, if they decided one boy was homosexual, then any boy who was his friend must be homosexual, too. As a result, the boy would lose his friends; no one would even talk to him. This "in" group picked on others as well. They called the short girl "Baby," the tall girl "Clumsy," the too-smart girl "Nerdy," the ones not as smart, "Stupid," and the list went on.

One day Mrs. Falante, the Spanish teacher, divided the class into groups to practice an exercise. One of the in-group girls was paired with one of the girls they called "Stupid." The in-group girl was laughing and getting her friends' attention to show them how stupid the other girl was.

Watching this, I started to breathe hard and became upset. I knew I would not forgive myself if I did not come to her defense, so I quietly asked her to change partners with me. We did, and I became the partner and we did the exercise. The teacher then asked for volunteers, "Who wants to give a demonstration?" I raised my hand for the first time. The in-girl turned and asked, "What are you doing? I am not going up there." I looked at her and said, "Yes, you are." I stood up, went to the front of the class, and waited. She stood and awkwardly followed me. I stood up straight, still angry, and then asked her as she came close, "Are you ready?"

She didn't answer. I started reciting the practice dialogue in Spanish, clearly and as rapidly as I could. The other girl looked at her paper and slowly pronounced a word at a time. Again, I gave my response rapidly so that she didn't have time to think. It took even longer for the girl to respond. Again, I very quickly recited the third sentence. She was way behind, looking at her paper and slowly opening her mouth as if trying to make a sound but not saying anything. She was like a fish out of water.

I said, "I'm sorry, but can you repeat that? I didn't hear what you said." I heard some kids giggle and she looked up from her paper. The next three sentences, I corrected her on every word that was not well-pronounced. The class began to laugh out loud. When it ended, the teacher was upset with me and made me promise to be more respectful next time. After that class, four girls, including the in-girl, approached me.

"Hey, who do you think you are?" She asked. *"Yo sé quién soy y sé quién es usted. Eres una estúpida,"* I said in Spanish. ['I know who I am and I know who you are. You are stupid.']

Another girl replied, "Let me refresh your memory: You are in the United States, so speak English." *"Por que?"* I said. *"Além de serem diotas vocês são ignorantes também."* ['Why? Besides being stupid you are ignorant too.']

That made them mad. They started to yell at me all at the same time until a voice behind them stopped the noise, "Hey, cool it girls, before you get in trouble." It was Brendon.

The in-girl complained, "Did you see how she humiliated me in front of the whole class?"

"I saw it," he answered. "But I also saw you trying to humiliate your other partner, Tracy, and it wasn't funny."

The in-girl turned to me and snarled, "We're reporting you to the principal." Then she stomped away. Brendon looked at me

41

for a second and I thought and hoped he would say something, but he didn't, and everyone went to their next class. Nothing else ever came of the encounter except that as time went on, Tracy and I became good friends. I learned that she was actually smart.

All through high school, I admired Brendon. Just about every girl in the school liked him. Although he never paid me attention, I never felt he was unfair. "How could Brendon pay attention to someone like me," I thought, "when he could have any girl in the school?" I went to all the school football and basketball games because Brendon played on both teams. But I was one of hundreds of students. Brendon was popular with friends and teachers and seemed to be involved in everything. I thought he was too good for me. I envied the beautiful American girls who got close enough to him to be friends.

I made it through high school somehow without serious incidents. Other than soccer, I wasn't part of school activities and I didn't go to dances, but as time went on, I made a few friends. During my junior and senior years, I also worked in a fast food restaurant after school. I managed to graduate as an honor student, but did not go to college right away. I was still an "illegal." Instead, I went to work full time. I stopped playing soccer because there were no teams for girls, and because Brendon wasn't on the sideline to watch me. I didn't know where he went.

But the One who writes our lives devises many twists and turns.

About a year after graduation, there was news about a new law that gave aliens with employment sponsors a chance to become "legal." Mother contacted Miss Lupe's brother, Don Fernando, and asked him about it. He explained it but said there was a problem: we didn't have the skills to qualify as "needed workers." Nevertheless, Don Fernando spoke with the restaurant owners where Mother worked, Mr. and Mrs. Adams. They understood the situation and decided to sponsor her as a "Brazilian cook." They even helped us pay the application fees.

The government approved our applications; Mother could work and I could become a foreign student while we became legal residents. I got into a community college nursing program. But as a foreign student, I was not eligible for financial aid, I had to pay out-of-country tuition, and I was not supposed to work. Again, I had to rely on Mother. Because of it, I did not want to go to school. It was too expensive and she would have to work two jobs again. But she was insistent, saying, "If you do not take this opportunity, everything I did was for nothing." So I went to nursing school and took informal jobs cleaning, babysitting, and tutoring for people we knew. It was a tough time but Mother never complained. I don't know how we made it.

Within two years, though, we became permanent residents. I got work as a waitress in the same restaurant as Mother. I was also able to get some financial aid that helped me complete nursing school.

Mother never said 'I love you,' but it was not necessary. Her love was all around me. She never thought only of herself. I knew it and did my best not to disappoint her. She never made me feel guilty for her sacrifice, but I felt guilty anyway.

After graduating, a hospital nearby hired me, and Mother cut back to part-time work. We could finally settle down and live a little more comfortably. We bought a two-bedroom home in Seabrook. Mother enrolled in a program to get a high school diploma. We often invited friends over and Mother would cook for them. Holidays, we always had decorations in the house. Overall, I could see she was finally happy.

In her spare time, Mother helped immigrants who were pregnant, ill or needed some other attention. She would take them to doctors, banks, insurance and utility offices, schools and other places, even to apply for jobs. She was popular among those who were illegal, who would otherwise have to avoid emergency rooms and other places where their status might be questioned. Many became friends and frequent visitors.

At home, it seemed we were living our best life and I was thankful for it. But my love life was perplexing. I couldn't settle with anyone. I never brought my dates home because I felt they were not good enough for me or Mother. So why should I disturb her peace?

As soon as we were eligible, we applied for citizenship. We took the tests and completed the requirements. This was the freedom we sought. Immediately, Mother registered to vote and awaited the presidential election with excitement. Finally, it seemed worth all the hard times. Life was going the way she wanted. I didn't want to change anything, but unfortunately, the best of times became the worst of times.

About three months after we became American citizens, I returned home from work and found Mother on the kitchen floor, breathing but unconscious. I called the emergency number, and an ambulance took her to the hospital. On examination, doctors said she had a stroke; they also said she had a brain tumor. Until then I had never thought Mother could die one day. Now, from nowhere, without warning, another tornado had arrived.

At first, to cope with the diagnosis, I denied its fatal consequences. I preferred to think it was just another bad storm that she'd recover despite what the doctors said. As a nurse, I had seen cancer before, but I knew it could not happen to us.

Soon I had to accept help. Our friends came to the house as often as possible so that someone was always with my mother. But this once self-reliant woman was becoming weak and fragile before our eyes. Even then, she worried more about me than herself, constantly reminding me to eat well, take care of myself, and never trust my heart in matters of love. For her, love was an illusion that only brought suffering.

The day came when the doctors took away all our hope. I began to pray. Although I had never seen it before, I now saw my mother praying many times. She was a woman of faith.

Through my desperation and fear, I thought I had enough faith for my prayers to be heard. Every day for weeks, I got on my knees by Mother's bed and prayed for God to save her. When her condition did not improve, I began to pray for mercy, "If you allow her to die, would you please allow me to die too?" I prayed this for many days.

On a cold blustery morning in late October, my beloved mother, Maria Celeste Medeiros da Silva, breathed her last. It was just over a year from the diagnosis and only days before the presidential election she had waited for with such hope and excitement. Mother was only forty-three, and I was twenty-four. It was her ultimate pain, and was devastating to me. I rationalized the idea that she had found peace.

Mother and I never talked about death. Some of our Brazilians friends suggested her body should be sent "back home" but I couldn't do it. There was no reason to send her back. I also knew that as a Catholic, she did not want to be cremated, so I arranged for her burial in a Seabrook cemetery.

After the burial, I took temporary leave from nursing and kept to myself, avoiding friends and neighbors. I ignored the telephone and knocks on the door. She was quiet and never a burden.

I became preoccupied with thoughts of death, God, and spiritualism. I wondered how they could be related and how a God that so many people trusted could let my mother die. She only wanted to live, and I didn't want to be left alone.

The first few days were the worst, crying and sleeping and hoping to see Mother in my dreams. But she wasn't there and seemed to be forever gone. All I sensed was emptiness, and it scared me. I felt that life had become worthless, without reason to continue. For sure, though, my own heart still beat and my lungs respired. Being alive, I started moving again.

After the crying and sleeping came the cleaning. I filled and discarded many boxes of things from every room in the house.

Then I washed clothes and rearranged the furniture. Cleaning Mother's room was tough. It was like invading her privacy and destroying her memories. A part of me wanted to leave her things alone while another part wanted to let them go along with my pain.

I would go over the facts: She was so young. She had to overcome so much in her life. And, when she finally was able to enjoy it without working so hard, it was time to go. Why? How unfair it was. Before, she was healthy and active. She only cooked and ate healthy foods. She never hurt anyone. Why was a woman who deserved to be happy cut down so soon? Why did Mother die so young? Why her? Without answers, I could not move on.

Elena helped me walk through grief. Inspired by her, and to keep busy when she didn't need me, I began keeping a journal, too. It helped me remember life with Mother, especially after emigrating Brazil. Instead of Elena's reams of loose paper in thick heavy folders, mine resided in a portable computer, the same one I used to translate and type her stories. In this way, you could say we were getting electronically bound together at the same time our physical lives were beginning to occupy the same space and time, and share the same household routine, food, atmosphere and circle of friends and family.

CHAPTER 5

It was a bright, blue and green morning in mid-May, and I had been working for Elena over a month. We went to daily mass at 9:00am, and afterwards, Elena asked me to take her to the beach. When we got there, she became silent and serene, much like the ocean before us that morning. In a way, I wished I could read her mind, the same as I often wished I could learn the secrets of these cold New England waters. Both Elena and the ocean extended beyond the horizon to mysterious worlds completely foreign to me.

Elena was a very intense woman. Even at her advanced age, she still had passion for life. I felt the opposite, never really part of life, not even my own. I had been living, learning, and feeling everything through other people's experiences. I didn't recognize myself and usually couldn't grasp my feelings. But watching and being with Elena, I knew I wanted to find myself and be free.

Back at the house, Elena asked me to resume working on her journal. I complied, not knowing what was to come.

When I left the bordel, I had nowhere to go. I wanted to get away from Julio and everything that hurt me. I never wanted to see him again. I never wanted to see my family again. I never wanted to be in that bordel or in any other again.

*I did miss my mother. Seeing Julio, I was so overwhelmed that I did not think of her until much later that night. I had sat down exhausted in the woods outside of town and felt ashamed that I didn't ask him about her, angry as I was. I decided to try to find her, to see her one more time, at least. I slept in the woods. They were dark but familiar. The next morning, I went to find Mother. Twice, I found rides in carriages/*carroças*, but in between still walked several miles. It was late Saturday afternoon when I arrived. It was* *summer and very hot.*

We used to go to fairs on Sundays, so I thought I might find her there the next day. At the fairground, the venders were getting ready. I hid and slept under a table that night. It was starry and I felt peaceful. Only the dogs noticed me and barked but I did not care. I quickly fell asleep.

It was already daylight when I awoke. Townspeople were appearing, and some had familiar faces. I didn't want anybody else to see me. I borrowed pencil and paper from the rice seller whom knew mother, sat under a tree and wrote a letter to her. I told how much I missed her, and I asked her to forgive me for causing any distress. I promised to write again, and then left it with the rice seller.

My mother was not literate. Before I learned to read, when she needed someone to read letters from one of her half-sisters in another state, she'd ask a local schoolteacher. They'd read, and then write her response. That's what I thought she'd do with my letter.

After entrusting the letter to the rice seller, I left quickly, like an animal running away from hunters. I was running from more humiliation. I had challenged custom and was punished. I was a young girl who believed in love; I had spent two years in bordellish hell. What was worse? Being in hell or being lost?

Oh, I was so young—

Suddenly, Elena asked me to stop. It was enough for her that day, and for me, too. My mind was full of questions. What was so important about a past that was no longer part of her life? Why waste time thinking about what could not be changed? Why did she care about those faraway Brazilians? They did not care about her, not if she lived or died.

Elena and Grace got to work preparing for Brendon's visit. Their whirlwind caught me up and didn't leave a moment's peace. They had to clear the attic of old clothes for Goodwill and the Salvation Army. They wanted to sort and select old souvenirs and photos for Brendon's parents. The list went on and on. After several days of it, I was ready for a break.

As if reading my mind, Grace decided to take Elena to their lake house in Maine, and gave me the weekend off. I took Elena's journal with me because I wanted to read it straight through without having to stop every few pages.

At home, the journal was only my companion. I opened it where I had left off with Elena a few days before:

What is happening now with those left behind?

I often wondered why my real parents abandoned me. I was hurt by the abandonment and maybe still am. It was the pain of a girl who always heard she was a "poor little thing" forgotten by her real parents. People looked at me with pity.

I could not ask to be loved by my adoptive parents. They never knew what love was. They gave me what they had to give.

After writing the letter to my mother, I was back as before, not knowing where to go or what to do. But I was seventeen years old and not so afraid. I took the road away from the bordel and avoided rides from men. Some nights, I slept in the squares, other nights in the woods, in the sugar cane fields, or wherever I felt safer. Eventually, I reached a town that had a train to Maceió, the state capital. I had never seen a train before, but I took it as far as I could afford to go.

I never knew there were places like Maceió. At first glance, everyone was elegant, polite, and beautiful. The main buildings stood upright and clean. I saw the ocean for the first time. From the harbor, it seemed to stretch to the end of the world. The breeze and salty smell made me feel as part of it.

The beauty of the town was superficial, however. Maceió was full of poor and homeless people and I was one more of them. For a few days, I lived on the streets near a city square and a store that sold used books among other stuff. I walked constantly, looking for jobs and somewhere to stay. Being poor in a city seemed worse than being poor in a backwoods village: at least in the village, there would be land for a garden, some fruit trees to pick, some shade to sleep under. In Maceió, the story was about money. If you didn't have some, you couldn't eat.

Many homeless people lived in flimsy shelters mostly made of sugar sacks or whatever else they could find. These clumped together by a river near one of the squares. It was a colorful, comic, yet tragic scene. But the tent people were always on the move. They were not supposed to stay in public places; the police constantly evicted them, and destroyed whatever belonging were left behind.

And there were the animals and the trash everywhere. In that part of the city life didn't have much value.

I saw mothers and fathers trying to comfort their crying and hungry children. I saw fathers going to jail because they stole a bit of food for their family. I saw desperation in many faces. I saw dead children. With all this around me, my own troubles became secondary.

*I befriended a young tent woman, Lili, who had two little sons. Her husband had promised to take her to São Paulo, more than a thousand miles to the south. In those days, many northerners/*nordestinos *migrated there for work and a better life. But Lili's husband was missing. Two months earlier, the police had thrown him and some others in jail for resisting eviction. Later, everyone was released but Lili's husband was not among them. She visited the jail repeatedly and each time got the same answer, "All those men were already released." Now they were alone.*

Lili let me stay with her and the boys in their tent. My money was almost gone. Nevertheless, I shared what I had with them and we ate for a few days.

When I was not looking for a job and a place to stay, I looked at used books in the store, or sat in the city square and watched the people. They moved and moaned to themselves, not noticing me, as if I were invisible.

Many nights, not being able to sleep, I watched the stars and felt I was invisible to them too. But I also dreamed about good things to come and other worlds that might exist. I thought about the fu-

ture and about what if I lived in another time. I often wondered how many more people would have to sleep there. I wished no other person would have to experience this kind of poverty. I wanted to prevent others from having a story like mine. Perhaps this is why I started recording what happened to me and what I saw happening to others. I also did not want to be lost in time. I did not want to be forgotten. Even now, I don't want to be someone who went through life without leaving marks.

I have no children of my own. I have no grandchildren with my genes. The beating that killed my child-to-be also killed my chance to have another. I do not know where I came from. Physically, I will leave no marks on Earth. I want you (whoever you are or wherever you find this to read) to know my story. I know that one day, someone – you – will find my writings. These are my marks. If you read my story, at least this did not die. I know that time separates us. But through these writings, we are as close as two strangers can be. I do not know in what time you are, but I know you are there. I hope that in your time the world is better.

I wish all women are free. I wish no one have to experience hunger. I wish all children go to school, and none have to work to survive. I wish the politicians stopped stealing from the poor. And I wish that parents did not have to abandon their children.

I walked through Maceió several times looking for work: businesses, residences, churches. One evening, I walked by a church with open doors. I went in and sat on a bench. There were statues of saints and pictures of angels all around. It was comforting, but I felt abandoned, orphaned. I looked up and asked, "Have you forgotten me? If so, why?" I had prayed many times before but my questions were never answered.

Sitting in the church, I remembered how Mother used to say, "We never suffered as Christ did," but I wondered if he suffered any more than me. I started to cry and tears trickled down. A crucifix was on the wall. I wondered, as I often did, why God allowed him to die that way.

If my life had a purpose, I couldn't see it. Mother told me that Christ died to save us, but it seemed to me the mission was not accomplished. I knew I had to eventually leave the church and go back outside to face the wretchedness of the street. I just wanted to stay there.

A young priest sat in the same pew, gazing silently ahead. I wiped away my tears with a handkerchief Dona Marcia had given me. She knew it was useful to women like us.

"It looks like it will rain soon," the priest said after a while.

"Yes, Father," I said softly, looking down.

"Are you new here? I don't remember seeing you before."

"Just moved, Father."

"Are you with your family?"

"I have no family."

"Where are you living?"

"By the river. I can't find a job."

"Can you write and read?"

"Yes, Father."

"What is your name?"

"Elena."

"Elena, I am Padre Jonas..."

As we finished talking Padre Jonas asked me to come back the next day to see if he had found me a job.

The next day, he told me two ladies needed help with their laundry twice a week, and if everything worked out, he would help me find more work. That afternoon I met the ladies in the church. When they asked where I lived the priest quickly answered, "Elena just moved from the countryside and is staying with a friend." I would never get a job if people knew where I really lived. Thanks to the priest, I got more work. He and I became friends and I went to mass at his church every Sunday morning.

As soon as I started working, I rented a room big enough for Lili, her sons and me. But she didn't want to move. She was still

52

hoping her husband would come back. I visited her often and gave her money when I could.

One day, they were gone and the whole area was empty. People said the police destroyed everything and evicted everyone. Many ran away, afraid of being jailed. There was no sign of Lili or the boys. For several days, I looked for them but never saw them again.

I often went to bookstore by the square as I waited for Lili. I spent hours there even though I couldn't afford to buy books. The owner gave me two long unsold: "Dom Casmurro" and "O Cortiço." They were the first I ever read.

One afternoon, I was sitting in the square, reading "Dom Casmurro" when an elegant gray-haired lady with a gray-haired dog approached me. I saw her occasionally at the square and at church, but I always sat in the back while she sat in front. She never talked to me before. This time she surprised me with a friendly smile and a greeting, "Good afternoon." No one of such high class ever spoke to me before.

She introduced herself as Dona Rosa. She was a nice, pleasant person. That first time, we chatted for about an hour, sitting on a bench. She said "Dom Casmurro" was her favorite book and it pleased her to see a young woman reading it. She thought Capitu, the main female character, was intriguing and she had many theories about her. I was surprised how a single character could make for so much discussion about a book.

The next day, Dona Rosa came back to the square with her dog and again sat with me. This time, she asked about me. She was curious why I was usually in the square. I gave her a quick summary, skipping the two years of bordel life, and said I always wanted to come to a big city. I told her about meeting the priest, and the laundry work he got me. I enjoyed having someone listen to me; it wasn't often that someone cared enough to hear a life story.

Dona Rosa listened with considerable attention, occasionally with tears in her eyes. At first, I thought she was sorry for me, but after a few afternoon conversations, I realized that she was sorry for herself. It was odd. Here was a person who seemed to have everything, but who constantly complained about the smallest issue. After a while, though, I think my story began to rub off on her. She started to feel guilty for not being grateful for what life gave her.

Our conversations in the square continued for several days. She wanted to know about my life and I wanted to learn about the books she read and the places she went.

One day, she said her gardener was ill and she needed someone to replace him. She asked if I wanted to help her.

We walked to her house—it was more like a mansion—and went straight to the back. I was curious to look inside the house, but she was more interested in showing me the garden. It was a beautiful spot. There were flowers of every color. I thought of Mother, who loved to keep flowers around our home.

With great pleasure and with Dona Rosa's guidance, I pulled weeds and cleaned around the flowers. She bent down next to me and we worked together until the dusk.

Ah! I remember that deep smell of the flowers.

After a while, she offered me a snack; I was hungry. We had chocolate cake and orange juice. It was a pleasant Brazilian afternoon (I feel as if I was there now). We laughed, and I was happy. I didn't know I could be so happy again. She was amazed at my skill with garden tools and she asked to see my hands. Holding them, she saw they were working hands.

Evening came. She wanted to pay me. I really didn't want to accept as she had given so much already. But she insisted. I needed the money.

I was still doing the ladies' laundry twice a week, and Dona Rosa continued hiring me for small jobs at her house. She paid me well. Slowly, I started to save some money.

Dona Rosa and Padre Jonas showed me a good side of humanity at a time when I doubted there was any goodness at all. They made me feel loved and worthy of kindness. They lit my shadowed world with a newfound hope that never died. From them, I learned that forgiveness helps people continue living. They told me each time I forgave someone, I gave myself a chance to look ahead with optimism. *Forgiveness is not a favor we do for someone else, it is a path to our own inner growth. No one can live "happily ever after" without forgiveness.*

Dona Rosa's gardener, Mané, never returned to work. He was very elderly. He and Dona Rosa were lifelong friends and company for each other from the time his parents were slaves of Dona Rosa's parents; a strange beginning to a friendship. They spent long hours together in the garden, especially after her husband died. Now with Mané leaving, she was even more heartbroken and lonely. I recognized the situation well.

Many times in my life, I felt that everything happened for a reason. It all has to do with our destiny, even when it is unknown. I had this impression again when Dona Rosa offered to hire me full time. I promptly accepted. I was tired of laundry.

For lodging, Dona Rosa gave me the small house in her backyard. It had two bedrooms, furniture and everything else I needed. It was as if I had finally found my place in the world. Ah! Dona Rosa, my dear good friend. I was a child in that new world. But I was ready to become part of it.

Except for Padre Jones one day in confession, I never told Dona Rosa or anyone else about my two years in the bordel. I'd rather those years never existed. I was determined to become the woman I wanted to be, not the woman others expected.

Gradually, Dona Rosa increased my responsibilities and my pay. With her help, I took care of the gardens, kept the clothes and did light housekeeping. Another woman, Clotilde, cleaned almost daily. Most of all, and unpaid, I enjoyed being Dona Rosa's companion. She was a constant and excellent cook, and I learned many kitchen skills from her.

The days went by quietly as we spent the afternoons in her garden and talked for long hours. I loved listening to her stories. She was like a queen at the other end of the sugarcane industry from me. While I came from the deprived and exploited side, she lived in the satisfied side, full of elegance and wealth. She had the kind of life we could not even dream about. The luxurious lifestyle of Dona

Rosa and her kin were attained on the bent backs and cut hands of husbands, wives and children who slaved in the cane fields.

She was the only daughter among four children of the most influential sugarcane mill owner in the region. She was her father's beloved princess and her mother's dream. To her brothers, she was the well-behaved sister, and to her husband, the chosen wife in an arranged marriage. She lived by the rules. She lived in silence. She lived in a world her parents chose for her. I did not know whether she was oblivious, or just accepted living without making her own decisions. She was never responsible for her actions. She just needed to say "yes" to everyone and hear orders without complaining. I compared Dona Rosa to Julio because both in the end accepted the rules and expectations of their parents.

However, Dona Rosa had sadness without definition in her eyes. She had a life without the vibration and passion that makes eyes sparkle and hearts pound. Something was missing in the woman who, others always thought, had everything.

While I liked Dona Rosa, I wasn't sympathetic to her sadness. Every room in her house, every jewel, every pair of shoes, every piece of clothing that rich woman wore derived from the labor of others who sacrificed their lives and health day after day in the cane fields of her parents and forebears. Yet I also was grateful and felt ashamed of my thoughts. She did not choose the life she lived, but simply accepted it regardless of what she wanted. I often felt sorry for "poor" Dona Rosa.

She married José Rosalvo, the son of a well-known farmer who was a large and rich supplier of sugar cane in Alagoas. She told me that at first she did not like her husband. He was an arrogant young man and everything was supposed to be the way he wanted. She also said he made her miserable and, a few times, he hit her. For some time, the husband too was upset because he had no choice in the marriage. She sensed he loved someone else. As a young couple, they seemed condemned to a kind of opulent misery. But as time passed, they became friends and companions, and within about five years, they had made a strong, loving relationship.

Her husband built the sugarcane mill and grew the family businesses. Dona Rosa managed the household and raised their two sons: Marcos and Vicente. Marcos was one of the directors of the mill; Vicente managed the farms. Marcos married, but had no children although Dona Rosa suspected he had a child outside the marriage. Vicente was also married.

Marcos would visit his mother about once a month. He always seemed busy, and was arrogant and rude. Most of the time, he did not acknowledge my presence except when we were alone. I hated him because he reminded me of a time that I hated myself.

Once when the family was having dinner, I was in the kitchen cleaning. Marcos appeared and surprised me.

"Do you have any fresh coffee?"

"Yes sir, I just fixed it."

"Serve me."

I served him and he tried it.

"It is not good. It needs more sugar."

With that, he grabbed the sugar bowl and held it up to me. I continued washing dishes.

"Elena, I need more sugar in my coffee," he said.

"Sir, you have the sugar-bowl in your hand."

Dramatically, he poured the coffee on the floor and said,

"This coffee was already too old. You need to clean up this floor; it is dirty."

He ignored a call to him from the dining room. "Do you know Elena? I have efficient ways to teach you to obey me." And then he left the kitchen. Fortunately, for me, he never had a chance to prove his threat.

I thought Marcos was an unhappy man. His friendships were measured according to wealth. Marcos himself was only a wealth object. Take that away, and he would have been a body without a soul. It was obvious to me that he was more attached to money than to life. Consequently, he was more afraid to lose the former than the latter.

Dona Rosas's other son, Vicente, was different. He was polite.

He often visited, usually once a week, sometimes more. He was a good man. "His only problem is his wife," Dona Rosa used to say. Suzana, his wife, was always complaining she hated living on a farm. They constantly argued about it. She wanted the excitement of the city, she loved shopping, partying, and the beach. By contrast, he was a quiet man who liked the country life. Yet they had a bond: two daughters, whom they adored.

That was Dona Rosa's predicament when I met her: widowed and alone, with two sons who were unhappily married. That summed up her life. "But," people used to say, "She has all that wealth!" Everything revolved around money. They were always talking about what belonged to whom. They belonged to money.

Once I was in my new job and received my first week's pay, I wrote to my mother again. I told her everything that had passed and sent some money too. She almost wrote me back, describing events from the village.

Some of it was shocking: one of my brothers was killed while resting in a field when a worker accidentally ran over him with a plowing machine. There was Julio's marriage. There was my mother's sadness for my father's continuing indifference to me. People were often moving in and out of the village. Those were hard times for farm workers. Jobs were scarce and Brazilians were forced to move constantly to find work.

But there was also good news: weddings and births mainly.

We began to correspond.

Meanwhile, I was working my way into a world where I did not socially exist. It was not simply that I didn't have it with me, but that no one ever recorded my birth or provided identification. So like many at the time, I was never officially born, I did not officially exist.

Dona Rosa was the first to explain the importance of and need for a birth certificate. She used her wealth and connections to help me get one. With what I remembered of my family, we calculated my approximate birth date and adopted my real mother's maiden. "Maria" was her first name and "Santos" her middle name. So I became "Elena Maria Santos." With this, I was issued a birth certificate stating my place of birth as Maceió. I was nineteen years old at the time.

Thanks to Dona Rosa's encouragement, I went back to school. She also taught me how to dress nicely, speak well, use makeup, have good table manners, cook and take care of a home. Then, she invited me to live with her in the main house. I did so, but with great reservations. As it turned out, the move was not accepted by most of her family and it was the cause of argument. Only Vicente supported it. But I did not care for their opinions. It was Dona Rosa's decision that mattered.

I became a teacher in Maceió when I was twenty-three. With Dona Rosa's introduction and recommendation, I was accepted to teach in a public elementary school. Public jobs were given only to those with connections.

I loved to teach. I felt at my best when I was in a classroom filled with children. By then, I had become quite different from the young village girl of several years earlier. People in Maceió respected me for my teaching and because I had Dona Rosa's support.

But during the time I lived with Dona Rosa, I was not able to avoid the jealousy of her daughters-in-law. They did not like the idea that someone who came from such a poor class/pobreza could earn such a big place in Dona Rosa's heart and home. They were also afraid that Dona Rosa would write me into her will. Also, Vicente's wife, Suzana, did not like my good relationship with her two daughters and that Vicente treated me the way he did.

As long as Dona Rosa was around, her son's wives tolerated my presence. But they really did not care for anyone. And for sure, they didn't care for each other.

One afternoon, Dona Rosa and I went to church to visit Padre Jonas but found he was occupied with confessions. We waited a while and then went back home. Approaching the house, we saw someone there and thought it was Vicente. But when we got close, I saw Marcos kissing and fondling Suzana. I tried to divert Dona's Rosas attention, but she saw them, too. I took her to the garden. We sat, in shock. I may have expected a lot of things from the family, but not that. Dona Rosa made me promise that I would never tell anyone. I did, but at the same time, I wished Dona Rosa was not there so I could laugh in their faces.

Then the whole drama intensified. We looked up and there was Vicente and the girls coming up the walk. Dona Rosa flushed red. To alert the two inside, I started to talk very loudly.

"Hello, girls! How you are doing? I haven't seen you two for about two weeks already," I said, hugging them and making as much racket as possible.

"Elena, do you know Sassy had puppies?" the girls asked me with excitement.

"No, nobody told me anything; how many puppies?"

"Nine!"

"Wow! And how are they doing?"

"They are good; Daddy is helping us take care of them."

"I am sure they are getting special treatment."

"Where is Grandmother/Vovó?" "She is watering the flowers. I forgot to do that side this morning. And you know how Grandmother is about her flowers."

"Oh, Elena. I think you are in trouble," Vicente said.

"Yes, I guess I am. She's a little upset. But I think they will be fine."

"Did you see Suzana or Marcos?" he asked.

"No, are they here?"

"Yes, they are inside. We came all together to see Mom. But she wasn't here and the girls wanted to go to the store, so I took them there and went to the post office while we waited. I got a letter from my friend Matthew in the United States."

"We just came from church. Dona Rosa saw that some of the flowers were a little sad, so we went straight to the garden."

Then Suzana appeared in the doorway. "Vicente, where are the girls?"

"They were just here. Ah, they are with Mom," he answered.

"I was wondering what took you all so long to come back," she said, approaching. Then, she continued, "You know I don't like your brother."

We all went inside. The rest of the afternoon was peaceful. Dona Rosa tried her best to forget the scene but I could see it was repeating in her mind. She knew that adultery was not only a sin, but a crime: if proved, it could put Suzana in jail, and the publicity alone would destroy the family's name.

Days later, she talked to Marcos and Suzana separately. The incident remained in the back of our minds, at least in mine.

A few more years passed. Dona Rosa grew older and worried I would never marry. She wanted me to have a husband and family, and introduced me to some young men who might have mutual interests with me. But they seemed to be more interested in Dona Rosa's wealth.

Also, I didn't feel ready to marry, or to love a man. I chose to stay alone; life was easier that way.

But Dona Rosa would not give up the idea that every woman should be married by a certain age. Thus, we accepted every social invitation. Even when she didn't attend, I had to represent her. She seemed to be invited to every event in Maceió, and I was never to miss one. I especially abhorred weddings. Young singles at weddings were easy targets for old ladies' questions. Dona Rosa would say, "You are a teacher now, a member of society, it is your duty to be there. What will people think if you don't go?" Or she'd say, "You are a member of the church, and everyone is going." Or, "You have to represent me there, I don't feel well. I can't go and they know you live with me. If you go it is like me being there."

One wedding was especially disturbing. As always, Dona Rosa and I arrived at church early and sat in front. From there, we had a close look at the ceremonies. First, the couples, friends and family would appear and give their testimonies to the marriage. Then the parents, the groom, and the bride.

This particular one seemed to be just one of the many usual weddings, but it suddenly changed when the third couple entered the church. I did not recognize her but I certainly knew him: Julio. He looked older. The church was full but I stared knowing that he would find me. And he did.

Julio was even more surprised than that night in the bordel. I could not look away. For a brief moment, I saw the friend, the boy that could only make me happy, the young man that made my heart beat harder. He and his wife passed by, and it was all gone again. Side by side, they found places near the altar.

During the reception following the ceremony, the bride's father introduced Julio and Luiza Valério to Dona Rosa and me. Luiza was the bride's cousin. Julio made look like we were new to each other. For the third time, he denied me. Politely, he left to talk to the groom while Luiza briefly spoke to me.

"The name 'Elena' is rather notorious in our village."

"Why? Are there many Elenas there?" I asked.

"No, not really. Just one whose story is often repeated. But we live in a small village and any little thing that happens becomes big news."

"What happened about this Elena?" I inquired.

"Ah, she did what many poor girls do to change their lives. They grow up like wild animals, and have no self-respect. I'm sorry, I shouldn't say that. I will not burden you with stories. You probably have no idea the kind of girls I mean. City life is so different."

"It's not a burden," I said, "just the opposite. Actually, I'm quite interested in small town stories."

But Luiza said, "I can assure you that a woman like you would not survive a week there."

Our conversation ended as Luiza's son Vitorio came over. She introduced him and said he was six years old. Though he seemed to be a sweet boy, he reminded me of his Grandfather Mr. Valério.

Julio and I had no chance to talk and neither of us sought out the other. I felt I could read his mind, but I also knew I could not trust my feelings. The passing years gave me better appreciation for when we were children. If I knew Julio, he was miserable with Luiza. Or maybe I never knew Julio at all.

Soon, Dona Rosa got tired and I was ready to leave. As we departed, Luiza invited me to visit their farm whenever I liked. It was just a formality of the moment.

Back home, I tried to forget the meeting, but something changed. Julio was no longer a dream. At the wedding, he became human to me. He was no longer above me. We were no longer the rich boy and the poor girl; we were man and woman.

Dona Rosa became ill, so much so that she couldn't keep up her busy routine. She needed help walking, and her physician became an almost constant presence. I took care of her with the help of a nurse that Vicente hired. She stayed with Dona Rosa mornings while I taught school from eight to noon. Vicente remained close to his mother and visited almost every day during her final months.

One afternoon, Vicente and I waited in the hall outside Dona Rosa's room while the physician attended her. Vicente told me, "Marcos was the absolute favorite of our father, everyone knew it, and Marcos was very proud of it."

"But," I said, "you are your mother's favorite, I'm sure."

"More for protection than for admiration and love alone," he replied. "She knew it was hard for me to live up to father's design and expectations when I was always compared to my brother. Marcos and my father really had a connection. Marcos knew how to please him in every way. He would absolutely obey his orders and acted exactly as was expected. I could not, and I had no desire to do it."

He continued, "The truth is that my family has been just an image. My mother wanted to believe my father was the ideal, perfect, loyal husband. But that was far from the truth. I think we never really knew my father. When I was eighteen, Marcos was twenty-one and went to France to live with an uncle for a year. My father wanted me to follow my brother's footsteps. Probably, he didn't want me around, he wanted Marcos back. Well, I refused to go to France; my brother had his history and I didn't want any of it.

"So instead, and even though he thought France would be more useful for family and business purposes, my uncle offered to send me to America where he had a friend at Yale University. That was fine with me, I just wanted to leave Alagoas. It was the best two years I ever had. It was the first time I had complete freedom."

"But weren't you scared to go so far away alone?"

"No. It was exciting! My mother was the one who was sad and afraid; she tried to keep me here. When I was overseas, I often thought about not returning. I spoke English well, I had a lot of friends. Life was so different and I liked it there even with the cold winters. I could have stayed. But in my second year at Yale, Mother started to send me persuasive letters. I knew I had to come back."

I said, "I am glad I don't have to go anywhere. Even though I never left Alagoas, I think I traveled enough. Besides, I have everything I need right here."

Vicente replied, "I think there are many places you would like to see."

"But," I said, "there are also many that I would not like to see and we never know what we may encounter on our way. I don't want to take the risk."

"Maybe that is why my mother trusts you so much," he said. "She knows you will not go anywhere."

"I wish she would not go anywhere either," I said sadly.

"I know. But there is nothing we can do any more, Elena. You heard Doctor Jorge." After a pause he continued, "When my father died I felt nothing but guilt for not being able to cry or feel bad. But my surprise was that Marcos didn't seem sad either. It made me wonder if either of us loved him. It also made me want to be a better father than he was."

"I never met your father so I can't say anything about him. But I can say something about you. Vicente, you are a wonderful father and you know your girls love you. I can even say they care more about you than about their mother. Please, don't tell this to Suzana, she would not like that."

He started laughing and then I did.

"I know I will miss Mom, and the girls will, too. I can't imagine, Elena, life without her. Marcos and I probably will drift apart and our only common subject will be the farming and sugar *business."*

"Don't worry Vicente. Perhaps your brother will change and you two will have a better relationship."

"Elena, you will see snow in Maceió in December before Marcos sees me as his brother. There is no reason for him to change."

On a beautiful September afternoon, Dona Rosa peacefully died. Only Vicente and I were there. Just before, she asked him to always protect me. She sensed that without her presence, everything would change; and it did.

Two days later, a local official read Dona Rosa's will before Marcos, Mariana, Vicente, Suzana, and me. Everything except a savings account was equally divided between Marcos and Vicente. I was the only other person mentioned. She left me a very generous sum.

Marcos and the two wives were furious. They told me that I should not accept "that favor" because Dona Rosa did not know what she was doing when she signed the will and she had give me enough while she was alive. Vicente told them he was present when she signed it, and that she knew what she was doing. He said if they tried to contest it, he would testify in my favor. Nevertheless, the three of them gave me twenty-four hours to leave the house. Dona Rosa, Vicente, and I knew that would happen, and so I already had found another place.

Later, I was alone packing when Suzana came. She wanted to tell me what she could not say in front of Vicente and Dona Rosa.

"Your days of rich-girl living in a big house are over. Your god-mother is gone and you can go back to where you came from."

I had no intention of replying and carried on packing. She continued, "I know what kind of woman you are. Do you think I haven't noticed how my husband and my brother-in-law look at you? You are a witch. But it did not work with Marcos and it will stop with Vicente because I will kill you if it doesn't."

I wasn't offended. In her, I saw a woman desperate to understand why her husband treated her the way he did, a woman asking for attention.

"*Look at you, so delicate; looking like an angel. But in reality, you are a demon. I cannot understand how my mother-in-law was fooled.*"

My silence was making her nervous. She wanted a reaction to feed her emotions and I would not give her one.

She yelled, "Do not ignore me! Look at me when I talk to you!" She grabbed my arm.

"*Let go,*" *I said firmly. She held on. I looked at her and said again slowly, "Let go."*

"*You deserve to be beaten like the dog you are,*" *she said, still holding my arm.*

"*If you do not let it go right now I will show you what a dog can do to your face.*"

"*Now you are showing off,*" *she said freeing my arm.*

"*Touch me again and you will see,*" *I said in a lower voice.*

"*Animal. You are an animal.*"

"*Touch me again and I will show you,*" *I repeated. I got closer to her face, and said, "We both know who is the woman two brothers share. Do you really think nobody ever saw you and Marcos? Poor Dona Rosa died knowing what kind wife Vicente has."*

I truly wished she had grabbed me again. I was ready. But she didn't.

"*You are not worth it,*" *she said. "Get out of our lives. I do not want to see you ever again. And, be careful with whatever you say. It may kill you."*

Early the next morning, Vicente helped me move my belongings. He was the only one who knew my new address.

During the next few months, it was hard to live in Dona Rosa's absence. I missed her company. Secretly, Vicente visited me a few times. Mostly, he talked about his parents and how it was for him growing up. I was uncomfortable talking about myself. When he realized it, he stopped asking. But I enjoyed his company.

I continued teaching, giving most of my time to the children and their families. They were from a poor part of Maceió, and many had a hard time putting food on the table. Hunger was everywhere.

Living by myself and not having Dona Rosa gave me time to be more involved with the children, and I could pay more attention to their needs. I used some of what Dona Rosa left me to help their families.

It was also a difficult political time. Brazilians could not freely express their opinion, afraid of being called "communist" and sent to jail. The father of one of my schoolchildren was jailed and tortured to inform on his brother who opposed the government. He didn't know where his brother was. With Vicente's influence and the help of the church, we got him released from jail.

When I learned what my schoolchildren were going through, I suggested that the church organize a daily supper, and Padre Jonas supported the idea. Most parishioners agreed and some of us helped financially. My days went from home to school to church to home. I was happy with it and did not ask for anything more.

One day, in Bible study, we discussed freedom and human rights. Suzana was there for the first time. She interrupted me, screaming that I was a "communist" and her "husband's mistress." She claimed I shouldn't be at church. Ten minutes later, she was still screaming when I just walked away.

Next morning at school, Vicente and Ms. Aline Cordeiro, the school principal and my friend, were waiting for me. They thought I should not work that day because the local authorities had sent someone to investigate an accusation of communism against me. They said the way things were going it would be very hard to prove I was innocent. I didn't understand, but the truth was that I didn't care to prove or not prove anything to anyone. If they wanted me, they could take me. I wasn't for or against the government, I just wanted a better life for the children and their parents. But Aline convinced me I would not do any good if I was dead, and then Vicente suggested that I flee the country.

That hit home. Evidently, Suzana was so angry that she would do anything to manipulate the situation. She had turned all the influential ladies against my being a teacher, a member of the church and Maceió society. Plus, now there was talk about the supposed relationship Vicente was having with the girl his mother had helped so much... a communist who wanted to organize poor Brazilians against the government. It seemed the authorities had put me on a list of political suspects, faster than lightning, just because of a word. Vicente said he couldn't defend me because every time he tried Suzana became angrier. And others were afraid to take my side for fear of being called communist too.

Vicente said he tried to convince the authorities of my innocence but they advised him to persuade me to leave Brazil because Suzana would get people to testify against me. Vicente, the mayor, and the police chief knew she wanted me jailed and tortured. Then she could visit me in jail just to see me defamed and deformed. In fifteen days, I had all my documents in order to flee to the U.S., while the chief police delayed the investigations.

Having studied two years abroad, Vicente was still in touch with a few friends. He sent telegrams and they all replied positively, saying they would help me when I arrived. After several messages back and forth, they decided I should stay with his friends in Boston, Massachusetts.

I did not want to leave Brazil. It didn't feel right. I was born Brazilian, and it was my country. At the same time, I did not feel particularly courageous. Once, my father had almost killed me, and I did not want to give someone else the chance to do that, and perhaps succeed. There was no reason to stay. The authorities knew I was innocent but would bow to Suzana just because of who she was. Once again, I gave up to what life offered. I didn't fight. I just did what I had to do: I left Brazil.

I did not know anything about America, I didn't speak English and didn't know the laws. But I trusted Vicente and put myself in his friends' hands. I thought, "Sometimes life takes us to strange places. It is time to go again."

The night before leaving, Vicente, Aline and Padre Jonas came to my apartment to talk for a while and say goodbye. I asked Aline to send two letters for me, one to my mother and the other to Suzana. Then I told Aline to donate the rest of my books and belongings *to the church. I hugged her and she left.*

Padre Jonas gave me his blessing and left as well.

And just before Vicente left, he kissed me and said, "I am sorry."

And I said, "I am sorry too."

That was it. It was all over again.

The next morning, taking only a small suitcase with me and my remaining money, I went to the harbor and boarded a ship. My life in Brazil was over. I felt I would never return, I felt displaced. At that moment, I wished I had my real parents with me and thought "If they knew me, they might had loved and protected me."

I turned another page in my life.

On the ship, I dealt with the unknown by trying not to think of what was happening, I stopped trying to understand the reasons behind life. Many days, I simply stood at the rail and stared at the sea. Once, I thought I would just jump overboard and end the constant running away. But that passed. Then, excitement set in, but that too waned. Most of the time, I remember looking out at the sea, towards the horizon.

That was the end of the first journal folder. It had become dark outside. Elena was with Grace in Maine, and I was on my bed reading by the lamplight. On balance, I wondered whether Elena was really forced to leave or if it were just easier for her to escape Brazilian society than fight it. It must have been around fifty years ago. While I couldn't judge her, it made me think of all the others who didn't have a choice.

CHAPTER 6

On Monday, I went back to Elena's house early, before she returned. I had borrowed her journal without permission and wanted to put it back in its customary place. The pages had probably never been out of the house, much less across town; yet the stories in them spanned thousands of miles.

Later that morning, Grace arrived with Elena. "It was a long trip," said Grace as she helped her mother over the doorstep and into an easy chair.

"But I am glad we did it," Elena replied.

"I know," said Grace, "Portland seems so different now. But it was good to see old friends…"

After some tea, Grace left Elena in my care. I noticed Elena was holding a black-and-white photo. Curious, I looked. There were two little girls, one about ten years old, one a little younger, and they were building a tall sand castle.

"Who are they?" I asked.

"This is Grace," Elena said, pointing to the older one. "And this is Sam."

That was a new name to me. Elena continued, "Brendon's mother. She died. Grace and Sam were very close."

"How did she die?"

"Oh Cecilia, I don't want to talk about it. And you know, Brendon is coming next week. Please don't mention Sam to him."

Elena was somewhat melancholic that day and, at times, even distressed.

During that week, I completed reading the first folder to Elena. Then, as if there were a deadline, she gave me a second folder to read aloud:

Emily and Matthew McGhee, two of Vicente's friends, met me in

New York City. Matthew and Vicente were at Yale together and took some of the same courses. They remained friends and often corresponded, even through the war, mostly in English but occasionally in Portuguese. As a result, Matthew and I could communicate a little.

From New York, we drove several hours to Boston where they lived. The drive was at times terrifying. I never saw such tall buildings. They looked like they were leaning over the roads and that they might fall down on top of us. In Maceió, we had a lot of cars and some buses but nothing like this! Everyone, including Matthew, drove so fast in the cities, even faster on the highway.

I lived with them for about a month while they helped me to find a place of my own in Charlestown in the northern part of the city. Through them, Vicente sent me some extra money for a few months. Thanks to Emily, I found some cleaning jobs. The pay wasn't much but the work was a start in a new and very different country. Emily also helped me find part-time work in a plant nursery. It was difficult, though. I missed everything Brazilian: the food, the music, the books, my friends, and the language. And my lack of English made it worse. It was so overwhelming that at some point I thought Brazil was all I wanted.

After the past few years, I thought I could handle anything and would be unaffected by external forces; but they still hurt. I felt like a child again. I felt like a leaf carried by a mighty river, without control over even the basics. It was humiliating to hear people talking and not understand what they were saying. I was overwhelmed by all I had to learn. Here I was, an accomplished schoolteacher feeling stupid and lost when people approached me. Also, to me, Americans spoke too rapidly. I was most comfortable in my jobs, especially working with plants and flowers. They didn't need conversation.

My apartment was near the route of Boston's elevated trains. They rumbled all day and evening, every ten or fifteen minutes. Only the width of the sidewalk three floors below separated them from me and when they passed, the building shook as if from an earthquake. If that were not enough, there was a neon sign above the storefront downstairs. It flickered red and white all day until midnight.

The trains stopped around midnight and let me sleep until a little after six in the morning. They became my alarm clock. On waking, I would make coffee and leave for work. It was about a block to the nearest station, then a brief ride downtown, then through a long tunnel that scared me half to death. I transferred to a train that went to Allston, a very different neighborhood to the west of the city. Then I walked for a couple more blocks to the nursery.

My first few trips, Emily rode with me and marked the stations and the changes on a "subway map." Later, I got lost a couple of times. When I asked some people, they just looked at me funny and walked away. Once, I asked a policeman for directions, but he didn't understand me. When I showed him the map, he took me to the correct platform, pointed to the location on the map and showed which train to take.

But the trouble of getting lost and the other things that went wrong in those first days were worthwhile once I got to the nursery. I loved the work. The owner and the workers were kind and helpful. Soon it became my full-time job. The people made my period of adjustment worthwhile. They helped with my English and taught me the names of the flowers. I liked the work as much as anything I had done before, even as much as working for Dona Rosa.

It wasn't that way with some of the nursery's customers, however. Once, a woman said, "You Puerto Ricans are all alike. You can't even speak English." She kept talking but I did not understand what about. Some regular customers even refused my help, so we decided that whenever they entered, I would go to the back of the shop and a white American girl would help them instead. In Boston society, there were the whites on one side and the rest of us on the other.

I sensed those walls being erected around me. I became self-conscious of my skin, my hair and eye colors. Once on the way home on the subway, a young man yelled, "Hey nigger lady! What are you doing here? Go back to Roxbury where you belong!"

There were times when I was accosted on the street and propositioned. Even black men did it. I did not understand what they said but I knew what they wanted. I just kept walking and fortunately was never followed very far.

I imagined all this as an invisible enemy, and I learned not to fight back. I learned to accept and go along with it as a means of protection.

Two years passed, through two full cycles of those distinct Boston seasons. I kept to my work, learned English and adapted to the culture. I became more and more distant from Brazil.

I was fascinated by the changing weather, and its impact on life in New England. I loved autumn. When summer was about over, the trees told change was on the way, with tones of green, red, and yellow. Humans were also susceptible. Winters, I was calm and enjoyed an afternoon cup of chamomile tea and a book – Hemingway, Steinbeck, Faulkner and others. Even now, the weather boosts me, the spring's happy sounds of the returning birds, then the bright summer mornings when I can walk on the beach and enjoy the crash of waves alternating with the serenity of low tide.

I enjoy all the seasons, but was definitely at my best during fall. It was during the fall months that I began writing this journal. At first, this made me miss some of the Brazilians I'd left behind. I thought I'd never see them again. Also during the fall, I could walk down by the docks in Charlestown. I could look across the water and see Boston's skyline, not quite as tall and dense as New York's. Emily taught me the subway route to the Public Garden, a place so beautiful with all its flowers and flowering bushes. I especially loved riding the swan boats in the Garden pond and feeding the ducks that swam alongside. I also learned the route to the Charles River and its Esplanade Park, and to the various museums.

During my first summer, Matthew and Emily took me to the Esplanade to picnic and to hear the outdoor music. It was July Fourth. The park was packed with all ages of Bostonians and tourists, lots of young people like us, some single, and many families. Each had blankets for the ground. The stirring music was played by the famous Boston Pops Orchestra, led by Arthur Fiedler. We were lucky enough to sit near the stage. Fiedler's long white hair bobbed wildly as he waved his baton. The stage was set into a large enclosure that looked like a big pink ball cut in half. Emily called it the "Hatch Shell."

This Fourth of July was during the Korean War. Because thousands of American soldiers were overseas, the audience was overtly patriotic. The evening opened with the "Star Spangled Banner", so everyone stood at attention and sang the solemn words. Then everyone cheered and clapped. It was very emotional. The conclusion of the concert was a Russian patriotic piece called "1812 Overture." Near the end of it, loud cannons were fired and church bells rung all around the city. Then came the fireworks! At first, I was startled but then when Matthew told me what they were and I just watched in amazement.

Matthew was a civil engineer and Emily was a nurse. Matthew's best friend, also his business partner, was George Woodard. I met Mr. Woodard and his wife at Matthew's house. They seemed a happy couple. She was as beautiful as an angel. Seeing her, my first thought was that some people were just born to be happy, while others had to struggle through life. She was perfect and seemed to have a perfect life.

One time, I accompanied Emily to Mrs. Woodard's house in Cambridge. Mrs. Woodard's baby was almost due to be born and Emily had just learned she was pregnant. It was a pleasant visit, both of them talking about their babies-to-be. They urged me to find a husband and have my own babies. We laughed, but I never told them I could not have children.

Three weeks after that visit, Mrs. Woodard died giving birth to their second child who was to be named Grace. Her other child, Michael, was only five.

Reading this, I paused and then continued. Elena had become

very attentive.

Mr. Woodard was devastated. Emily helped him with the children. For myself, I felt guilty having previously envied her good fortune in life. Maybe if we had never met, she would still be alive, I thought.

Mrs. Woodard's sister, Doris Parker, also helped with the children for a couple of weeks. But she had her own family and that made it impossible to also care for a nephew and baby niece. And as Emily was pregnant and busy at work, she couldn't handle things by herself. So she asked me, and I agreed.

At first, Emily took care of the children during the mornings while I was at the plant nursery, but soon I became the full-time nanny. Grace, so small, was a beautiful baby; Michael was a great help. He loved to care for his baby sister. They were very close from the time she was born and came home. nanny → step niece

Michael was shocked by his mother's death. He did not understand where she went and why she didn't come back. Many nights, he was too agitated to sleep, so I read stories to calm him. He was a sweet boy. He helped me in the garden and watched me prepare dinners. We invented a routine to help him through the next few years. At bedtime, he'd pray for her to visit him in his dreams. For months, I thought he did not even know my name. Slowly, Michael became attached to me and I felt close to both of them. I knew Grace's cries and when she was tired, hungry, or just wanted love. Fairly soon, they were not just my job but the most important people in my world.

Mr. Woodard was almost never home. For months on end, he became married to his work. Often, he stayed in his office overnight, and many days I did not see him at all. As there was no one else to stay with the children, I ended up staying at the house. If I needed to go to my place, I would either leave them with Emily or take them along with me. During this time, Mr. Woodard seemed to be a selfish, miserable man. He completely neglected the children. At first, I gave him the benefit of the doubt. I thought his behavior was understandable given the terrible loss. But then weeks went by without a word or a touch from him to Michael and Grace. In a way, they had lost both their mother and father.

I was angry at him. I thought no one needed affection more than Michael and Grace, but he chose to feel for himself first. Soon, I wished he wouldn't come home at all, and that wish was pretty much granted by his long absences. He would be home only late evenings after everyone was in bed, and then he'd leave the next morning before anyone woke.

Because of it, Emily arranged for me to stay with the children until they found someone who might be better qualified. But that someone was never found. I moved into the house despite the uncertainty of who would eventually care for them.

One night, Mr. Woodard came home earlier than usual. Michael and I were having dinner and Grace was in my arms. I got up and put an extra plate on the table, with Grace in her highchair. Mr. Woodard sat down and for the first time had dinner with his children. I didn't go back to the table because I suddenly felt out of place.

After dinner, I put Grace to bed; then Michael. I read him a story and kissed him goodnight. Turning off the light, there was Mr. Woodard in the doorway. He looked at me and then left. When I went down stairs on the way to my bedroom, he was waiting for me in the living room, a drink in his hand.

"Who are you?" he asked.

"Sir?" I did not know what to answer.

"I asked, who are you?"

"Sir, my name is Elena Santos. I am the housekeeper and I help Emily take care of your children."

"How long you have been here Elena?"

"About five months, sir."

"Then, why don't I know you?"

"I don't know, sir."

"Where are you from?"

"Brazil, sir." After a silence, I asked, "Anything else, sir?"

"No."

I went to my bedroom hoping that he would not be at home the next day. I did not know how to act in front of him. It was extremely uncomfortable. I felt he wanted to show me some kind of superiority, and I was worried he might want me to leave. But I didn't want to leave Michael and Grace. We three had become attached in many ways.

The next day, I woke early as usual, and had coffee before the children rose. Before I finished my coffee, there he was again.

"Good morning."

"Good morning, sir."

"May I have some coffee, please?"

I served him. Then, I began Michael and Grace's breakfast.

"Can I get you anything else?"

He was reading the newspaper. "No, thanks. I'm fine."

I went upstairs. Michael and Grace were awake. I changed Grace's diaper, took her in my arms and went back to the kitchen for breakfast. Michael was excited to see his father but Grace didn't notice him.

Mr. Woodard touched her head and, "Hello, you. How have you been?"

At that, she smiled. Then to Michael he asked, "Michael, what do you want to do today?"

"Elena promised we would work in the garden today."

Mr. Woodard looked at me blankly. My blood turned cold as ice. Then he said: "Okay, how about Elena showing us what has to be done in the garden and we can do it together?"

"That would be fun, Daddy," Michael excitedly answered.

"Okay," Mr. Woodard replied. "That's how we'll spend the day."

We were all in the garden, busy as bees, when heavily pregnant Emily came with groceries for the week. Emily was surprised and glad to see Mr. Woodard with the children. Everyone was happy, the happiest in a long time.

Before I could tell her about my short conversation the night before, Mr. Woodard took Emily to the porch. They talked for a long time. Again, I was afraid they'd make me leave. I started wonder-

ing if I could get my job at the nursery back again.

I was fixing everyone's lunch when Emily came into the kitchen: "Hi Elena, how is everything?"

"Fine. Does he want me to leave?" I asked, almost crying.

"Who?"

"Mr. Woodard. He doesn't seem happy with me."

"No, that is not what is happening. He just doesn't know what to do. He's afraid to be a single parent.

"He acted as if he didn't know I was here taking care of the children."

"He knew you were here, but he didn't know how to approach you. He is trying to put his life back together."

"What does he want me to do?"

"We will change a few things. I cannot do the groceries any more. I am feeling too heavy to do anything like that, so you will do all the shopping and house cleaning. He also wants you to help him with the children. He wants to be closer to them. He wants some time alone with them. He knows his children love you, and he is thankful for it. He does not want to separate you, but just needs some time alone with them."

"Michael is very happy to have his father with him."

"I saw that, too. It's a good sign." Then she began talking about her pregnancy. She was radiant, more beautiful than ever…

The next five years went by. We established a routine. Michael grew up quickly and Grace had become a beautiful little girl. Mr. Woodard was home every evening at six. After dinner, he played cards and games with the children. He wanted to know about their day. Michael and Grace enjoyed the evening routine, especially during winters. Summer weekends, they'd go to Revere beach for walks and amusement rides. Other times they played in the yard. Sometimes after school, Michael would have friends over to play, and other times he'd visit them. He always called to let me know where he was, and came home before dark and on time for dinner. I knew that I was not officially part of their family. But when nobody else was around, I was one of them. I didn't have to please Michael and Grace to have their love. Maybe that was the first time I felt unconditionally loved.

Meanwhile, Mr. Woodard was still very reserved with me. Our conversations were limited to things about Michael, Grace, and housekeeping.

One day, Emily came to the house and said Mr. Woodard invited a woman to dinner with the family the next Saturday. He wanted me to talk to the children about it. I was surprised, but suspected what was going to happen. As he was still young, everyone expected him to remarry. That was the thought I had, and my heart was broken. It meant I would have to leave; everything would change again. Dutifully, I told Michael and Grace to expect a guest for dinner.

Saturday evening, Mr. Woodard introduced me to Judy. She was polite but I was distressed; this woman was going to usurp my relationship with the children and everything in the house.

I prepared and served dinner but I was not part of the family. I dealt with the situation by stayed in my room for most of the evening.

For the following Saturday, Judy invited them to have lunch at her house in Portland, Maine. It became a big event for them. Mr. Woodard gave me the day off. For hours, I just wandered around town, shopping a bit but feeling strangely exposed without the children. Later I went back to the house and spent the rest of the day cleaning the kids' rooms and preparing their favorite dinner.

One morning a week or so later, Emily called and asked me to come see her. I took the bus and walked the quarter of a mile to her house. I knocked, and she opened. And there was Vicente suddenly before me. He looked much older. For the first time, I could see he was ten years older than me, although still very handsome. The three of us chatted for a while, then Emily excused herself to work in the kitchen. Vicente and I spent the afternoon on the porch talking about Dona Rosa, Brazil, Vicente's family, and my new life in Massachusetts. Emily joined us from time to time while doing chores.

At one point, he asked me, "Do you want to go back to Brazil?" I seldom seriously considered returning. His question made me at least briefly consider the possibility.

When I did not answer immediately, he continued, "Officially there is nothing prohibiting you from going back. Besides, you do not have to live in Maceió. There are plenty of towns and villages that always need teachers."

"Vicente, I will always be thankful to you. You are the best friend anyone could have. I know you worry about me, but I am fine here. I do not want to go back to Brazil and I cannot go back."

"Elena, are you sure? Brazil is your country. There you can have your own place and see your mother."

"Vicente, you know I loved to teach and would love to be with my mother again. But from what I hear Brazil is in crisis and if I went back, with my luck"—we laughed— "sooner or later someone would accuse me of something. I want to avoid that. Besides, Michael and Grace are here and I can't leave them."

"I heard you have been like a mother to them."

"And they have been like angels to me."

"Elena, no matter what you decide, you know I will always be there for you."

"I know. Having your friendship makes me feel like the luckiest person."

When it came time for him to leave, Emily called a taxi. In a few minutes, as it approached, Vicente asked, "One more thing: did you send Suzana a letter?"

"Yes, I did."

"It seemed to have had a great effect on her, at least for a while. She even burned it. And as far as I know, you two are the only ones who know what was in it."

"And, we will keep it that way."

"I understand."

The cab was there; it was time for him to leave.

"Good-bye, Elena."

"Good-bye, Vicente."

He kissed me and left. Even though we kept in touch for years later, that was the last time I saw him. — Vicente

Emily gave me a ride back home, but we did not talk much.

Many times, I wished I could control the events in life. Vicente was one whose mere presence calms one's heart. I wished I could have kept him close.

That night after dinner, Mr. Woodard asked about my afternoon at Emily's. I replied, "It was lovely."

"Why?" He again asked.

"Because an old friend visited me."

"Must be a very close one to have come all the way from Brazil."

"I never said he was from Brazil. How do you know?"

"You said he was an old friend," he said laughing.

That struck me as the most intimate conversation we had had in five years. Mr. Woodard was an interesting man. But once again, I was associating with someone above my class. I had my place and he had his. To him, I was like the air we breathe: essential but taken for granted until we have trouble breathing. He had his house cleaned and in order, with beautiful flowers in the summertime, food on the table on time, clean clothes, children who are healthy and well cared for, and with no one to ask where he slept on Saturday nights.

For Mr. Woodard visited his girlfriend every Saturday for about a month until Grace suddenly caught the flu. I took her to the doctor who gave a prescription and ordered bed rest. That Saturday Mr. Woodard's girlfriend, Judy, came for dinner again. She asked if she could take care of Grace and told me I could take the time off. But Grace heard it and cried, saying she wanted me to stay with her.

"I'm sorry," I said. "I cannot leave her."

Judy said, "It's okay Grace, I'll stay with you." She patted the girl's blanket.

"No, I want Elena to stay!"

"Don't worry Grace, I will stay with you too," I said

Judy said, "Okay, I will be downstairs with your daddy. I hope you feel better soon, my dear." With that, she went downstairs to the living room.

About an hour later, Grace was sleeping quietly. I went downstairs. Mr. Woodard and Judy were talking. I was tired and intended go to my room.

"Elena!" Judy called out. "Grace seems very attached to you," she said.

Mr. Woodard said, "Elena has taken care of Grace since she was born. It's natural she would feel that way."

I said, "I'm sorry but I'm really tired. I'll go to my room."

Judy said, "I understand and I'm sorry to burden you. I know you work hard here. You must be exhausted. Good night, Elena."

From that time, Mr. Woodard spent Saturday evenings at home. Judy never returned to visit.

Late one night, I went to check on Grace. Mr. Woodard was in the living room by the phonograph, listening to his favorite song, "As Time Goes By." I tried to pass without disturbing him when he called out: "Elena, would you like to dance?"

"Sir?" I said. I couldn't believe my ears.

"Please, would you like to dance?"

He restarted the song, came over to me, and we danced. I was not sure if it was a dream or reality—but I wanted it to last forever. I could smell his scent and feel his body. I felt safe and secure in his arms. He controlled my senses, but I didn't care. It was suddenly a perfect picture, a portrait of my ideal life.

While we were dancing, though, I suddenly imagined Julio, and remembered that the most beautiful moments were fleeting, temporary. I could not stop the clock. So before the song ended, I pulled away and ran upstairs. I spent the rest of the night with Grace.

A couple of weeks later, Emily dropped her son Max by the house to play with Grace while she went shopping. When Emily returned, we shared a pot of chamomile tea.

"This may be a severe winter," Emily commented while looking out the window.

"I think Grace was sick because of the weather."

"I know. How is she doing?"

"Much better now. But I was very worried; I never saw her so sick."

"I'm glad it's over. George was worried too."

"I know."

"Elena, when Judy came to see Grace, the visit didn't go well."

"She came but it was a bad time," I said. "Grace was sick and she is not used to other people."

"It was a difficult situation for Judy. She did not mean to offend you or upset Grace, but just to help."

"I understand."

"There's a bigger picture, Elena. Judy and George have been close for a long time. He was her only love. They went together all through high school and were going to get married after he graduated from college. But then George met Mary. Judy was devastated and never married. And then the War came. Her brother was an Army officer and went missing in action. They declared him dead but he was never found."

"I'm sorry," I said.

"Do you know that George and Matthew were Army engineers, building bridges and things like that so that the Allies could attack the Germans? They did it under some harsh conditions. George saved Matt's life when the Nazis attacked their bridge, and the abutments under Matt collapsed. George risked his life to save Matt."

"I did not know that."

"Matt's brother served as naval officer during... But back to Judy. A few months after Mary died, George called her. They talked on the phone several times, then he went to see her in Portland. She was with him when he needed someone to talk to and then to share affection. All these years, she was waiting for him to bring her home as wife."

"I'm sorry."

"Only Matt and I know this."

"Why doesn't he marry her?"

"Because of you."

"Me? I never did anything."

"It's not your fault. I think the truth is that he never loved her the way she loves him. She is, was, his 'safe harbor,' but that's all. He goes to her when he feels alone."

"But why is it because of me?"

"You made a big change in his life."

"Emily, please. We hardly even talk. You and I both know that Mr. Woodard sees me only as his servant. I know who I am for him: I am the woman who cares for his children. He doesn't even see me. Anything else is nonsense."

"Elena, you're wrong. George is your biggest defender. Maybe I shouldn't tell you this… The business has not been doing as well as Matt and George anticipated. They are working hard, but just few days ago a customer and his wife went to George's office to tell him that they wouldn't do business with him because he was keeping you here. George immediately terminated their contract and only later told Matt."

"Oh! Emily. I don't know how much more sorry I can be. I seem to be a plague for everyone, everywhere I go."

"No, Elena, it's not true. You have been a light for Michael and Grace. You have been helping Matt and me so much by seeing after Max, too. Everything is easier for us because you are here."

"This is of no help if they are losing business because of me."

"Elena, it's only a few clients, and they won't lose their business just because of that. I just told you so you'd understand how much George thinks of you."

"I love Michael and Grace but I know my time here may not last…"

"Don't say that. What would George and the kids do without you? Don't even think about it. This is exactly what George doesn't want to happen. He's afraid one day you'll leave them. Besides, George has no prejudice."

"Emily, my dear friend, he does. You must know it. He's probably suffering because of it." I continued, "I know this is going to stay between us; this is why I am trusting you with my heart. I think Mr. Woodard doesn't know what to do. He thinks he needs to choose between going on with his life and keeping his children's life the way it is. You are wrong when you say he's defending me. I know I'm not one of his kind. He may defend what I do or what I represent but not what I am. If wasn't for my childcare and housekeeping, he would be the first to ignore me as he would other immigrants and Blacks in America. Mr. Woodard has his own convictions: he's a white man."

"Elena, why do you talk that way? George is not the color of his skin."

"Why not?" I asked. "Isn't it what we are all made to be?"

"You might be right. But you're wrong about George. I hope you'll learn that. We don't have to accept prejudice from anyone."

"Emily, I'm sorry, but it is easy for you to say. You don't have to deal with this system. You are not in my skin. The worst is to deal with those who are so close that it gets to where they don't even know what to do with their preconceptions."

"What are you trying to say?"

"It's not important. I know that sooner or later Mr. Woodard will marry again and everything will change. I am ready for it and I hope the children will be too."

"I think you are underestimating your importance to George."

"Underestimating? Emily, please. For five years, he has shown me how important I am. I am as important to him as any other servant that may come to this place and love his children."

"You do not understand. Without intending, in five years you became what Judy always wanted to be... essential to him."

"Emily, I don't understand. How can I be essential to a man who does not need me? I'm confused. What are you trying to say?"

"Elena, when George married, Judy believed it wouldn't work because Mary was not a good match for him. She thought he would always think about her, Judy, as the perfect woman instead. Judy loved George too much. She believed Mary and George were a mistake because they were completely different people. George wanted to marry, have children, work as an engineer, and have a simple life. Mary was the gorgeous and talented woman who passionately wanted to be a singer. She absolutely enchanted George with her beauty, and he captivated her with his intelligence.

"You know," she continued, "Mary's parents kicked her out of the house when she was eighteen because they did not like her lifestyle. That's when she moved to Boston. Meanwhile, George had a poor relationship with his father who was very dominating. He told George that Mary was not someone he should marry. So George married her almost in defiance. After a while, neither George nor Mary was happy. They thought it would help to have children, but nothing improved."

"They seemed to be happy," I said.

"They kept up the appearance. He didn't want his parents to say anything. When Mary died, George felt guilty because she did not have the chance to pursue her dream. She gave it all up. Then, he went back to his safety net, Judy. But soon after, you came along and everything changed…"

"Emily, you asked me to help him with Michael and Grace."

"I know and I am glad I did. They love you. You brought happiness to this house that it never had before. George was grateful to come home and see Michael adapting so well to the situation and Grace growing healthy and happy. This was the happy, simple life that George always wanted. He says you are an excellent cook and gardener. He enjoys coming home after a long day's work and having dinner with you and the children. He enjoys reading bedtime stories to Grace and playing games and talking to Michael almost as an adult. He's enjoying it all. He also knows that if he marries again it will mean that you would have to leave, because no woman, even Judy, would accept you in the house with the relationship you have with the children. He would not let Grace and Michael lose you because of that. Judy came to visit when Grace was sick because she wanted to prove a point. But she was not thinking clearly."

"I'm sorry, Emily, really; I didn't mean to interfere. I love Michael and Grace and I didn't realize how much it would affect Mr. Woodard's life."

Emily concluded, "George is a decent man. I am sure he is doing what he feels is best. "

The long conversation with Emily told me more than I ever knew about Mr. Woodard, but at the same time, it left me very confused. I felt I never knew what he was thinking. Although I saw him daily, he seldom talked to me, and when he did, it was never about himself or about us. Emily was sort of our go-between.

Even though Mr. Woodard was often vague with me, knowing he needed me was satisfaction enough. Once more, I gave myself up to what life had to offer. I tried to not think about him, and instead concentrated on the housekeeping and the children. That was plenty.

That morning came. The yard was green and we had some windows open. Elena was excitedly awaiting Brendon, but I just wanted to avoid him. Everything about me was wrong that day: My clothes were uncomfortable, my hair was wild, I felt shorter, my hands seemed bigger, and I was not sure when to speak Portuguese and when to speak English. Through the morning, I wished he had decided not to visit. Meanwhile, neither Elena nor I could stop looking at the kitchen clock.

It was 11:08 when I heard a car drive up. I looked through a window. It was Grace, John and Brendon. For a moment, I stared, knowing he could not see me. He hadn't changed, just looked a bit stronger and taller. His smile was still there, the reason why girls constantly fell at his feet. I felt that way all the time, too, but I admired him just like now - through a glass window.

Elena was in the living room and I didn't know if she heard the car. Grace's voice announced the visitors as they all rushed inside. Brendon went over to Elena and hugged her while the rest of us looked on.

"Oh, Brendon, how much we missed you. I am so happy to see you."

"Grandma, I missed you too and I am happy to be here."

"Tell me, how's Abby?"

"Abby is fine. Busy, but she'll be here this summer. Grandma, I'm glad to see you looking so well," said Brendon.

"Sorry for breaking the moment, but I can't stay. Golf club's waiting," said John.

"Oh, John you play golf every weekend. They won't mind if you miss today," Grace said.

"Of course they would. I'm their only competition."

"Oh, please. I didn't see 'competition' last week."

"That was different; I wasn't feeling well last week."

"Sure…"

"What?"

"Don't worry, Uncle John. Go on to your game. I'll keep the women company."

"You'll be fine without me. Brendon, these two did not stop talking about you the past couple of weeks. I'm glad you are finally here and I think you should stay the whole summer."

"Such selective hearing you have," said Grace. "I didn't expect you were listening to us."

"Honey, not even my selective hearing was able to ignore you. But I love you anyway, you know that. And I'll see you at home later. Brendon, can you give your aunt a ride home?"

"Sure, Uncle John."

"Elena, I'll see you tomorrow. 'Bye Cecilia," he said while leaving the house.

"Oh, Cecilia, you were so quiet there that I didn't even notice." Grace asked, "Brendon, do you know Cecilia? You two went to high school together. Do you remember her?"

For a second I thought he wouldn't. But he said, "Hi Cecilia, how are you?"

"Good, thank you. How are you?"

"Good. Good to see you again. I think I haven't seen you

since graduation."

I was going to say, "I thought you didn't see me at graduation, either" but I caught myself and said, "Yes, it's been six years."

"Do you still play soccer?" he asked, smiling.

"No. Not since high school."

"Cecilia, you played soccer?" Elena asked

Brendon jumped in. "Grandma, she was the best soccer player in the whole school. Cecilia, you didn't tell them? She was like a star. Everyone came to see her play..."

Was he talking about me? I was afraid to correct him.

"But I remember you all were very good at sports. I always heard good things about your and William's coaches. And, Abby, my goodness she was a fantastic dancer. Do you remember?" Grace asked.

"Of course I remember. We were up to our ears in activities, and much of that we have to thank you and Grandma. But Cecilia was really talented. Every game, she surprised us with a new play no one expected. I really thought you would try for one of the big teams. I followed the World Cup just to see if you were with Brazil or the U.S...."

Elena was listening, trying to read between his words. I was listening too, doubting this was the Brendon who never talked to me directly through all of high school. I didn't know how he even knew I was from Brazil.

"Oh, Brendon, my goodness, you exaggerate. You're embarrassing Cecilia."

"Please Cecilia," said Elena, "forgive Grace. For her, if it's not Brendon, William, Abby, or Claire, it's not good enough. She's always been this way."

"What do you mean?" Grace asked, as if Elena had hurt her feelings.

"Sweet Grace, don't take it badly, but you do this all the time. Brendon probably remembers better than I do. Whenever other parents said how proud they were of their kids in sports or school, you always said how much better Brendon was, or William or Abby or Claire. You could never accept that anyone was better than them in anything.

"That's not fair. I am proud of them, sure, but I'm not that bad. Cecilia, I didn't mean to be rude. I'm sorry."

By then, Brendon and Elena were laughing and I was feeling sorry for Grace.

"Don't worry Grace, I didn't take it that way" I said.

Grace continued, "Brendon, yesterday I saw Steve McCarty and he asked about you. He's renting a place on the beach with his girlfriend. Can you imagine they already have four kids? They are adorable, but my lord, they are busy bees."

"I know he loves that girl," replied Brendon.

"I am sure he does. But I was surprised he knew you were coming. Are you still in touch with him?"

"Of course. Not just with Steve, but with a lot of others from school."

"Sure. I just didn't know."

"My dear Aunt, there is a lot you don't about us... I mean, about me. Now, what do you all think about going out for lunch?"

I was happy to be included. We went to their favorite restaurant in downtown Hampton. I felt as if we were all in high school again where everyone knew everybody and I was the outsider who only had outsiders for friends. In the restaurant, I knew two people: Peteco, the dishwasher, and Soninha, one of the girls who cleaned the tables, and the kitchen after hours. But it was not by coincidence; most of the restaurants employed someone I knew or had heard about.

The hostess greeted Elena and Grace and welcomed Brendon.

Showing us to a table, she said, "Brendon, you will never guess who's here."

"Cindy?" Brendon guessed.

"Right! Have you seen her already?" The hostess seemed like

she wanted to keep the conversation going.

"No, just a guess, considering her father owns the place. How is she?"

"She's fine, beautiful as always. I'll tell her you're here. I know she'll love to see you all."

I remembered two Cindys in high school. Of one, I just knew her name. The other, besides her name I also knew she was close to Brendon. With all my heart, I wanted 'Cindy' to be the first one, but it was the other.

"Oh my gosh! Hi, Brendon! It's so good to see you again," said Cindy as she approached.

Brendon stood and gave her a high-school kiss, "Hi. How are you?"

"I'm happy to see you."

"Do you remember Grandma?"

"Of course. How are you, Mrs. Woodard? Mrs. Andrews, always so beautiful. How's Abby and William?"

"Very well, thanks. She's still in school, studying to be a veterinarian. I hope she'll come back and open a clinic in the Seacoast. William is very busy in Florida.

"That's wonderful. Brendon, please sit. I won't bother you. Your waitress is coming. Brendon, call me. I want to see you again while you're here."

"Cindy, do you remember Cecilia?"

"Yes, I was trying to remember from where. How are you? I didn't know you were still in the area."

"I am," I answered. "How are you?"

"Good, thank you. Just very surprised see you here. I thought you returned to Mexico."

Everyone paused and looked around. Then Grace said, "Cindy, you know Cecilia is from Brazil right."

"From Brazil? Silly me. I always thought it was Mexico."

"Cecilia's been our lifesaver. When Mom had the stroke, John and I didn't want her to stay alone, and she refused to leave the house for a nursing home. Thank God, we found Cecilia.

She's taken such a good care of her." I don't know why, but from Grace it sounded like an advertisement.

"You look very well, Mrs. Woodard," said Cindy.

"I feel well," Elena said.

"Here she is," Cindy said. "This is Liz. She will be your server today and I will let you enjoy your lunch. Brendon, call me?"

"Sure. I'll see you." He kissed her again and she left us to lunch.

I was afraid that encounters like that would happen all day until the whole high school class would be reunited in kisses and pleasantries. But the rest of the afternoon went without further incident. After lunch, we dropped Grace at home and everyone else went to Elena's.

Elena and Grace made sure to keep Brendon busy. Daytimes, he patiently abided by their plans as if he knew what to expect and how to make them happy. Evenings he had to himself, however. He would usually go out and then return after midnight.

The fifth night, he came home earlier. Elena was sleeping and I was in the library transcribing her journal into the computer. I heard his car drive up and hoped he wouldn't look for me. We had never talked alone and I was not ready for it now. Of course, I always dreamed of being alone with him at some time, and in the dream, I had the perfect words ready, and the perfect manners. But the words I cast out into the real world were never that flawless.

Brendon walked into the house and came straight to the library. "Hi Cecilia, I'm glad you're still wake. Steve, Cindy, Colin, and a few others will get together tomorrow at Cindy's. They asked if you'd like to come, too."

The last thing I wanted was to see Brendon and Cindy together. I said, "I don't think I can. I have to stay with Elena. But thank you."

"If you want to come, I'm sure Aunt Grace would watch Grandma for us."

"Brendon, thank you, but I don't want to burden Grace or

Elena. It is very nice of you all to think of me."

Brendon said, "I decided to stay a while longer. This week went by so quickly that I had no chance of doing everything I wanted."

"I am sure Elena will be very happy."

"I know she will... Good night.

"Good night."

I couldn't go back to transcribing that night.

CHAPTER 7

The next few days, we all grew used to having Brendon around. He was left to manage on his own, spending days with his old friends. I resumed reading the journal to Elena:

That winter was harsh, with several snowstorms. It snowed almost every other day. Schools were frequently cancelled. Mr. Woodard spent more time home, as many of his construction projects were delayed. Usually I would do the snow shoveling, but Mr. Woodard would sometimes help, and he made sure we had enough wood for the fireplace. Somehow, the cold, crisp weather also started to bridge the distance between us. Shoveling together, winter cups of hot chocolate in the kitchen, sledding with the children and other small times we shared. The weather, though, began to be more than I could handle. Hard times I could live with, but my body wasn't built for constant, bitter cold. There was never snow in Brazil, only two "weathers"—hot and cool. Never cold. In Boston, the frigid, damp weather cut to my bones. I became ill with something that slowly took me over. At first, I tried to keep working: Michael and Grace needed me and I had nowhere else to go. What would I do if I couldn't keep working? I thought if I became useless, Mr. Woodard would let me go. I believed I had a verbal contract: a salary and a place to live in exchange for taking care of his family. His children's love was also immense payment. I was afraid he'd put me in a hospital and hire a replacement. The thought depressed me. It sapped my strength and started to take away my reason to live.

One morning, I couldn't get out of bed. I had a high fever. I lost track of time and where I was.

I had all kinds of dreams and hallucinations that weighed me down and dominated my mind. I couldn't remember much afterwards, only an impression, like mere fragments of a jigsaw puzzle. It was as though I was living my life over and over again, without an end or beginning, and without logical sequence. I was powerless, without desire. An image I remember was of a healthy and beautiful baby in my arms. Suddenly, the baby started to bleed until its whole body dissolved in blood. I screamed in desperation, but to no avail. The image repeated and repeated until a child appeared and took me from the scene to somewhere brighter and more peaceful. When at one point I looked at the child's face, it was little Grace. Right then I realized it was a dream and I knew I had to wake because Grace needed me.

I opened my eyes, confused and weak. I was in a hospital. The dream subsided; reality returned. Emily was with me, just like always. She said Grace and Michael were well, but missed me. She also assured me I just needed to rest. I was exhausted. Even breathing was painful.

I was hospitalized for a week, but it felt like a month. Mr. Woodard visited me every day. He did not replace me; instead, he cared for Michael and Grace himself. When I was well enough, he and Emily took me home. Riding along, I thought, "Home for me is where Grace, Michael and Mr. Woodard live." They were my family.

Once home, I recovered quickly while the house itself got back to normal. But some things changed forever. Mr. Woodard and I spent more time together talking about ourselves, our favorite things, books we read, music we loved to listen to, places we'd been and people we met. He taught me to enjoy a glass of a good wine while listening to music on quiet evenings by the fire.

My life was sweeter and warmer than ever. The following two years affirmed our friendship. We took Grace to her first day at school. We watched Michael play baseball. We had good moments and wonderful memories from a time when we learned to trust, support, and love each other.

I knew how important I was for them, but it was sad to see how uncomfortable Mr. Woodard became when "church" and "Elena" were spoken in the same breath. On Sundays, I helped Grace and Michael get ready for their father to take them to church. The rules of the institution were strict and the gossip was inevitable. Emily and I thought it humorous when the women chattered about my "living with" Mr. Woodard. They had many names for me. But they were so hypocritical. One of them was cheating on her husband and she thought it was a secret. And the same married men who claimed I had no self-respect in front of their wives would then proposition me for dinner or other private trysts. One of them "wanted to learn more about Brazil." Clearly, this church was an institution that led people to become hypocrites and betray themselves.

Mr. Woodard's company was not doing well. There were not many construction contracts. Our lifestyle became restricted. I no longer took a full salary; instead, I drew on some of my savings to help with the household. The more involved I became with the family's problems, the closer I got to Mr. Woodard.

Although their business had once been good, Matthew and Mr. Woodard realized things were slowing down, and it was time for a change. They decided to sell the company and the land it had accumulated before it was too late. Also, Emily had a good job prospect in Florida, and she was tired of the New England winters. Matthew wanted to try the construction business in the South while for Mr. Woodard it appeared there was new construction starting north of Boston, especially in New Hampshire.

They sold the business but remained close friends. Matthew, Emily and Max moved to Florida and Mr. Woodard decided to sell his house in Boston. Having already made up his mind, he wanted to move northward; he looked first in northeastern Massachusetts and then along the New Hampshire seacoast. He searched for months for something that would satisfy the family, be affordable and yet be close enough to Boston. One Sunday after church, he said he wanted to show us a place he liked. We drove northward from Boston.

Now, neither Michael nor Grace wanted to move from Cambridge because they liked their house, their schools and their friends. To compensate, Mr. Woodard wanted to make sure the children would like the new place. But during the drive, they seemed un-convinced. We drove by many towns along the coast with beaches and scenery, and they complained when we didn't stop. Then we passed farms with cows and horses, but those were only minor dis-tractions.

As we went farther north and inland, the beaches faded from view and the complaining increased. They found something wrong with every town we passed. One was too small, another was too crowded, one was too old-looking, another had nothing of interest, another looked dumpy, another had too many trees.

Then Grace suddenly shrieked, "Michael look, the beach!!" "Daddy, please stop. I'm hot!"

"Just a couple more minutes," he said. Then anxiety turned to excitement. For them, a beach compensated for the old home, the old schools and the old friends.

After some turns, Mr. Woodard stopped the car in front of a dark-red house with a wooded yard and flowers all around. Imme-diately, I could picture us there. Michael and Grace began listing all that was good about it: the woods, the big backyard with enough room for a garden, a ball field and a play house all at the same time. Inside, the kitchen was larger than the one in Cambridge. To my surprise, Michael and Grace didn't find anything wrong with the house.

Grace asked energetically, "Daddy, when can we move here?" We all looked him, waiting for his answer. He looked at me. I smiled. Then, he said,

"Soon, very soon."

It crossed my mind that moving to New Hampshire was also a way to escape the gossip about my presence in the Woodard's home.

From the first day at the new house, I knew this was where I wanted to live. The community was much smaller than Cambridge. It was easy for Michael and Grace to adapt. They could walk or ride their bikes to school, and there were so many children around that they were always busy playing or planning what to do next with them. There was a candy store nearby they visited at least once a week. Besides that, they could have their friends over and play in the yard or in the house. They could run around and mess the whole place and I didn't care until it was time to clean up. Then everyone pitched in. They were happy.

I loved to garden and loved the beach that was close by. We had much more land than in Cambridge, so I was able to grow a lot more vegetables: tomatoes, lettuce, cucumbers, corn. I also planted apple trees. My gardens helped us save money. I loved to work outside, especially early mornings or late afternoons; it reminded me of when I was younger in the woods of Brazil.

We would often spend summer afternoons and sometimes all day at the beach. I found it interesting how these towns changed during the summer. What might be a quiet town in the fall, winter and spring, with their storefronts all boarded up, would become an overpopulated, busy, and noisy town in the summer, both exciting and fun. It energized me to see so many happy people together, swimming, riding bikes, eating, jogging, sleeping, talking, building sand castles. There was so much to do.

Remembering my mother, I'm sure she would have enjoyed being with us, away from the fear of hunger, sacrifice, and humiliation. But maybe not. Hers was a completely different world and, for Mother, the village was where she belonged.

We stayed in touch and I received a few letters from her during those years. Mostly she wrote me about new babies or recent deaths. At first, there were more babies then deaths, then over time the news reversed. I also corresponded with an elementary school teacher, Mrs. Marta Peixoto, the one who actually wrote the letters for my mother. That's how I kept in touch with the past. But as the years went, I became less and less connected to it.

There was something new for me, the future. I was becoming part of a family.

I admit I had become as interested in editing Elena's journal as she had been in writing it. In my mind, I thanked her for everything she had committed to those pages. Often, as she described her experiences, I compared her life with other immigrants that I knew. At the time she immigrated to America, Elena was able to avoid some of the problems of more recent immigrants. Even though it was a struggle and she faced prejudice as most of us did later, Elena was never alone, or on her own. She had the support of those around her, and she had their love. And, when Elena arrived, there were not as many non-white immigrants except from Puerto Rico, and they were not as visible as today.

My mother and I went through a long process to become citizens and we were still among the lucky ones. There are so many men, women, and children living in poverty and completely anonymously in America. There are those born here who are the children of illegals and thus under constant threat of their parents' deportation. These children will be stateless displaced persons if forced to move to their parents' home country. Undoubtedly, they will experience exactly what their forebears suffered before they decided to flee. But so many more are arriving every day that it would be impossible to simple legalize everyone who arrives. It is not one government's problem, it is a global issue. But it can only be solved where it starts.

Illegal immigration had become part of the national debate. For some, it was the cause of all problems. The economy was bad because of illegal immigrants. Welfare programs did not work because of illegal immigrants. The tax system was broke because of illegal immigrants. Teenagers were consuming drugs because of illegal immigrants. For some, illegal immigrants were criminals, did bad work, and their kids crowded the schools. Still, illegals were cleaning Americans' homes, cooking meals, growing their crops, and taking care of the children. Some were even inventing new technologies and building houses.

For that moment, I was glad Elena's writings were keeping my mind busy enough to not think so much about Brendon.

The house was fuller with Brendon there. He had a guest

bedroom upstairs, but slight traces of him appeared elsewhere...
a jacket in the hallway, a cup in the sink, a chair moved closer
to a table. He still puzzled me. I was happy to know he would
come through the door at any moment.

Grace came to see Elena and Brendon almost daily. She
seemed to have much more free time. "Not as many people are
renovating their homes," she would say. As the home improve-
ment business took less of her time, she spent more of it taking
care of the people around her:

"Cecilia, do you know if Abby called Brendon today," Grace
asked one day.

"No, Grace, I don't."

"It seems easier to know about her from Brendon than from
anyone else," Grace said, almost complaining. "I miss her so
much. I just wanted her to come at once."

"Isn't she coming next month?" I asked.

"Yes, so she said. But I hope she'd come sooner because
Brendon is here. It would be nice if William and Abby were
here, too, like when they were children."

"That's a sign you're getting old!" Elena laughed. "Cecilia,"
Grace continued, "This evening, John, Mom and I will go out
for dinner. Will you tell me what medication to bring and what
else I might need to do? We want you to take the afternoon and
evening off and spend some time with your friends." She paused
and then said, "We have not been fair with you about using all
your time."

"Grace, please, don't worry about me."

"Cecilia, take the evening off and enjoy yourself. You are
young and you need to be among people of your age." Elena
suggested.

"Good morning ladies," Brendon said, coming into the
porch. He kissed Grace and then Elena before taking a seat beside Elena.

"Good afternoon," Grace replied. "How did you sleep?"

"Well," he said.

"We were telling Cecilia that she can have the evening off. John and I will take Mom out for dinner and then I'll stay with her tonight."

"Isn't today Wednesday?" Brendon asked.

"Yes, why?"

"Because they'll have fireworks on the beach. Cecilia, would you like to go and watch them?"

I looked at Elena for an excuse to say "no" but I didn't find one.

Grace chimed in, "Yes, Cecilia. That would be nice, wouldn't it?"

Unwillingly, I agreed. "Sure, it would be nice."

The rest of the day I could think of nothing else but the awkwardness of going out with Brendon. And would it be just the two of us or the group of friends I was never part of?

Brendon came for me later and at seven we arrived at Cindy's family beach house in North Hampton. Actually, it was a small cottage that fishermen used years ago. When we arrived, everyone noticed us. Brendon introduced me to the group. The party continued its course. There were about fifteen of us, some old acquaintances and some newcomers. Everyone was drinking except Brendon and me.

"Brendon, slow down with that alcohol-free beer or you'll get really drunk!" somebody joked when Brendon reached for a drink in a cooler.

A young woman asked, "We know Brendon is driving tonight, but Cecilia, why aren't you drinking?"

"I have to work early in the morning," I answered.

Another asked, "Cecilia, where have you been since high school? We haven't seen you for a while."

"Just going to school and work, you know. I've just been busy," I said.

"My sister wants to become a nurse but at the speed she's going, by the time she graduates she'll be old enough to retire," a young man called Steve said.

"Steve, yesterday I saw your mom in the store. Is that her new husband?" one of the girls asked.

"Yes, that's him, and it's a funny story. When they met, he told her he had a lot of money but it was all tied up in investments. So right from the first, she started spending her own money whenever they went out to eat or drink or shop. In her mind, she thought that eventually she'd win big-time. Well, two months passed and he asked her to marry him. He gave her a ring that he said cost five thousand dollars and that later when he got his investment money she could pick out an even more expensive one. The same story about a place to live. He suggested they live in her apartment for now, and then later she could pick anywhere she wanted. All this time, Mom was in heaven. She thought she won the lottery and wouldn't listen to anyone.

"Of course, we were all kind of jealous of her good fortune. But just a week after the wedding, he came up with an incredible story that he had lost all his money in the stock market. Then the rent came due and Mom had to pawn the engagement ring. That's when she discovered it wasn't worth but a hundred dollars. Then he came up with a story that he had health problems and couldn't work.

"So now she's thinking about getting a divorce. It would be her fifth. And she's already talking about meeting the next love of her life." Everybody laughed, but I was surprised by the way Steve talked about his own mother.

At nine o'clock some called out, "Fireworks!" and we all went outside.

The whole sky light up like it did during saints' days and church festivals in Brazil. Back then, we used to wait a whole year to see the fireworks and attend the carnival, then we would spend all day watching the carnies setting up the rides and games. Those days always started with the hope that only childhood holds. And then it would always end with my father's drunkenness and with the despair that could only come from a hopeless child.

I looked for Brendon. He was beside me. I felt happy.

Darkness followed the fireworks and we went back inside. Brendon and I sat together while everyone else smoked, drank and watched some bad singers on the television.

"I'm glad you came," Brendon said, smiling.

"Thank you for bringing me," I replied.

"I have to tell you, I was really surprised when Aunt Grace called about you."

"Why would Grace call you?"

"It was about your application to be the live-in nurse. I remembered we graduated together. She was curious to know if I knew you."

"I've always been here. But the strangest thing to me in all is that until this week, I had never heard you say my name."

"Don't you remember me repeating it many times? Didn't you ever hear your soccer fans screaming your name whenever you touched the ball?"

"But you never talked to me."

"You didn't seem interested in making friends."

"That's not true. I had friends; just not your kind."

"Cecilia, you're smart and tough like nobody else."

"Right. While the other girls were sweet and beautiful."

"No, no," Brendon said. "They were afraid of you."

"But I never did anything to them."

"Cecilia, please. Don't you remember?" He signed to Steve to come over. "Steve, who was the girl, the one whose leg Cecilia almost broke in one of those games?"

"You mean girls," Steve said. "There were more than one." Both laughed. "One was Emma and the other Justine. Their parents were really angry."

I couldn't stop laughing.

"Kevin!" Steve called another friend to come over. "Kevin, do you remember what the soccer coach used to tell you guys to make you all play harder?"

"Of course I do. He'd say, 'I'll bring Cecilia to show you

guys how to play soccer!' We all were afraid he'd do it and embarrass us in front of the whole school."

They seemed to enjoy making me laugh. All the stress in high school suddenly seemed childish. I was glad to let it go and relax, at least for a while.

Someone caught Brendon's attention. I looked, too. There was Cindy standing in the doorway of one of the bedrooms. She was on the phone to someone. Brendon and Cindy saw each other.

"I'll be right back," he said to me, and went over to her. Then they disappeared from view. One moment I felt special, the next insignificant. As always, I tried my best to hide my feelings. I turned my attention back to Steve and Kevin.

About eleven o'clock, Brendon and Cindy returned. Her eyes were red as if she'd been crying. Brendon informed us, "We're going to the restaurant, Cindy wants to get something there."

"Slow down Cindy," said Kevin.

"I wasn't drinking alone..." Cindy defended herself. She seemed drunk. "But if I ever needed to drink, today beats any day."

"Who else wants to come?" Brendon asked.

"I do," Steve said.

Brendon said, "Cecilia, you come with me, too."

I didn't argue.

The four of us drove to the restaurant. It was already closed. Cindy grabbed her keys and Steve followed her to the door while Brendon and I stayed in the truck. I asked him, "Can you drop me at Elena's, please?"

"You're not having fun?"

"I'm just tired, and I still have to work in the morning. Besides, Grace is waiting for me."

"Okay, I'll take you home." While we talked, a van drove up and parked in front of us. We watched a man and a woman get out of the vehicle, look at us, and walk to the entrance. As they came under the light from a street lamp, I recognized them.

"Rubens! Camila!" I yelled, getting out of the truck and running to them.

"Cecilia! Que qui cê tá fazendo aqui menina?", they asked.

["What are you doing here, girl?"]

"Tô com uns amigos. A Cindy, a filha dos donos veio buscar algo."

[I'm with friends. Cindy is the owner's daughter, and she came to get something.]

"De novo!! Essa menina sempre vem depois que tá fechado, faz uma bagunça, atrasa todo o nosso trabalho, e deixa pra gente limpar," ["Again! This girl always comes after it's closed. She makes a mess in there, delays our jobs, and leaves everything for us to clean up,"] Camila said putting her hand on her belly.

"Are you okay?" I asked.

"Meu estômago tá doendo um pouco. Mas eu tô bem."

[My stomach hurts a little. But I'm fine.] Rubens added, *"Americano num tá nem ai pra gent."*

["Americans don't care about us."]

Then Camila suggested, *"O Peteco tá ai, vem dizer oi pra ele."*

["Peteco is here, come and say 'hi' to him."]

I walked back to the truck and repeated the conversation to Brendon. He got out and walked with me into the restaurant. Cindy and Steve were in the bar deciding what to drink and Peteco was vacuuming the floors. After I introduced my three Brazilian friends to Brendon, he went to the bar as if he had no time to spare.

Peteco said, *"Essa moça vem quase toda noite pra pegar bebida. Só vem depois que fecha e deixa toda a porcaria pr'eu limpar."*

["This girl comes almost every night to grab drinks. Only comes after is closed and leaves a mess for me to clean."]

Rubens added, *"O gerente tá percebendo que tem bebida sumindo. Ele tá pensando que somos nós que tamo levando."*

["The manager knows there's liquor missing. He thinks we're stealing it."]

"Ele falou isso para você?" I asked.

["He said that to you?"]

Rubens explained, *"Não diretamente. Mas disse pra dona da companhia que tinha garrafas sumindo e que era quando o restaurant estava fechado. Eles acham que so nós tamo aqui depois que fecha. Eles pensam que é a gente."*

["Not directly, but he said to the company's owner that there were bottles missing that could only have disappeared after closing. They think we're the only ones here then."]

Camila hugged me and said, *"Cecilia, você sumiu depois... Aparece lá pra ver a gente."* ["Cecilia, you disappeared after... Come see us."] *"Deixa eu ir limpar os banheiros."* ["Now, let me go clean the bathrooms."] She grabbed the cleaning stuff and went toward the back.

Rubens added, *"Eu vou pra cozinha. Prazer ver você Cecilia, e aparece lá."*

["I'm going to the kitchen. It's a pleasure to see you Cecilia. Come visit us."]

I nodded, *"Apareço sim."*

["I will."]

On his way to the kitchen, Rubens said to Peteco, *"Peteco termina ai e vem me ajudar."*

["Finish what you're doing and come help me."]

Suddenly from the bar, Steve yelled, "Can you bring the mop, please?!" Peteco looked at me, waiting for a translation.

"Eles precisam de um mop." I said while gesturing as if I was using a mop; I didn't know the Portuguese word. He nodded and went to get one.

I walked to the bar. Brendon was propping Cindy up on a stool and Steve was holding her hair back. Brendon gave her some napkins. Peteco came with the mop and Steve showed him where Cindy had thrown up. Even though visibly sick, she laughed and said, "Steve, he doesn't understand what you're saying... He doesn't speak English, look." Looking at Peteco, she said "Hey, just clean everything and don't tell anybody that we are here tonight."

Peteco, who only knew Portuguese looked at me, wondering. Cindy, triumphant, laughed even more.

"Cindy, that's enough…" I said.

"Cecilia, why? It's funny. You used to do the same with us, don't you remember?" Not paying attention to her, I showed Peteco where to clean.

"'Good thing we have Cecilia with us. What we would do without her?" Cindy said.

"Cindy, stop, that's enough," Brendon said.

"It's high school all over again," she continued, resting back in the chair.

I told Brendon I wanted to go home. "If you can't take me, I'll call a cab."

"We're all going back," he answered. "Cindy, can you walk?"

"Sure, if it will make Cecilia happy…"

"Instead of thinking about me," I said, "you should do the right thing. Tell your parents that you've been stealing drinks from the bar. Don't blame innocent workers for what you've been doing." I left the restaurant and waited in the truck. Brendon dropped me at Elena's, then he and the others went back to the beach house.

I was tired but so angry that I couldn't sleep. I went across the hall and checked on Elena. She was sleeping peacefully. I went to the library and brought down her journal. Then I heard Brendon come in. He walked over to me.

"Not tired yet?"

"No."

"'Sorry for how it all turned out tonight."

"That's okay, it's not your fault."

"Don't mind what Cindy said. She was drunk. Normally, she's a nice girl. I know she didn't intend to hurt you or your friends."

"I don't know what her intentions were, but what she's doing is wrong. Those people spend every night cleaning restaurants. In her family's place, there are four big stations to do every night. Do you really think they have time to go around the place following her orders and mopping up after her drunken vomit?"

"No, and we didn't intend to get in their way. And I thought Cindy had her parents' permission to use the bar."

"Well," I said, "it turns out she doesn't have permission because the manager thinks the cleaners are thieves."

"We didn't know that. But don't worry, Cindy will square it all with her parents and the manager." He paused, then said, "I know it's late but there's a photo of my mother that's mine. It's somewhere in one of those old albums on the bookshelves. Can you help me find it?"

I brought down all the photo-albums and placed on the big desk in the center of the room. We looked them over. I didn't know what I was looking for, but wanted to help.

"What photo is it?"

"It shows a beautiful woman," he said, "with a little boy on a beach."

"Okay. Let's see what we can find. "Here's one." I showed him.

"No. That's Aunt Grace with William. But it should be in the same album. Can I see it?"

"Sure." I gave him the album and he looked, page after page. He stopped at one and stared. I knew that was it. He smiled. "This is my mom," he said.

"She is beautiful."

"She really was. She died in a car accident when I was three."

"I'm sorry."

"It's okay. Thanks for your help." He kissed me. I didn't know what it meant. He went up to his bedroom. The house was silent. I went back to Elena's journal.

One day, there was a letter from my mother after a long time without any communication. For some reason I left it unopened for a few days. What could I expect? Probably someone's death.

Finally, I opened it. Yes, it was about Julio's death.

That was when I realized life doesn't last. And I want to tell my story. I want it to live after me. I want other girls to read and to avoid my mistakes. So I began to write this journal the day I read that letter.

According to my mother, Julio was caught in a fire during the seasonal burning of one of his sugarcane fields. While able to escape alive, he was badly burned and later died at the hospital. Before that, he asked to speak to my mother. Workers found her at home and brought her to the hospital. When she saw him, he was already dying. His last words were, "Me perdoe, e peça a ela pra me perdoar também." [Please, forgive me, and ask her to forgive me too.] *In the letter, she wrote, "I was alone with him as he died the most terrible of deaths." Continuing, she wrote that up to then, she hated Julio, but there, she couldn't hate him anymore. She said she felt sorry for him and his family. Until that letter, I didn't know what my mother really felt about him. She never told me. I cannot imagine what it was like for her to see him die under those conditions.*

That afternoon, after early dinner with Grace, Michael and Mr. Woodard, I just wanted to be alone. I walked on the beach. It was early autumn, still daylight. I took the letter and, from the rocks of North Beach, I read it a few more times. I wished we could go back to our childhood again, just once more. I wished I could tell Julio to go in peace, without pain or fear. With love.

Watching the sea, time had no meaning. I don't know, I guess I fell asleep right then and there and began dreaming. Julio and I were playing together again, just as in our childhood. It was sweet. I remember telling him, "Julio, I thought you were dead," and his answer came, "No, Elena; we will never die." Then I heard someone call. The dream of Julio started to fade but I had the feeling he would always be there. When I woke up, there were Grace, Michael, and Mr. Woodard.

Hugging me, Grace asked, "Elena, are you okay?"

I answered, "Yes, sweetie. I'm fine. What time is it?" I had been sleeping more than an hour and it was already dark. They had begun to worry, and went to the beach to find me. We walked home together.

After Michael and Grace went to bed, I invited Mr. Woodard for a glass of wine, and then we talked for hours. He was the man that I loved. I knew everything about him. I could read his thoughts. I knew when he was happy or sad, when he wanted company or just wanted to be alone. I knew when he was upset or frustrated. I could identify his needs and feelings. All this kept me in love with him.

However, through all the years until then, we were both together and apart, because I never told him about my experiences with men. Until then, I was still living in two worlds. That night, however, I opened my heart and told him everything. And, as I talked, my world became lighter and the circumstances that once were reasons for sadness became part of the past.

Only one subject is still unresolved: the baby that might have been born. He or she did not have a chance. I don't lay guilt on anyone; not even on my father. I know there was nothing I could have done to save its life. My baby-to-be was the real innocent, and would always be in my heart.

Mr. Woodard listened patiently. What I didn't tell him yet was that he was the one I wanted for the rest of my life.

Two days later, after the children had left for school, I was watering the garden. Mr. Woodard came from the house and approached me with a look that was part serious and part relaxed. "Elena, please, do not say anything until I have finished. I think you know my true feeling about you. I do not think that I could care for Michael and Grace without you. You've helped me to be a better father and a better man. For a long time, my feelings about you were confused. I wasn't sure, if I actually loved you or if I was just overwhelmingly grateful for your presence. But now, Elena, I love you and I love who you are. If you feel the same way about me, will you marry me?"

It was everything I wanted to hear from him. It was then that

I found a safe harbor and felt my destiny was complete. Yes, I was supposed to be with him, in that place and at that time. My life before this was over. My future began when Mr. Woodard proposed marriage.

I kept my silence. I could not hold the tears. Then, he got in one knee, held my hands, and again asked, "Elena, will you marry me?"

Finally, I said, "Yes, I love you too. And, I will marry you."

And just like that in the middle of my garden, Mr. Woodard became my beloved George, the love of the rest of my life. He was the man who loved me beyond any barriers and who would respect and encourage me to be the person I truly was.

There is no better feeling than to be loved for who one is, not for who one should be.

A few days later, a minister married us in the same garden. Michael, Grace, our neighbor Mrs. Smith and the minister's wife were there. The ceremony was simple and straightforward. Michael walked beside me, and Grace was our flower girl. After the ceremony, we had dinner at home. Mrs. Smith stayed with the children at our house the rest of the night. George and I went to a hotel on the beach. It was a happy day.

I was at the same time overwhelmed by Brendon's sudden attention to me and intrigued by the constantly secret signs that Brendon and Cindy were together. I could not understand why he needed to keep something like that secret.

CHAPTER 8

It was late one afternoon about a week after the incident in the restaurant, when my Brazilian friends phoned me. Immigration officers had arrested twelve illegals in six restaurants. Among them, there were five Brazilians—Peteco, Rubens, Joel, Carmen, and Soninha who had a three-month old baby whom she breastfed. Camila, Rubens wife, was feeling worse that evening and didn't go to work. Her illness saved her.

After the call, I went to the porch where Elena and Brendon were talking. I looked him straight in the eye.

"Cecilia, what's wrong?" Elena asked.

"Brendon," I asked, "where is Cindy?"

"Why? She went to New York for few days. What's wrong?" He seemed confused.

"Do you know what she did? She is evil."

"Cecilia, what are you talking about?"

"She called the immigration service against my friends."

"You must be mistaken. Cindy would never do that."

"Immigration arrested them, including the ones who work at her father's restaurant." I took a deep breath and continued, "Who do you all think you are? Right now one of the poor women is apart from her three-month baby. And just because Cindy wanted to prove a point."

"Cecilia, calm down," Elena implored.

"No, Elena. These people think they can treat us any way they want. To them, we're not human. You know that better than I."

"Cecilia, this is a misunderstanding," Brendon said.

"Brendon," I said, "how can you do this? You know what Cindy did. How can you defend her? Elena, I will call Grace. I need to help them."

"Brendon, go with Cecilia," Elena said.

"No, Elena," I said, "I don't want his help."

"No, you don't. But your friends do. Remember, Brendon will soon become an attorney. I am sure you can use his help to find the right people."

"Why, Brendon?" I said again. "Why didn't you stop her?"

"Cecilia, I swear I don't know what's going on."

Soon, Grace arrived to stay with Elena while Brendon and I went to investigate. The immigration office said that only a licensed attorney could talk with the detained workers. After many calls, we found one in Boston who was fluent in Spanish and Portuguese. He took the case and visited them. Soninha was suffering the most. Besides being away from her baby, she was in terrible pain because her breasts were swollen from not nursing.

After three days, many miles of driving between the Seacoast and Boston and many phone calls to friends and families in the U.S. and Brazil, I became resigned to the immigrants' fate: deportation. There was nothing more I could do for them, so I went home. I absolutely believed that Cindy was the cause of it. But I also felt guilty that I may have started it. Maybe if I hadn't interfered that night in her parents' restaurant, the arrests and deportations wouldn't have occurred.

I don't know if it was from guilt or friendship that Brendon became valuable to me during that time. Certainly, without him, the workers wouldn't have had any assistance at all. The only moments of stress were when Cindy came into our conversations. Brendon was sure she never called immigration, and I felt just the opposite. Over and over, I asked him, "Please, if you have any proof that it was not Cindy, then show me." He always answered, "I can't prove it, but I know it wasn't her."

After some days off, I went back to Elena's and was touched by everyone's sympathy for my friends. In fact, the family helped us pay for the lawyer.

The first opportunity Elena and I had to be alone, she asked me, "Why are you so sure Cindy called immigration?" I told her about the night in the restaurant bar. She listened without emotion and then asked again, "Do you really think that's proof?"

"I really do."

"Don't you think she deserves the least doubt?"

"No, she doesn't. Do you know how much they are suffering? Soninha is desperate because she can't see her baby. Rubens and Camila have never been apart since they married. Peteco has a son with leukemia in Brazil; he was working to pay for the medical treatment—"

"Cecilia—"

"No, Elena. She had no right to do it."

"Cecilia, immigration fined Cindy's father twenty thousand dollars for having two illegals working there."

"Do you think this proves she did not do it?" I asked.

"It only shows that she deserves the benefit of doubt," Elena said.

"She probably did not expect her family to be affected by the situation."

"I don't know," said Elena, "but I trust Brendon's judgment, and he has reasons to believe she wasn't involved."

"His judgment could be blinded by his feelings for her."

"What are your feelings for him?"

"What do you mean?"

"Cecilia, I am eighty five years old. I have seen many things in my life, enough to see how uncomfortable you are when Brendon's around and how you look at him."

"Elena, please, you know it is impossible."

"What's impossible? My dear, you are a smart and attractive young woman. Why would it be impossible?"

"He is a young man with a perfect life. Soon, he'll be an attorney with an ideal family… while I will always feel like an illegal immigrant girl. Why would he ever feel anything more than friendship for me?" I said it with some bitterness.

"Because love is not a set of rules. I don't know how he feels about you and neither will you if you never ask him."

"I can't. I couldn't handle learning from him that he loves another woman. He believes in her unconditionally even though he saw exactly how she was that night. He probably just used me to make her upset and now feels guilty for doing it."

"That doesn't seem like Brendon."

"I'm tired, Elena. I wish with all my heart that my friends are released and given a chance to stay."

"Cecilia, the immigration officers could have acted on their own without anybody."

"It's not likely. The restaurants they hit were the ones Rubens had contracts to clean. Why was that? Besides, they have no criminal records. Immigration would not go after them for any reason."

Elena tried to comfort me. "Let's pray that everything goes well," she said.

The five Brazilians arrested and their families became the focus of our attention. The tension around their fate increased as the days passed. The five become people with real names, not just nameless "illegal immigrants," and they had stories of their own.

Elena's church collected and donated ten thousand dollars to Peteco's family in Brazil to help with his son's leukemia treatment. Others offered their hopeful wishes that the five would be freed as innocent people. Despite this, some simply maintained that illegal immigration was a crime.

Locally, the arrests changed things. Employers, afraid of fines, fired most of the illegals. This meant the workers had to find other jobs. But they still could rent their homes and apartments, shop for food and other necessities, register their vehicles, send their children to school, and pay taxes.

Brendon's interest in immigration law grew as he worked with the attorneys to ensure that our friends would have the fairest possible judgment. He always mentioned how contradictory the laws were and how they would never function properly in practice. One morning when I went to fix some coffee, I found him reading in the kitchen.

"Good morning," I said to him.

"'Morning. You are up early."

"No, you are up early. I wake up every day at this time. Would you like some coffee?"

"Yes, that would be nice, thank you. I couldn't sleep."

"If you tell Elena that," I said, "she'll make you drink chamomile tea. She swears it's good for everything from insomnia to colds, to headaches and allergies." We laughed.

"I wish I could find a way to help them. But it seems there aren't many windows open."

"All the same, I know they appreciate what you're doing."

"Cecilia, in our yearbook you said you wanted to be an attorney, and I know with your intelligence and talent you could have done it. Why didn't you pursue the law?" He asked. I thought of many answers but I choose the one that was truthful and easy.

I said, "My mother and I were illegal immigrants at the time and, as you know now," I pointed to his book, "I couldn't apply for college."

"So, how did you change your immigrant status?"

"Through an amendment that allowed my mother to work, and because I was unmarried and under twenty-one, I was allowed to stay with her and have foreign student status."

"Is that why you are so angry about this case?"

"No, I am not angry because I know what they've been going through. I'm angry because there will be no consequences for the one who started it."

Brendon frowned. "I wish I could prove to you that Cindy didn't do it... I have something to ask you... Abby is arriving this week—two weeks early—as a surprise for Aunt Grace. No one is supposed to know it. Now, Abby and Cindy are very close friends, so can you please avoid commenting about Cindy in front of Abby?"

I put his coffee on the table, grabbed mine, and went to

drink it on the porch. To me, that was all he had to say to put me in my place.

That morning, Mr. Lawrence the immigration attorney came to see Brendon and to spend the day at the beach. He told us that the court dates were scheduled for the second and third week of July. He also said that even though hoping for the best, we should be prepared for the worst. We learned that the only thing we could hope for Peteco was deportation. This was because the group he was originally with had been caught by the border patrol in Texas while crossing over. They had been set free, with later court dates, but disappeared into the country and never showed up for court. He might even be sent to prison.

During his visit, I had the opportunity to ask Mr. Lawrence some questions about the cases and the day of the arrest.

"Brendon, didn't you tell her? The officers received an anonymous call. That is how it usually happens."

Hearing that, it was unnecessary to look at Brendon.

I avoided being around him and talking about my friends. Elena's journal was my perfect excuse.

Adapting to my new role in the Woodard family was a bit of a challenge, even though I was already a dona da casa [the reigning woman] *there. Becoming George's wife changed my world in many ways. I got out of the shadows.*

The next Sunday, as usual, I helped Grace and Michael get ready for church. George, Michael and Grace all looked at me with a question on their faces.

"What?" I asked.

"Aren't you coming with us?" George asked.

"Oh! Yes, of course." I said, surprised. "It will only take me a minute."

I dressed quickly and we all went to church together for the first time. When the service concluded, the minister presented me to everyone as 'Mrs. Woodard.' They all applauded. I was embarrassed, yet so proud. I think I had more love than ever as I looked at

George and then at the children. At the same time, all the attention was more than I could imagine and I knew I was crying. 'Mrs. Woodard' sounded so different to me. It was the first time I had ever been called that except when George said it after the marriage ceremony. But that was more in fun.

Later, I thought it seemed that with my birth and status, I could never have a place in society on my own merits. It seemed unfair that only after marrying a man did some doors open. Just a week before the marriage, I was not supposed to appear at church. When I did, the ladies wouldn't speak to me, and they looked at me as if I were an alien from the most distant of worlds. Suddenly, all that changed when a man accepted me as his wife. The title, 'Mrs. Woodard,' changed everything.

About three months after our marriage, another letter came from Brazil. This was from Mrs. Marta Peixoto, the teacher. It brought devastating news. My mother had died. The angel of my life was gone. She was the last connection I had with Brazil. In a brief period of time, the two most important people of my childhood, Julio and Mother, had gone. Even though we hadn't seen each other for years, it was always important for me to know she was there.

The letter said that Mother passed away peacefully. She went to sleep one night and then didn't wake. She was a healthy woman who never went to a doctor in her life. All her children were born at home. If she had symptoms, she treated them with different kinds of teas. If there is a heaven, my mother is there. She supported her family's tribulations with strength and had an unquestioning faith in God. She did not know how to read or write, but she was knowledgeable. I will be eternally grateful to her. The only reason I survived all those years is because I had her. She used to say, "God would never give you a cross you cannot carry."

The day I learned about her death, I knew I would never go back to that village or to Brazil again. I liked to think of my mother as a place to which I could always go back. I dedicated more time to helping others. I made sure that at night I was so tired from working that I fell asleep easily. I became even more active in church and kids' activities. I liked to see my house full of children. They have such good energy. I had to cook more and clean more, but it kept me busy.

When our friendly minister moved away, a new, arrogant one came to replace him, someone who only cared for how much we pay him. I did not like him at all but kept going to church to please George and the children.

One Sunday, a few minutes into the sermon, a young baby began to cry. The minister stopped and looked sternly at the parents. The baby stopped crying, then the minister resumed preaching. A few minutes later, the baby resumed crying, to the minister's discomfort. Curious, I looked over at the parents and realized it was the minister's own son and daughter-in-law! Grandfather-minister stopped altogether and changed his theme. He talked about how it used to be with his own children when all he had to do was look then straight in the eye for them to understand his meaning. "But these days," he continued, "the new generation of parents don't know how to raise their children."

Right then and there, the minister was humiliating his son in front of the whole church. I couldn't believe it. I was so angry, I was shaking. I rose and started to leave. Before I reached the door, he called to me:

"Is there any problem, Mrs. Woodard?" Why he did that, I don't know. But I could not handle any more.

"Yes sir," I said, "there is a problem. It's you." My answer finally freed my heart. By then, everyone was looking my way. I kept going. "I have a problem with your sermon because you are a bad speaker. I have a problem with how you talk about children. I also have a problem with how you treat your own family in this place. I have a problem with you trying to get as much money as you possibly can from the members of this church. As you see sir, I have a problem with you and this is why I am out of this church." I said it as loud as I could. I put my hat on and walked out.

I felt proud of myself until I thought about George and the children. This might become our first fight. As I walked out, George,

Michael, and Grace followed. We all got in the car. George turned the ignition and looked over to me.

"What just happened?" he asked.

"I don't know," I was looking through the windshield, not at him. "I lost myself when I heard that man humiliating his son. I..."

Then, I finally found courage to face George. He was laughing at me.

"Why are you laughing?" I asked, confused.

"Because many of the people in that church wanted to do what you just did. Nobody had the courage to give that fellow a piece of their minds. I wish you'd seen his face when you walked out the door. Boy, was he angry! And, do you know what? I am damn proud of you."

So it wasn't our first fight. But one came soon enough, this way: after our wedding, I began writing George's parents, John and Louise Woodard, who lived north of us in Maine. I wrote how much I wanted them to be closer to George and their grandchildren. In the letters, I also said that it would be a pleasure to meet them.

Those many years I kept house before we married, George's parents never visited. George just wanted to stay away from them. He said, "All my life, my parents wanted to control my decisions. I was never good enough for them. So I don't want them to do to my children what they did to me." He also said that his parents told him if he married Mary, he was not going to be their son anymore.

More than anything, George wanted Michael and Grace to live in an environment where they could be themselves. George had had a restricted and unhappy childhood. He married Mary only because he wanted his parents out of his life, and he got his wish soon enough.

It was sad that the grandparents were never part of Michael and Grace's childhood. That had gone on for too long. Michael and Grace should at least know them. So after a few letters, they invited us to visit them in Portland on an upcoming Sunday.

I intended to talk with George about this, the same afternoon when I caused such an uproar in church. But I completely forgot.

The next morning, he raised the idea of finding a new church. The conversation about future Sundays reminded me about the invitation. So I said we couldn't go to church the next Sunday because his parents had invited us to Maine. Well, I was not expecting his reaction:

"What? What are you saying?" he asked with the maddest face I ever saw.

"George," I said, "it is not that big a deal. Your parents just want to talk with us and meet the kids."

"How do you know my parents?" I said, "I wrote to them and—" "Elena, who do you think you are? You don't know anything about my parents. You don't know what you're doing, and you have no right to do it!" "George, they are your parents." "Parents, you never had parents. What would you know about them?" he replied.

His words profoundly hurt me. I retreated to the kitchen for a cup of tea. What else could I do? Soon, my tears were flooding down.

"I'm sorry, Elena. I didn't mean to hurt you. I never ever want to hurt you. But you had no right to contact my parents behind my back," he said.

I kept silent.

"You have to understand," he continued, "there are things and people that have to stay where they belong."

"I'm sorry, George, it was a bad idea. I just wanted to help. I should have asked you before I wrote them. I am so very sorry." He hugged me and I knew our fight was over.

Still, we had to decide about the invitation. We had a long talk and, that time, he had the last word: we had no choice but to go to Maine.

During the week, George and I talked at length about his parents and his childhood and about what he was expecting from a reunion with them. It was especially hard for him to imagine talking with his father again. As Sunday approached, he became more anxious.

In contrast, a trip to "Grandma's house" was all that Michael and Grace talked about. John and Louise Woodard had lived there ever since getting married. It belonged to John's father, George's grandfather. At first, John rented it by working with his father on the family's fishing boat. Louise stayed at home. She had four miscarriages before giving birth to George, their only child. The parents worked hard to send George to college in Boston.

By ten o'clock Sunday morning, we were ready for the trip. It was a pleasant drive north on U.S. Route 1. We went through many towns until arriving in Portland.

After few turns here and many turns there, we arrived at the Woodards' home. It was small and white, Cape Cod style, with black trim. It clearly needed a handyman's attention, first some painting, then some windows replaced, and there were shingles missing from the roof.

We got out of the car slowly and walked to the front door. I looked at George and asked him to ring the bell. He said, "No, you do it." So I rang. We heard sounds from the inside. I stepped back with Michael and Grace. An elderly woman already in tears opened the door.

"George!" she said, hugging him.

After a moment, George said emotionally, "Mom, here are my wife Elena, my son Michael, and my daughter Grace." She hugged each of us and we went inside.

Mr. Woodard was peeling potatoes in the kitchen. Mrs. Woodard called, "John, George is here." Mr. Woodard cocked his head, grabbed a dishtowel, wiped his hands, looked at George, and walked out the back door. It was like being in a picture: we all froze until Mrs. Woodard found the words to put us in motion again.

"George, I'm sorry. You all stay here and make yourselves at home. I am going to talk to John." She started to walk through the kitchen and out the back door when George said:

"Mom, stay here with Elena and the kids. It's about time for Dad and me to have a talk." Then he went out the back.

The rest of us finished preparing the meal and setting the table for lunch.

The two men were outside in a shed in the back yard for a long time. After a long wait, we started to eat and were almost ready for dessert when they finally returned inside. They both had grease on their hands, faces and shirts. I thought they might have been fighting but they were talking about problems fixing a car.

George and his father were talking again. Grace and Grandma were acting as though they always knew each other. Grandpa John showed Michael his collections of coins and cards. Most of the time there was Grandma, Grace, and I in one group; Grandpa, Michael, and Dad in another. On our way back to New Hampshire, George seemed relieved. The children were excited talking about their next visit to Grandma's house. But by the time we went through York, Grace and Michael were sound asleep. "It seems you and your father had a good time together," I said.

"We did."

"I was a bit apprehensive when you decided to talk with him."

"I was too."

George seemed as if he didn't want to talk about it, but I was equally determined to know what happened.

"It's good everything went well."

"Yes, it is."

"George, please, just tell me what happened."

He laughed.

"We just talked about our differences, that's all. We didn't yell at each other—I thought we would. I guess I was as stubborn as Dad was, and thought the problems between us were bigger than they were. We have more in common than I thought. All said, they are my parents and they love me, and I love them and want to take care of them."

I was silently crying. He turned to me and said, "Elena, thank you for forcing the issue and not giving up... You know, now they are your parents, too."

After that, George visited his parents every other week and once in a while they visited us. George repaired their old Cape nicely. He and his father had their projects, and they repaired the steep roof. I was alarmed when I saw where they had been working, and warned George not to be up there, but he just laughed and said maybe I shouldn't be visiting when he was on the roof. They also repaired or replaced most of the windows, painted the whole exterior—the painting was not so dangerous because they had high, strong metal staging to stand on—and remodeled the basement. They also remodeled the kitchen—I came to love it even more than my own—and the bathroom, and then added a bathroom downstairs. There were lots of other improvements.

One day when I visited, they were arguing about the basement. They were yelling at each other and George's father stomped up the stairs. Mrs. Woodard took hold of him and called George, and then made the two apologize. Peacemaking was probably new to her, but she did it well. Later, George told me that as he was listening to his mother's complaints about their arguing, he began to see how much they had changed. It was more than the color of their hair. They were heavier and a little stooped. Their veins stuck out, their skin was blotched, their faces had become deeply lined, their necks fleshy. Most of all, they moved much more slowly. They were old now.

George said he had been stupid for spending so much of his life arguing with his father and then being estranged from both of them. I understood that while he was helping them repair the house, he felt helpless about repairing his parents. They were much different than before. Of course, George wasn't the same person, either.

As for his parents' relation to Michael and Grace, George still wondered how that could be so different, pleasantly so. And he was often taken aback when Michael said things like, "Dad, I wish you were more like Grandpa John."

For several years, we celebrated Thanksgivings, Easters, and Christmases together. Michael and Grace loved "Grandma's house" and they spent many weekends there, too. Either George or I would drive them.

Michael and Grace made friends with the children of Adam and Molly Foster who were neighbors of Grandma Woodard. Adam was George's childhood friend. He and Molly had four girls and two boys. The youngest daughter, Samantha, was about Grace's age. They became close friends, and "Sam" occasionally came down for weekends with us. The two girls played together as children, and later as teenagers dreamed and talked together incessantly.

For Grace's twelfth birthday, we decided to have a party at our house. All her classmates were invited. Among them was Joseph, a schoolboy the others ignored. I learned that he and his family were transients of a sort, renting at the beach during the winter off-season and then in a trailer park in the summertime. I thought the children were being cruel and wondered why. Over time I learned there were many coastal residents who were prejudiced against poor families in the area. But at the time of the party, I was still naive. I asked Grace, "What's the matter with Joseph? Why aren't you all playing together?" She answered, "He's just different."

Before I could react, Samantha went immediately over to the boy, took him by his hand and for the rest of the day she was his pal.

It was after that party when George suggested that we ought to build a new and bigger house on the land behind our current one. He said the kids were growing, and we were starting to need more space for family, friends and weekend guests. Also, he wanted to add some room for his parents when the time came.

So, during that fall and winter, we sketched our dream house. It was our project together. George handled most of the details but let me mostly design the kitchen. I liked what he had done at his parents' house and I got other ideas from magazines. I talked with friends, especially a woman from our church who had recently had a house built. She helped me imagine what a kitchen should have and where appliances should go.

George and I agreed to put the laundry right off the kitchen; no more carrying clothes and linens up and down the stairs. And I surprised him when I asked for a sun room to grow plants in all year. He laughed at first but then added one, also off the kitchen. Together, the laundry, kitchen and sunroom made up much of the south side of the house. We also planned a TV room on the first floor, and a recreation room that filled most of the basement. As it turned out, the 'rec room' quickly became a favorite of the kids and their friends. We also made space for a 'Jacuzzi' the brand of hot tub that was just becoming popular.

'Our House Project' became a major preoccupation. It was the subject of our conversations everywhere, at home, in church and with friends. It became the talk of the neighborhood, from the name of the architect to the size of the bathrooms. Some imagined that President Kennedy's architect had designed it! Some said our bathtubs were going to be so big that people could swim in them! All of this added to our excitement.

By spring, we had begun construction and by the middle of fall we moved out of our old house and into the new one. Then we tore down the old house and made a driveway to the back, and planted trees alongside.

The Sunday after we moved in, we had a church service in the house. Most of the congregation came from the new church we had joined It wasn't perfect, but we were comfortable with its doctrines and atmosphere. Also, I wanted to be part of one and help in the community. From the beginning, our new house was often a place for church events, and from time to time, it sheltered many of our friends in the community.

The following summer Matthew, Emily, and Max came to visit, and stayed a week. Emily and I had a lot of free time together. Children and husbands seemed to fill our conversations even though the men were gone most of the week. Emily talked about Max's achievements in school, and about the ups and downs of Matthew's business in Florida. She said he hoped to have George as his business partner because there was a big new housing project starting that he couldn't handle alone. Matthew wanted a partner he could trust.

This Florida housing project quickly became like another person in the house, requiring our total attention. It was as if Matthew were an actor on stage giving a singular performance on which all the world depended. The task was to build a community for senior citizens where the residents would have small homes adapted *to their needs and with easy access to shopping, entertainment and recreation. It seemed that nothing escaped Matthew's eyes. His preliminary drawings had a main building for offices, enclosed swimming pool, and rooms for games, parties and light exercise. There also were walkways through a somewhat wooded area. It seemed the perfect place for seniors, and Matthew was determined to have George at his side. By the end of the week, it was settled: George and Mathew were partners again.*

The time came when Michael graduated high school. Then he went to college in Florida and worked part-time with Matthew. I had to accept the children were getting old enough to make their own decisions. I wanted them to need me all the time. But I was also proud of them even if I wasn't happy with some of their choices.

I tried to be especially close to Grace and Sam. On the one hand, I worried whom they would fall in love with. I did not want their young hearts disillusioned, and I wanted to keep them away from all the miseries of the world. On the other hand, I didn't want to prevent them from enjoying all they could while they were young.

With Michael, we did not have any problems—or maybe we did not worry about him as much as we did Grace. It was different with her: she was a beautiful, immature girl, and quite fearless. At some points, I felt she hated me. Even though I thought I knew everything about life, I knew nothing about raising a teenager and a young adult. Also, it was America in the 1960's and 1970's; freedom in those times seemed dangerous to me.

I never thought that too much freedom could be harmful, but reality set in the day I found some marijuana while straightening up Grace's bedroom. When I tried to talk with her later, she yelled at me, "It's none of your business what I have in my room or anywhere. You're not my mother. You're just my daddy's housekeeper who married him!"

I was shocked. I couldn't speak. I kept what I found and went to my room. Grace left the house, slamming the door behind her.

When George came home, I was still lying on our bed. And

without a better explanation for it, I showed him what I found and repeated what Grace said. She hadn't returned home.

We ate without her and then George waited in the living room. He was so mad that I became afraid of what might happen. So when I heard her come in, I sat beside him and we waited together. Grace entered slowly and seemed surprised to see us. George asked her a lot of questions that got nowhere. Then he scolded her and concluded by saying sternly, "Listen girl, Elena may not be your biological mother but she is the one who kept you alive when nobody else wanted to. She's the one who cared for you when you were sick; the one who fed you; the one who always made sure you were clean and safe; the one who comforted you; the one who put your happiness before her own when no one else would. And you are a stupid girl who's just hurting yourself and your parents."

That was the man I loved, and at the moment I also admired his ability to reach her in a way that I couldn't. Although at first she behaved as though untouched, Grace later apologized, saying, "I killed my mother. I don't want to lose you, too."

Samantha was even more troubling than Grace. During high school and beyond, she took up with a married man from Portland. Her parents were devastated. There were other occasional boyfriends, but she would always go back to the married one. Sometimes, she stayed away for weeks without a word. Then she dropped out of high school in her senior year and left with him, to points unknown. Her parents simply decided to ignore the situation and her existence. Despite all, I hoped the man loved Sam and was making her happy, but George's parents thought Sam was destroying her life.

Eventually, Grandpa and Grandma Woodard sold their house in Portland and came to live with us. John had developed heart trouble, and he and Louise could no longer take care of themselves. A little more than two years after they moved in with us, Grace met John Andrews, one of George's managers. At the time, Grace was also working in the company. John and Grace fell in love the first time their eyes met. He was a smart, responsible and hardworking young man. He had completed business school while working full time. Although Grace worked for George as receptionist when the position became available, she was more of a homebody. From me and Louise, she learned to cook, clean and decorate. She was our main helper after John and Louise arrived, and her love for Grandpa helped her start to care about the people around her.

As we all expected, John Andrews proposed marriage and, of course, Grace said "Yes!" For her, this was a surprise that left her smiling for days after, as if a dream of her life had become real. Soon, the wedding and after-wedding arrangements were the new topics in our house and the center of our lives.

The weeks before the wedding, everyone seemed nervous. Even though we had prepared for months, there still seemed to be things to do. Grace was always complaining she'd be too fat for her dress, but actually I had never seen her thinner. Our phone rang incessantly and our home became one big storage space for the blessed event.

Finally, Wedding Day arrived and everything seemed to miraculously fit together on schedule. The wedding was in the church. Just prior to the ceremony, an usher escorted me to the very front row, the attendants arrived, and then everyone stood up as George brought Grace down the aisle before coming to stand beside me. I was among the ladies whose tear-filled handkerchiefs were constantly in motion.

Becoming married, Grace had become a woman. All the years before then came to mind. I wondered if I was supposed to be there, or if it was accidental. In the end, it didn't matter; I had been with Grace from the beginning and I was proud of every moment.

The reception was at the house. We were happiness personified. The months of preparation were worth it.

For more than a month afterwards, though, we tried to make sense of the expenses. They were twice as much as we intended. George rationalized by saying, "Well, it's not every day that a daughter gets married. And, you know, Grace is our only one…"

The newlyweds were having their own house built, so they stayed with us for about two months before moving. I had just begun to get used to the idea of having a married daughter when she told me I would also be grandmother soon! Even though I had raised children, I didn't know anything about pregnancy. Now, seeing Grace slowly change, and knowing she had an infant growing in there, it was like witnessing a miracle.

We all wanted to protect the miracle. Maybe we were overly protective. I wanted to do all of Grace's cooking. George did not want her to have to work in the company anymore. Our son-in-law hired a cleaning lady. Grandma helpfully reminded everyone almost daily that she had miscarried four times before George came along.

Poor, pampered Grace. By the end of her pregnancy, she was screaming at us, "Let me do something!" "I'm not in a cocoon, you know!" She yelled at her husband, who was also overwhelmed by our protectiveness. We just wanted Grace to sit still and wait for her baby to appear. Then about two weeks before the expected day, Grace began to have contractions. We all raced to the hospital, but it wasn't time yet. We looked for signs the next several days. Every discomfort had us on alert. A day before her due date, she had them again. John drove her to the hospital, with George and me right behind them.

A few hours later, William was born.

William was two when Grace became pregnant with Abby. That's when Samantha came back into to our lives. She appeared one day, homeless and three months pregnant. When she said that her parents did not want her with them in Portland, we offered her a place in the house. There was plenty of room.

Sam told us she had a terrible fight with the baby's father when he learned she was pregnant. In anger, he hit her repeatedly, blackened her eyes, cut her lip and cheek and broke her left arm. Then he left and went back to his farm and family in Maine. I knew how brutal a man can be toward a woman, and how lucky I was to have married George.

After Sam recovered from her injuries, she and Grace were two *beautiful, pregnant women. Except for their condition, they were like happy teenagers again. It seemed that nothing was a burden; they often laughed for no apparent reason. Sam was back. We all loved her very much. She was loving soul who had loved the wrong man.*

While with us, Sam met Billy, the grandson of our neighbor Mrs. Smith. Billy was a hardworking young man. He was fascinated with Sam and asked her to marry him. It was hard for her to decide. Sam told me once, "Billy is the best friend a woman can have. I just don't know if I would ever love him as a man." Eventually, she decided based on what was the best for the child she was expecting. Sam was about eight months pregnant when she married Billy at his grandmother's house next door. We gave a catered reception as part of our wedding gift to them.

A month later I got the phone call: Sam was a mother. She had given birth to a healthy boy. They named him "Brendon." I went to the hospital and there I saw a proud father holding his newborn son.

About three months later, another call. This time Grace was in the hospital to give birth to her second child. George and I rushed over. We waited two hours for the news. It was a girl, "Abby." When I saw George holding Abby, it was like seeing him holding Grace for the first time.

Following Michael's college graduation, he entered the Navy as an officer. First they sent him to Japan and then to Vietnam. We were very worried and wrote him almost daily. He wrote frequently but had little to say either about what he was doing or much else except he was fine and what the weather was like. After three and a half years, he returned to us for two months then moved permanently to Florida.

One Sunday evening Michael called to tell us he was married. He put his new wife, Sandy, on the phone. She seemed very nice but we were so surprised that George and I could barely talk. We could say little more than "Congratulations, best wishes," and that we looked forward to meeting her.

About seven months later Sandy gave birth to Claire. George and I flew to Florida. My Michael was a father. It seemed unbelievable. They said Claire was born prematurely, but when I saw her, she seemed quite healthy, big and beautiful.

Those four children were the love of my life as a grandmother. William was just like his Uncle Michael. John had to share his role as father with Michael. For William, Uncle Michael was his idol. Vacations were all about Florida for William; he was such a happy child. Sam's Brendon was a prince. He cared about everyone. He could have been a sad person but he chose to make the best of his life. He was strong and sensible.

Abby was electric, independent, and talented. It seemed that for her the world had no limits. Abby played the piano and loved to sing. Brendon and Abby were nearly inseparable. They were almost always together at school and at home until Abby went away to school after the eighth grade.

Claire was my sweetheart. She was just like Grace, and for her, everything was about her Aunt Grace. A couple of times I laughingly suggested that Michael and Grace should switch William and Claire. When Michael and Sandy divorced, Claire spent the whole summer with Grace.

With this, the second folder of Elena's journal concluded.

CHAPTER 9

The temperature was rising to the upper nineties; the town was busy and the traffic intolerable. Elena and I preferred to stay home where it was cool. Even though we didn't always agree, I loved talking with her because she did not just talk about the past or the present, but also about what she thought would always be.

It was twilight when Brendon returned. Elena and I were drinking iced tea, talking and laughing. It was the only time I remember not mentioning the immigration issue.

At some point, Brendon sat with us and Elena motioned to a book on her coffee table. She said: "No book will ever be more exciting than real life. You can read a whole library and feel knowledgeable, but then you go to places, talk with people, listen to their stories and you quickly learn that what you know from libraries is relatively little."

We listened quietly.

"We are writers of our lives, and I wish I knew it sixty-five years ago. Our choices are like chauffeurs driving us to the next stop. We can ride and pay no attention, or we can pay attention and watch where they take us."

I wondered, "Is she talking about herself, or to us, or both?" She spoke slowly, all the while watching the plants and flowers move in the evening breeze.

"We may suddenly complicate everything by just taking a wrong turn. It could be a detour or we can get truly lost for a time, but in the end what really matter is that we get there."

Between her sentences were moments of silence.

"Other people also influence the direction we take, just as we influence theirs. We will influence the lives of those who are not even born yet…"

She now looked at us and continued, "You are both young.

Don't let pride and fear take you away. You don't want to wake up one morning thinking about what you didn't do or about what you will never know."

She kept talking and we listened, but I didn't comprehend all she was saying. Later that night before she went to sleep, she said, "Cecilia, open your heart and don't be so afraid. Being hurt is as much a part of life as happiness. There are people who need you and your love. I hope you know that."

Abby and Grace came to the house mid-afternoon the next day. Grace was unusually excited. It seemed that for her Abby's visit had meaning beyond its significance to Elena and Brendon. By her appearance and composure, Abby seemed to be right out of a fashion magazine. As much as I tried to find something ugly about her just to put my mind at ease, I could only find the opposite. Her eyes were deep, deep green, intensified by long eyelashes. Her hair had synchronized waves, while her golden, flawless skin told us she was truly sun-kissed.

After the greetings, Abby said, "Grandma, the house looks much bigger. Are some things missing? Where are all the pictures?"

"Your mother has most of them," Elena answered. "But tell me, how are you doing? We really missed you last Christmas."

"I missed you, too, Grandma."

"How long can you stay with us?"

"One or two weeks."

"I don't understand," said Grace. "Why can't you stay with us and then leave with Brendon?"

"Mom, please. But Grandma, how are you feeling? You look well."

"I'm fine sweetheart, happy to see you again."

Grace said, "What about we go out for dinner this evening? I can call John and ask him to leave work early today."

"Mom, not today. Brendon and I already have plans."

"Where're you guys going?" Grace asked.

"'Out with friends."

"With whom?"

"Grace," Elena interrupted, "let them be. I'm sure they want to spend time with their friends. Sweetie," she continued to Abby, "how's school? I can't believe you'll be a veterinarian soon."

"In less than a year, Grandma," Abby said. "And Brendon will be a lawyer, and from what I heard, he'll be a very good one."

"Yes, he is already practicing for us," Elena mentioned.

Brendon managed to change the conversation. "Abby," he asked, "have you heard from William? I called him yesterday but it went directly to voice-mail."

"I talked to Claire. She said William went to a party and the guys threw him in the pool. His phone was in his pocket," Abby said, laughing. "He's supposed to get a new one today."

"William. Life for him is a constant party," Grace snapped. "When will he grow up?"

"Mom, my brother is a fine, happy man. He works. Uncle Michael says he's the best for the business. Just because he doesn't fit your conservative idea of life doesn't mean he's not grown." Abby looked defiantly at her mother.

"You two, please, stop," Elena interjected. "How long has it been? Two, three hours, and you're already starting in?"

"'Sorry Grandma, but Mom is so judgmental."

"Judgmental?" Grace questioned. "It's called parenting. You'll know it when you have your own children."

Elena said, "If you two want to keep going, please do it in the library. Close the door and argue as much as you want there. The rest of us shouldn't have to listen."

"I'm going out with Brendon." Abby looked at him and asked, "Are you ready?" Then, she got up, kissed Elena, and said, "I love you Grandma." Brendon grabbed his keys and they left. Grace looked at Elena and it was like they were communicating telepathically. Elena shook her head.

Grace announced, "I have to go, too. I'll be home if you need me." Then she left.

Elena and I were alone most of the next few days. Brendon and Abby were always together and always busy with their own affairs. Brendon didn't come home a few nights, and I wondered what would be keeping him away. And Elena did not show me her third journal. Even though I asked for it many times, her answer was always, "Don't worry, Cecilia. I'll give it to you when I'm ready." This continued for some weeks, while I wondered what the third volume contained.

During those days, I heard Cindy's name mentioned a few times, mostly by Abby during her five-minute visits. But Brendon always managed to keep it brief. He was good as peacemaker; it seemed he was always trying to keep everyone in place. He was as perfect now as I remembered him in high school.

The week of the court cases was stressful and agonizing. We had some hopes the judges would allow our friends to stay in the country as legal residents. Brendon helped us write letters of recommendation but that was about all we could do to support them. We thought Soninha had the best chance because she had an American-born child. But, no. The court discovered she had used false documents to hide that she had been jailed at the border, the same as Peteco.

After the judge's decisions, the immigrants all signed letters of voluntary departure. Soninha had to go without seeing her baby again. One by one during the next twenty days, the government sent all five of our friends back to Brazil.

One day, as soon as Grace arrived at Elena's, I went to the restaurant where it all started. It was about three in the afternoon. I knew it would have been better to wait to talk with Cindy in private, but my emotions took over. By the front door, there was a sign, "Now Hiring," in uneven handwriting. Inside, I asked a waitress for Cindy. She wasn't there. I guess it was for the best. Frustrated, I drove to the cemetery and visited Mother's grave instead of going directly back to Elena's house. Again, I felt I was inside a tornado, as when Mother and I first arrived in Florida.

From the cemetery, I drove to Elena's. Grace and Elena were in the living room watching the news on television. They seemed absorbed in it and weren't interested in talking. I went around the house doing some chores just to keep busy.

As I was getting Elena's medications ready for the next week, I heard a car stop in the driveway and saw Abby was driving. She got out and walked around to talk to someone on the passenger's side. I recognized Cindy. Abby gently touched Cindy's face and said something. Cindy shook her head as a negative. They look at each other and smiled.

Abby was walking towards the house when I went through the back door, then around to the front and straight toward Cindy. I had no idea what I was going to say; I was just following my body, with the fresh memory of my deported friends. She saw me and looked right at me as I approached. If she was trying to keep me away, her stare wasn't going to be strong enough.

I said loudly, "How can you live with yourself?!"

"Please, just stay away from me," she pleaded. Then in a lower voice, "I didn't do anything."

"How can you be such liar?" I said. "You're evil! You destroyed their lives! And then you go out with your friends to enjoy the day as if nothing happened." I paused. "I just don't understand why you did it! You don't even know them!" I was becoming louder.

Then Abby's voice behind me, "Leave her alone!" I turned and snapped back at her, "You don't know what she has done!"

"Leave Cindy alone. She has nothing to do with your friends," Abby said.

To my surprise, Cindy intervened, "Abby, don't. Let's go."

I continued, back at Cindy, "You seem so innocent and unprotected now. Why can't you show your true colors to everyone?"

"Do you really think everyone is like you?" Abby asked me.

"Abby, please, let's go," Cindy begged.

"Cindy, no. Not anymore," said Abby. Then she turned to me and continued, "You don't care about anybody else but you. You go through life hurting people and you don't even realize it. Do you really think that your people are the only ones who have problems? We didn't ask them to come here. They came because they wanted to. They could have stayed in their country and made it work. I'm tired of hearing your stories and knowing that you are always talking badly about Cindy and about anyone who doesn't pity your stupid problems."

After a pause, she continued, "And I just wish Brendon gets tired of you, too. You think you are the only person in the world who has a reason to cry. Stop feeling sorry for yourself. Your friends have been deported because they were here illegally."

I was speechless. Abby continued, "But Cindy didn't do it." Then we noticed Grace and Elena on the porch looking at us intently. Abby continued as if she had to do it. "Cindy wasn't even here when it happened. We were both in Florida. And, we didn't even know that you or your friends existed. So, take your problems somewhere else; we have our own." Then she got in the car and drove away with Cindy.

I wanted to vanish. I didn't want to face Elena and Grace. But worst of all, I didn't understand half of what just occurred. I looked around. Grace was helping Elena back inside the house. I followed, but went directly to my room.

Later, Brendon arrived. From the living room, I heard the conversation between Grace and Brendon becoming louder. I opened the door to listen and try to make sense of it. Grace was asking, "Why didn't you tell me they were together in Florida?"

"If Abby wanted you to know what she was doing, she would have told you," he answered. Grace replied, "I trusted you, Brendon."

"Aunt Grace, Abby is not my responsibility, and she's not a child. She's a woman and knows what she wants. Aunt, you want to see Abby as you imagine, but not as she is."

"Brendon, Abby's destroying her life and you're helping her!"

"I'll always support her," he said. "Abby came here to talk but she was afraid of disappointing you. Aunt, I love you but I hate the way you treat her sometimes. You just want her to be perfect so people can tell how good a mother you must be. I'm sorry Aunt, but I can't sympathize with that." He paused. "I have to find Abby." He walked out.

Elena was sitting across the room the whole time. Grace murmured to her, "He never talked to me like that before."

Grace stayed another half hour or so. After she left, I went to the living room. Elena was staring into the fireplace. Being summertime, there was nothing burning.

"Do you know what is amazing about life?" she said. "When you get comfortable thinking you know everything, something always happens to show how little you know." While I was turning over her words in my mind, she asked, "My dear, what's for dinner? How about some spicy hot beans?"

During dinner, there were many silences between us. Our own thoughts overrode the need to talk. Finally, I ventured, "Is it time for me to go?"

"Go where?" She replied.

"I'm wondering if I should leave. I don't know what's going on here, but I don't want to interfere."

"Cecilia, you and Grace have something in common. You both overdramatize everything."

"I don't."

"My dear, you do." Then she continued, "No, you don't have to leave. This thing is not about your job. Now that you gave Cindy a piece of your mind and heard what you didn't want to hear from Abby, it's best if you just let it go. All will be fine." Then a pause. "Don't worry so much," she said with a bit of sarcasm.

I couldn't be upset with her; she was right. After dinner, I waited for Brendon awhile, but he didn't come home that night.

When I awoke the next morning, it was still dark outside but strips of light were breaking through. The only sound that disturbed the silence was the old battery-powered wall clock in the hallway. It must have been there at the beginning of my time in the house. Except for this morning, the ticking never bothered me. For few minutes, I was preoccupied by it. Then for some reason, I got out of bed and went down the hall to remove the batteries. The clock was a bit too high on the wall, so I took a chair, stood on it, brought the clock down and turned it over. In the center was the battery cover. I opened it and removed a cell. The relief was like magic.

When I moved my fingers around to place the clock back on the wall, I saw tiny, handwritten words on the side of the case, "*To you, the woman I will always love as my Mother, with gratitude, Sam.*" Seeing the words I felt as if I were disturbing something sacred. I put the battery back in the case. The ticking resumed and the silence ended. Defeated, I went to the kitchen, fixed coffee, and found a place in the porch to catch the early morning fresh air before a hot summer day arrived. I gazed out over the garden. My mind got hold of an idea that seemed as clear as the view before me even though it did not fit with the image I had of Abby and Cindy. Were they in love? I laughed at myself for even asking the question. Of course, that was ridiculous. For all I knew, Cindy was interested in Brendon, not Abby. But why was Abby so angry at me?

I was drawn from my thoughts when Brendon drove up in Elena's car. He pulled into the driveway and then into the garage. Closing the garage door, he came over to me.

"Hi. What are you doing up so early?" he asked, sitting in a chair beside me.

"'Couldn't sleep," I said. "And you? What are you doing here so late?"

He avoided my question. "I'm leaving today. I want to have my stuff ready before Grandma wakes up so I can spend some time with her."

"When today?"

"Around noon."

"Are you coming back?"

"Not anytime soon." A couple of small birds drinking from the garden fountain caught our eyes.

I started again, "Thank you for everything. I wish we could show you how much we appreciated your casework."

"Just take care of Grandma. She always took care of everyone. It's time for us to give her some peace."

"I'm sorry for yesterday," I started.

"Woman, you have been out of control!" We laughed and he continued, "You have been making hasty conclusions."

"Can you tell me what is happening?"

"No, but I can tell you Abby had her reasons."

"That's exactly how I felt when I approached Cindy. I had my reasons."

Again, silence. We turned back to the birds.

"I was glad to see you again, Cecilia," Brendon said. He stood up and was already opening the door when I forced a sound,

"It was good to see you, too."

The already-bright day was more than I could take at the moment. A gray-snowy one would have been a better fit for my soul.

When Elena awoke, she asked to see Brendon. I had a terrible desire to eavesdrop on them but felt ashamed at the thought. His luggage was in the living room. He was ready to leave. As if I were a captured soldier, I prepared myself to be strong, to show no weakness, and to share no secrets. At 11:50, Brendon's ride arrived.

Brendon and Elena came out of the library. He gave her a kiss, then grabbed his stuff. He looked at me and said goodbye. "Goodbye," I answered, and he left. It had happened again, out of nowhere. Brendon came into my life and then left without knowing my feelings. Like always, I continued to live deep inside my head and expected people to read my thoughts or catch the occasional clues.

"He reminds me so much of his mother," said Elena. "She must be very proud of him."

"Is he mad at me?" I asked her, hoping to hear more than the question would require.

"No. He just doesn't understand your attitude."

"Why am I now the bad one? I didn't say a word to your granddaughter. She was the one with the attitude." I continued, "Elena, do you know what? I don't care anymore. And I just wish I don't have to see any of them ever again."

"Cecilia, when I was a girl, having a homosexual in the family was a horrible thing. I often heard people say, 'In the worse case, it is better to have a prostitute daughter than a homosexual one.' I never really thought about it until yesterday. I love Abby very much. I do not care what other people think of her. She is and always will be my girl."

And, just like that, as if it were the natural thing to say, Elena dropped the truth on me that no one else wanted to mention. It cleared part of my mind, but added some confusion. I felt I knew less now than before.

"Cecilia," Elena asked, "did you know that Cindy and Abby were like that?"

"No. Until yesterday, I had no idea."

"They think you knew it, and thought that's why you didn't like them."

I said, "No, Cindy and I never got along because her crowd was always picking on us, the people in Seabrook. Her crowd was rich and we were poor, and they liked to rub it in. They used to say we Seabrookers were all brothers and sisters and cousins. In other words, that we were immoral and inbred. Did you know that?"

"Yes, but I never paid it any attention," Elena admitted.

"To them, our differences were never because of who we were but about where we came from."

"Maybe you should tell them that."

"No. I'm sorry Elena, but I don't have to tell them anything." We paused.

"Cecilia, I think Brendon likes you."

"It doesn't matter anymore. We're too different. Besides, I dislike Cindy the same as I did before." There was something still unclear: who led the immigration officers to the restaurant? I thought it could only have been Cindy.

Then Camila learned the truth.

A couple weeks after Brendon, Abby, and Cindy had left, Camila called me to tell about her plans to go back to Brazil as Rubens was already there. She also told me about Sandra, the woman who owned a cleaning company. She said Sandra bragged to some friends about "solving a problem" with Rubens. Sandra had restaurant contracts and she gave the ones she couldn't handle to Rubens. But she was receiving the money and wasn't forwarding it to Rubens because she knew there wasn't much he could do against her. He accused Sandra of not paying their wages, and threatened to go to the authorities. That's when Sandra, a Brazilian legal resident, tipped off immigration.

Oh, if only I had not judged Cindy so rashly, I could look at her and say, "I am sorry." But it had gone too far and it was too late.

I told Elena everything. She said, "When you're ready, you'll need to tell Cindy."

Soon, summer ended and the town became quieter again. I was glad to hear Elena say she wanted to go back to her journal. Life in her journal was much more settled. We chose to stay in her past.

Elena also slept for long hours. I could tell she was becoming tired and physically weak. We had more trips to hospitals.

One day, she made a living will and signed it in the presence of Grace and the attorney. She divided most of her belongings between Michael and Grace. Her house would go to the community to become an assisted-living home for the poor. There also was a letter to be opened only after she died.

Elena prepared to leave once more, but this time willingly and at peace, not forced to flee. During those days, she was also remarkably single-minded about reviewing the journal and going to daily mass.

Fortunately, Elena's memory was still sharp. I read the journal to her every day. As we went along, she added several episodes of importance, especially about her Brazilian childhood experiences. Despite all the early hardships, Elena seemed to miss her childhood the most. For others, and considering the circumstances, it would be impossible to long for that time, but I shared her feelings. I missed my early home as well, but it now was too far in the past and too far from New Hampshire.

More months passed. Every so often we'd have a visitor. But mostly, it was just Elena and me.

One snowy afternoon, when Brendon was three, Sam came to our house to pick him up after she went Christmas shopping. Our lives were about to change again.

She had pulled into the driveway. Another car pulled in behind her. I went to see who it was. A man was standing at the driver's side of Sam's car and the two were arguing loudly through the door's open window. Suddenly the man yanked the door open and dragged her out. I ran to the phone and called the police. When I went back to look again they were gone, with only Sam's empty car in the driveway.

Frantic, I phoned George and Grace. Then I remembered that little Brendon was with me; there he was, still looking through the front window. I hugged him. "Hi, sweetheart. Come stay with Grandma."

"Grandma, where did Mommy go?" he asked.

"I don't know, I don't know," I said, still hugging him.

The police arrived quickly, with George was right behind them. He talked with the police. Grace arrived and took Brendon to her house where he and Abby could play together, away from the sudden crisis.

About three hours later, we received terrible news. The car had crashed on the highway to Boston and both were dead. The police said it appeared that the man had shot and killed Samantha and then did the same to himself after the crash. There was whiskey in the car and a gun on the seat. There were no witnesses. Nobody really knew what happened that day, but we lost them both... the only ones who could explain. We were destroyed. If I could return to the day, I would have never let him take Sam from us.

Beginning with Samantha's, funerals became too much a part of our lives. We cremated her body and set her free over the North Atlantic. Then George's parents died, first Granddad and then Grandma. We buried them in Portland. A year later, Mrs. Smith died. But my life didn't stop, and I learned to keep going with those who remained.

Young Brendon stayed with me for few days after the crash. He cried many nights for his mother. I felt terribly hopeless, with little I could do or say but try to comfort him. I wished that I were God for a moment so I could bring his mother back to life. But I knew that Brendon would soon be fine with his father. Billy was good and loved his son. They always have been part of our family. When Billy was at work, Brendon was either at school, at our house or at Grace's. I'm glad Billy let us to be part of Brendon's life. He felt like a grandson, just the same as William. I was at my best when all the kids were home, and my life revolved around them. I was happy when they were happy; and I wanted to be there for them whenever needed.

Brendon was about eight when Billy remarried and moved to a new house. Billy and Emmy met when he was working on her house in Seabrook Beach. She was single, never married, and without children. Emmy's a wonderful woman and has been good with Brendon. Billy deserved to find someone who would love him and Brendon that much. The twins Sarah and Eve were born from their marriage. Overnight, Brendon became the most proud and helpful big brother. When we offered to help send him away to a private high school after eighth grade, Brendon refused, saying he "wanted to stay with his family." Everyone respected his decision.

That was the first time Brendon and Abby made major choices, although different ones. Abby went to a private high school and Brendon went to the public one in Hampton. Both of them were good students. They participated in and volunteered for many teams and clubs. Brendon was excellent in basketball. He was also an animal lover. When Brendon and Abby were children, I had dogs in our home and Grace still does. Brendon and Abby pretended they were their doctors, taking care of the dogs and enjoying accompanying them to the veterinarian. I never thought that what began as child's play would eventually become Abby's career.

As for William, even before he graduated high school, he already had his tickets to Florida. He was in such a hurry.

Claire was living with her mother; she was good in school as well, and Grace wished she would come to live in New Hampshire after graduation.

Every once in a while I would hear about them falling in love. The kids were so close in age that what happened to one soon also happened to the others. But the love affairs were brief and not very serious, and they passed through them without harm.

Then George decided to retire. All the time I was busy with the family, church, and friends, George was running a successful business. He was proud of himself and I was proud of him, too. His hard work, persistence and deserved success enabled our children, grandchildren, and great-grandchildren to enjoy a comfortable start in life.

Matthew decided to retire the same year, leaving John, Billy, Michael, and Max responsible for the company.

For George, retirement was difficult at first because he loved his job. For me, I had to get used to him being home all the time. For a few years, we traveled around the country and saw much of it for the first time. But we loved home and always returned to it.

Our traveling ended when George had a heart attack. It was time to take care of him. His heart had weakened and for the first time since we married, I had to think about losing him. I wasn't ready for it; we are never ready to lose those we love. But after many months of medicine, doctors and hospitals, my love, best friend and partner in life died. The last few days, we remembered our early years in Boston. We laughed.

Someone once told me that we could measure the good one did in life by the number of people who attend the funeral. By that measure, George was a very good man. More people than I ever knew arrived to say good-bye. Later, many more came to the house to tell me about his help and kindness. One widow had a desperately leaky water pipe and couldn't pay for the repair because she was alone, supporting several children. She said my husband fixed the pipe and when she asked where to send the money, George told her, "You may put my family in your prayers." The widow said that after that, whenever someone needed construction or repairs, she referred them to George. There were many stories like this, all new to me. My husband put people before business; he was a humanitarian in the business world.

Alone now, my life changed again. The nights were too long, our home was too large, and the people around me were always too busy. I missed George all the time. I also went back to the Catholic Church, to the local daily mass two or three times a week. It was like being home again.

I also found happiness in helping local charities. And, it was satisfying to work in the garden, watch flowers and vegetables return, spring after spring.

The grandkids scattered. At first, Brendon decided to attend college nearby. Later, he transferred to one far away and, after graduating, moved from New England altogether. Billy moved to Florida with his family because Michael and Max needed him there, and because the northern winters were wrecking his health. When Abby decided to travel for a year, Brendon joined her. I first thought it was a crazy thing to do but they were young and said they needed at least a year of their lives without the pressure of adulthood. They persuaded me; so I supported them. At least they were together again. Later they attended the same university. Claire went to

147

teaching school; I believe nobody could be a more dedicated teacher than she. William definitely loves the Sunshine State but has also become a smart businessman down there.

One summer, few years into his college studies, Brendon saw my journal in the library. But being written in Portuguese, he couldn't understand it. I told him that if someone translated my journal to English, some secrets would be revealed. After I had a stroke, he suggested I hire a nurse to live with me and who was fluent in Portuguese and English to translate my journal. We began to look. A few nurses came. But they didn't know Brazilian Portuguese. Only my friend Cecilia Maria Medeiros da Silva was perfect for the job.

Gradually, I was going back to my early years. Those memories were so bright. My childhood was coming back to me once again. I just wanted to go back home to run freely through the wild, chase frogs in a rainy day, and feel the same breeze that soundly made waves in the ocean of sugar cane. I wanted to fly. I remember hearing the lush songs of birds in the forest and seeing the colorful contrasts of trees and flowers. To feel the fresh air was like feeling the life in my lungs. To swim in the rivers in the wild was like flying in the hands of freedom. Those are such vivid memories. I remember the wild. I miss the ability to be anywhere and everywhere when I closed my eyes. I still wish to fly.

However, the passion for life that once accelerated my heart is missing. My heart lacks the feeling necessary for survival. Actually, I don't feel much now. Most everything is absent, as if in a vacuum. I can only live in my memories.

My life is complete, although I'd like to go back home.

Elena and I went through that fall and winter well even with the heavy snow and constant plowing. She was waiting for another look at spring. By the end of winter, Elena was starting to complain about the eternal cold as Grace was making sure everything was ready for Elena's garden again, the tools, the seeds, the watering can.

In one of the last days of that March, Elena asked me to

put fire in the fireplace. I found it strange as it wasn't cold that day. But I did without making any comments. When the wood was burning, she asked me to give her journals to her with all its pages. I did, thinking she was feeling nostalgic and wanted to feel those pages. I put them on her lap. She asked me to leave her by the fireplace. "Why?" I asked. She just looked at me. "Please, don't," I said. *burn journal*

"I don't want to leave it behind," she said. I placed her chair by the fireplace and took a few steps back. It was one of those pictures that are burned into one's memory and it will never leave mine. She took page after page and sent it to be burnt. She was crying. I was crying. I would never see it again. And, nobody else ever read it again. I wished I had never seen it before so I didn't have to feel its lost. When there were no more words left to be burnt, she tossed the folders in the fire and watched the flames rise.

"Why?" I asked.

"What else should I do?"

"I don't know."

"You have the translation. When it is ready, give it to Grace, Michael, and Brendon. Brendon needs to know what happened to his mother. It is not fair that we know more about him than he does. I still wish I knew who my real parents were."

"You didn't have to burn it."

"I had to. You can't live in my past. You have your future."

"I feel like I lost someone. I have nothing left, Elena. I lost everything and everyone."

"Oh, my dear, you have your whole life ahead of you. As you live, you will know the answers. Remember my friend Lili? I often feel she was an angel. She stayed around until I was settled with Dona Rosa. She was a link between what was and what had to be. I knew her for such a short time. But if I hadn't met Lili, I might not have been in that bench meeting Dona Rosa. You are very special, Cecilia. Your life has not been easy but I know there is a purpose to it. You and Brendon are so much alike. I wish you both could see it."

By mid-April, Elena's garden was already colorful. Grace had done it all by herself. Often, Elena supervised the work through the window. Her breathing was slowing down. Arrangements were being made.

April 18th was quite pleasant. It was the day before America's traditional Patriot's Day. Grace and John spent the day with us. Elena wasn't like herself anymore, even though she was still alive. At night, they decided to stay over. It could be at any time.

Elena stopped breathing at 4:18 in the morning of Patriot's Day.

It was heartbreaking to see Grace. It was the first time I saw her cry. She had lost her mother and best friend. Hugging Elena, she said, "Mom, I loved you so much. Thank you for taking care of Michael and me and our children." She continued, "There was no one else in the world I would have for my mother." By the end of the day, the whole family had arrived. John, Grace, Michael and Brendon took care of everything. Elena wanted to be buried. There was a church service. I never saw so many people there before. At the cemetery, there were even more, including friends and acquaintances. I asked Michael, "Who are they all?" He answered, "Everyone she touched and welcomed and smiled on, I guess."

For many, Elena was a hard-working angel who fed them and their children in tough times, without questioning their hunger or the causes. For others, Elena was the warm-hearted woman who helped keep them warm during harsh winters. To me, Elena was the friend who guided me out of the dark. Before me, while Elena's body went to rest, Brendon hugged and comforted Abby. I heard Grace's sobs. I threw my flowers to Elena and said goodbye, but I didn't leave. Where could I go? I could return to Elena's where my things were, or to my house, but neither appealed. So I stayed at the graveside and waited, though I did not know what for.

Everyone was leaving the cemetery and going back to their

families and problems. I had neither family nor problems. In my mind, the present and future were blank, so I went back to my bedroom in Brazil and to my mother's presence. I remembered that when I wanted to avoid my father or my friends, I would hide behind my bedroom door or under my bed. Then my mother would come and say, "Cecilia, they are looking for you."

A voice brought me back: "Hi, Cecilia."

I had a sense of confusion, imagination versus reality. I looked around and saw Brendon. Surprised, I said, "Hi."

"How are you doing?"

"Okay, I guess"

We were both standing there looking at Elena's grave. The last time we looked at something together, it was those two birds in her fountain.

"She was special." I said.

"Yes, she really was… Did you drive? If not, I can take you home?"

"No, thank you, I drove."

"Is there anything I can do for you?"

"No. But thank you for your concern."

He turned to leave when I called after him, "I know now that Cindy didn't tip off immigration. I just wanted to say that you were right."

He came close, kissed me on the face, said, "Take care," and then left. Again, all the strings had been broken. My tears were still falling; I thought I had shed them all for Elena.

I stayed at home for about a week, isolated by choice. Most of the time, I slept because it was painful to stay awake and know she was gone for good. I just wanted to be alone. I knew that one moment or another I would soon have to pick myself up and get a new reason to live.

Thankfully, the reason found me. One late morning, there was knocking on the door. I opened, and it was Grace. Not someone I was prepared for.

"Hi Cecilia, I've been calling you for days."

"I'm sorry, Grace. I've not been feeling well the last few days."

"I understand." Then a pause while she looked around. "This is a cute house."

"Yeah, small but comfortable." I offered her a chair and asked, "How are you doing?"

"Okay, I guess. It's hard. I feel like mom's still home and I can go see her if I want."

"I know what you mean."

"You know, she cared about everyone. It didn't matter if they were strangers. At the same time, she was very reserved; often, we never knew what she was thinking. A little like you sometimes."

"Me?"

"Yes, you. It's like we know everything about you and nothing at the same time. She was the same way; a bit of a mystery. When we asked her questions, she might answer with another question, or else change the subject. Sometimes we gave up asking. She was very brief when talking about herself. As children, we thought she was a fairy. Her origin was always a mystery." Grace continued, "Anyway, it is because of her that I'm here. She left something that's only supposed to be opened by you, with me, Michael and our attorney present. Michael is waiting for you to open it; and he needs to go back to Florida tomorrow afternoon."

"Do you have any idea what it is?" I asked. "No, it was between her and our attorney."

"Where are we supposed to meet?"

"At her house, tonight or tomorrow early in the morning. What's better for you?"

"Tomorrow morning is better."

"Okay, I will let everyone know. I have to go now. I hope you feel better. And I'll see you tomorrow." She said standing up and walking to the door.

"Oh, one last thing. You were working to translate her journal. How are you doing on it."

"It is almost done. I left everything at her house." I paused. "But she burned the originals."

"It sounds like her. I tried to read it, but I can't read Portuguese." She laughed.

"I will give to the translations to you once it is ready. She told me to give to you to Michael and to Brendon."

"Oh my! She always wanted Brendon to know it. I guess now you know more about us than we know about ourselves. Do as she wished. Thank you."

"Sure."

She left.

The next morning, I went to Elena's house. Grace, Michael, and their attorney were already there, and we went into the library. The attorney explained the reason for meeting and gave me a small box. I placed it on the desk. It contained 'O Cortiço,' 'Dom Casmurro,' and a sealed envelope. I knew how special those books were to Elena. Now, I treasure them.

"These books have been with us as long as I can remember," Grace said.

I saw some disappointment in her comment. "Grace, do you want to keep it with you?" I asked. "I know you will take good care of them."

"No, Cecilia. They are yours now. We don't know what it meant to her. She always knew best and if she left it for you, it's because you must have it," Michael said.

"You need to open the envelope," the attorney said. I opened it. There were three things inside: a bank check made out to me as a gift, a handwritten note saying how much she appreciated my "dedication and friendship in the last months" of her life, and a typed letter asking me to fulfill her last wish.

The wish was that Elena wanted me to go back to Brazil and spend the money remaining in her savings account on projects I would create at the hospital in town, at the school in the village, and among the poor people where she lived as a girl. She also asked Michael and Grace to be involved in whatever projects I'd create and develop.

According to her terms, I would receive half of the money after I got there and the balance two years later if I decided to stay in the area for two more years, so a total of four years. She wrote it was my choice. She expected it would be difficult but would appreciate if I accepted.

To me, it was the hardest decision anyone ever asked me to make. On the one hand, I could continue my life in another country, with all my expenses paid. On the other hand, though, I had never seriously considered returning to Brazil. But there we were in Elena's house, with Michael and Grace and the attorney waiting for my answer:

"I don't know. I need some time to think. What would happen if I don't do it?"

The attorney answers, "In that case, Michael and Grace would distribute the money to charities here in the Seacoast."

Grace added, "Cecilia, we all understand this is difficult. Why don't you take a little time to consider it?

"Thank you Grace. I need to." I said.

After that, I cleared my things from the house. Before leaving, I stopped by the garden. It was definitely the most beautiful place of all; Elena was very proud of it.

Someone said, "It is an amazing place." Surprised, I looked around. It was William, from the porch. "I'm sorry. Did I scare you?"

"No, that's okay," I answered. "You just surprised me."

He walked over. "Mom intends to name this place "Elena's Garden" before turning the house into assistant-living."

"I like the idea. This is a special place because of Elena; everyone should know that."

"I just heard you are in charge of Grandma's last wish," he said.

"It is more like doing a friend a favor."

"I heard that Brazil is a beautiful country." He said, clearly trying to keep the conversation alive.

"I bet it is," I answered.

"You bet? Aren't you from Brazil?" he asked, showing some confusion.

"Yes, but I left when I was a child. I can't say much about Brazil today."

"Actually," he said, "I met some Brazilians in Florida and there are many in Massachusetts and New Hampshire. I believe the people who clean our office in Portsmouth are Brazilians. Do you know any?

"Some."

"Do you still have family in Brazil?"

I stopped for a second before answering, "No. I don't."

"Wow. It must be exciting to think about going back there."

"Yes. But I am not sure I will go."

"Me, I'd jump at the chance," he said.

"But you can be anywhere you want, can't you?" I asked.

"Oh, that's what you think; I wish it were the case." He laughed. "I work hard and long hours in the family business. There's not much time off. But I enjoy it… It is just that sometimes I wish I could be free of all the responsibilities I was born with. Don't you know? Getting high grades in school, being good in sports, being responsible for the company, and all the other high expectations that come along. Looking back, I feel that I got too many responsibilities at too early an age. I don't remember spending much time playing and enjoying things when I was young. I was so busy and locked into a schedule, that I didn't have time for it. Say, are you okay?"

"Yes. Where is your mom?"

"Inside, talking with Uncle Michael. We'll leave in a couple of hours. They're just finishing some business."

"Just a minute, William. I want to talk to them; I'll be right back."

I went to find Michael and Grace. They were in the living

room:

"Excuse me," I said.

"Yes, come on in," Grace said.

"I've decided to do what Elena asked."

"I'm glad," said Grace. "But are you sure you don't want to think about it some more?"

"No, I've decided to do it," I said.

"Okay, we'll do whatever is necessary to help," Michael said. "Thank you, Cecilia. I am sure this meant a lot to my mom."

"We can get together one day in the next couple weeks, and discuss how you want to proceed," Grace said. "You know, I'm excited about this; I wish I could go, too. It would be interesting to see where mom came from."

"Well, why don't you go with her and spend few days?" Michael suggested.

"Oh, Michael!" Then to me, "Don't you know my husband? He wouldn't last two days without me to tell him where to find his car keys." We laughed.

"Okay, I have to go now," I said.

"Call me," Grace said.

"I will. 'Bye Michael"

"'Bye."

William was still in the garden.

"Hey. I just told your mom I will go to Brazil."

"You decided quickly."

"I know… But I don't need to be here for anything. It is time to go."

Over the next few months, Grace and I planned it all out and I was ready to stay in Brazil at least for the next two years. She made sure the money was there when I reached the village. I had to apply to renew my Brazilian passport and for my first American passport. Then we bought my air tickets. As the travel date approached, I become anxious, but I redoubled my thoughts about the trip. I refreshed what I knew about Brazil's history, government, geography, diets, traditions, people. Although I was still in the United States, the domestic scene was no longer my concern.

The excitement of going to a completely new place superseded my emotions about returning to Brazil. All the same, I was apprehensive about the living conditions and afraid of the violence that might be there, especially in Elena's old community. I had a sense of insecurity. My Grandma warned my mother to never return to Brazil, and here I was, going back to where my mother worked so hard to escape.

Of all Elena's family, by the time I was ready to leave, I was only still in touch with Grace. The day of my trip, she drove me to the airport. Part of me was sad. Years ago, my mother took me from Brazil and now I was going back there alone. Then I remember, the two books in my purse are also going back.

It was time to go. The airplane ascended, leaving Boston Logan far below. I wanted to do what Elena did, give myself up to life. Could I? Did I have her resilience? Once again, I was up in the sky away from everyone. The flight was to Miami, with a connection to Brazil. From that point, I was not consciously in the situation, I was just following the orders. I was doing what I was told. I couldn't control events. I was walking in the dark where I could only see a few steps ahead.

From Miami, the eight hours of flight to Brazil were clearly a transition. The plane's cabin had a loud mix of English and Portuguese. I just wanted to fall asleep and avoid thinking, but it was too noisy. For the first time, I was sorry I knew both languages. For the most part, these were mundane conversations, but screamed as if to make their seatmates understand better.

The wanted peace only came after about three hours of flying, after everyone tired and their excitement dissipated at least for a while. Strapped into my seat toward the back of the plane, I was as scared as an unprotected child who just wanted to hear someone say, "Everything will be fine." Finally falling asleep, I wished for and then thought I felt my mother holding my hand.

PART 2

CHAPTER 10

Overwhelmed —
return
to Brazil

Pátria amada, mãe gentil.

In Brazil, it was the end of spring and it was hot. My first stop was São Paulo, at Guarulhos Airport. From there, I took a flight to Maceió in the state of Alagoas. To see it from above and as we landed, Maceió had beautiful white-sandy beaches with warm green-blue surf, just steps away from exciting beachfront music, bars, restaurants and shops. Once I landed, however, violence was evident; the newspaper stands in the airport displayed image after image of grisly crime scenes and twisted dead bodies.

On the taxi drive into town, the view was busy, noisy and dramatic. My breathing became shallow. Everything seemed "too much" and "too many." Too much brightness. Too much heat. Too much color. Too much confusion. Too many people on the streets. Too many cars, motorcycles and bicycles clashing.

I stayed in Maceió a couple days until I finally found a way to reach Terra-do-Mato, the closest town to my destination, Village Aveverde. Transport was by an old van tightly packed with passengers. They were talkative, even welcoming; but I was really scared on the journey —it was just an old one-lane road and the driver was recklessly passing vehicles at very high speed. This continued for almost two hours. Luckily, there were green fields alongside the road to grab my attention. Here was part of Brazil's inland ocean of sugar cane. Then, toward the end of the trip, instead of the terrestrial green against the blue sky, there was nasty, dark gray smoke across the road. I thought the world was burning up. What we passed through was a hellish smoldering scene. On this very hot day, dozens of Brazilian workers were cutting burned sugarcane in large stacks of thin, dark, long sticks. It was strange as it was too early for the harvest season.

The ones who toiled over the stacks wore several layers of clothing, as much as we would wear on a winter's day in New Hampshire. The workers looked like scarecrows with discarded clothes draped over them. Elena had once lived here under these conditions, and at that moment I was angry that her final request had now put me here, too.

To my surprise, there were many women and children working. I looked at my watch and it showed 10:28am. By my standards, these kids would have been "in school," not "at cane." As we passed, I saw workers of all ages using sickles to slash the cane sticks from their roots. What a cruel, repetitive task! I closed my eyes until I heard the driver say, "Terra-do-Mato!"

The only hotel in town was really a large family home. I got a room and was grateful it was clean and private. It had a bathroom with shower, an air-conditioner, and the bed was comfortable. I took a cold shower; and with the air-conditioner on high, I slept through the afternoon and into the night. I woke up early the next morning, somehow content to be in Brazil even though it felt like a dream – as if I was a time-traveler.

While dressing, I noticed details in the room that I missed seeing the day before. The large bed sheet was a gorgeous handmade cloth with colorful flowers and full of wonderfully-fine needlework. My grandmother used to make those kinds of sheets. It required a lot of time, patience, and persistence to finish. A vision came to me of my grandmother on a rocking chair in front of her house working on a fabric.

The room also had handmade curtains and rugs like someone's home might have. But to me, it was still a strange place. I tuned the air-conditioner on low and went downstairs to find a map. The hotel's owner, Maria Angela, told me she didn't have one, but that there were many in town who would happily give directions. I said it was strange that so many Brazilian women were named Maria, including me.

"It is an honor for someone in the family to have the name of Jesus' mother, Maria. It is also a way to remember Maria's suffering as the mother of Our Savior," she said.

"Are you Catholic?" I asked.

"No, but my mother is," she said, "and I like my name."

"Where can I have a good breakfast? And do you know where Village Aveverde is?"

"I'm going to serve breakfast in the kitchen in a few minutes. You are welcomed to eat with us. And for travel, you can ride a moto-taxi to any of the town's villages."

"What is a moto-taxi?"

"It's a motorcycle used as a taxi," she answered, laughing.

"Is it safe?"

"Oh, yes! Very safe—depending on who is the driver." She said curiously, "I suppose you are not from here?"

"No." I didn't volunteer any more information.

Breakfast was excellent. The scrambled eggs with vegetables were delicious. There was fresh-squeezed orange juice with nothing added... a perfect morning drink. There were homemade cakes and breads that smelled good and tasted great. There were lots of fruits in bowls on the table. And a fresh cup of coffee made my morning. I was delighted.

I was the hotel's only guest. Maria said it was common to have weeks with only one or two guests, or even none. Maria and her husband had a son of fifteen and two daughters, seven and thirteen. Maria's mother, Mrs. Joana, also lived with them. Altogether, the family had lived in Terra-do-Mato for more than fifty years.

While Maria Angela ran the hotel, her husband Luiz managed a sugar-cane plantation in a nearby village. The couple was also politically active. He helped the local and state politicians get elected.

The women and girls were talkative. Luiz asked, "So, where are you from?"

"I live in New Hampshire, United States."

"Did you say United States? Is there a town in Brazil called United States?" Luiz asked, confused.

"I don't know about that, but I come from the country United States."

"Wow! You are our first international guest. So, what are you doing in such small town?" Angela asked.

"Well, I am a nurse and am learning about the health care system in Brazilian villages." I had nothing else to say. I did not plan to explain everything so early in my trip.

"Ah, is that why you want to go to Aveverde?" Maria Angela asked.

"Yes," I said. "I would like to see some villages before deciding if my research is working well,"

"Luiz, can you ask your brother to take Cecilia to Aveverde?" Angela suggested.

"Sure," Luiz said.

An hour later Luiz' brother, Marcos, was driving me to Village Aveverde in a silver newer Fiat Palio .

Leaving Terra-do-Mato, Marcos turned onto an old dirt road. There were so many holes that we were bouncing and dancing uncontrollably. Suddenly before us there was an even wider and deeper rut across the road. I tightened the seatbelt and shut my eyes as Marcos drove through it. For the next ten minutes, his little car shook, rattled and rolled, falling into every hole and rut and then climbing out again. Finally, Marcos said, "Cecilia, you can open your eyes now."

"What was that?" I exclaimed. "Why did you take this road?" My heart was racing and my head pounding.

"It's the fastest way to Aveverde. And the others are worse. Actually, this is the main road."

"How old is it?" I asked.

"I don't know, but thirty years ago this was the only way from Terra to Aveverde." I realized then this must have been the road Elena used when she walked away from her village.

There were many people - mostly adults - walking along the roadside. Again, sugarcane was growing everywhere. The green, sweet ocean of grass spread along both sides of us, all the way to the horizon.

Marcos slowed and stopped alongside a woman who was walking with a young child in her arms. The woman was about seven months pregnant. Both she and the child were sweating and seemed tired. Marcos offered them a ride. She quickly opened the back door, placed the child in the seat, sat, and then closed the door gently. I was about to ask her to put the seatbelt around her child but kept the idea to myself. Marcos asked where she was heading.

"Fazenda Alegria," she answered, trying to control her rapid breathing. "Four o'clock in the morning we were in the hospital. We waited all morning but there was no doctor to see me."

"What's wrong?" I asked.

"Sometimes, I feel tired. I saw a doctor once, that was four months ago. No more. I'll go back when I'm ready to have my baby."

It was a busy local road, in bad need of repair, but the fastest way for people to reach town. It also brought sugarcane from the fields to the mills; there was a detour to avoid the hills. I wondered to myself why the road was so neglected, but I really didn't want an answer and I didn't want to get involved in local problems.

Marcos left the woman and her child at her home, five minutes out of our way. Then we continued on to Aveverde.

The sugarcane gave way to a kind of bush country. We passed a few scattered houses before entering a large open area surrounded by buildings and trees, with people throughout. It resembled a scene from the 1800s. "Here we are," said Marcos. "This is Aveverde."

I looked around. I felt in another world, as though that long dirt road had taken us into the past. Here, I was the alien, and felt the villagers knew it.

Marcos was a patient guide. Driving slowly around the village, he answered all my questions. There were about eight hundred inhabitants, two churches, an one-room health clinic, a school with four classrooms, a soccer field, a square, and three drinking places – one of them in the center of the village.

Most of the houses were made of clay. Electricity had arrived twenty-five years earlier, but water came only from wells or from a farm pond a half mile away. I was amazed at the large number of children and dogs. It seemed that too many people were sitting on their porches and in the square in the noon sunlight. Again, I wondered if the children were not supposed to be at school and the people at their daily work.

Later I learned there were very few jobs in the village: in the cane fields, at the school and clinic, and as housekeepers in the homes of teachers and other school employees. In the sugarcane, workers were employed by the farmers or by the mill. The town employed some school and health workers. Residents chose their housekeepers by their abilities to clean, cook, and care for children. Most men worked in the sugarcane, but it only offered jobs for half the year, mid-September to mid-March. Sugarcane workers were paid weekly based on daily wages, Government employees were paid monthly.

The price of food, fuel, clothes, everything was high compared to the United States. I could not imagine how these Brazilians could survive with such low incomes.

One house caught my attention. It was big and white with a large porch around it. I pointed it to Marcos and asked him, "Who lives there?"

"The Valério family," he answered. "They own most of the land here. Vitor Valério runs the farm and the hearts of the girls." I didn't ask for details as I wasn't quite ready to know the Valério family. Until now, I thought they only existed in Elena's past.

We returned to Terra-do-Mato and had lunch in the hotel. Again, the food was good. There was something called *feijao the corda* (some type of beans) with *farofa* and rice and *churrasco*, the best steak I ever ate. During lunch, I made a deal with Marcos to be my driver until I was able to get a Brazilian license.

Marcos was eighteen and had just graduated high school. He did not know what to do with his future and, sad to say, he did not have many choices. He was frustrated by this and blamed it on the legacy of military governments. Many young adults never completed high school. I liked him immediately, and I thought Marcos could help me understand the lives of the people here.

The next day, he took me around town, to the hospital, the town hall, some schools. There were many small public schools. They opened from eight in the morning until noon for one group of students, and then again from one to five in the afternoon for a second group. Two schools were also open in the evening from about seven to ten-thirty for students who worked during the day.

On the third day, we went back to Aveverde to visit the school. The principal was a young woman Marcos knew, named Marta Candido. The school was old, with a brick wall surrounding it. Marta gave us a tour. When we entered the kitchen, the cooks were still outraged by a robbery earlier that week. Because the robbers had taken their tools, appliances, and a lot of food, the cooks were debating how to feed the children. According to them, theft had become common and the mayor promised to hire security guards for the schools.

"What do you normally do when this happens?" I asked Marta.

"We bring food from our homes. But if we don't have any, the kids go hungry."

We looked in the classrooms. There were big, open windows. As we passed one room, I glimpsed a young girl whose eyes were the color of honey. Her skin was light brown and her hair was slightly curled. I thought Elena might have looked like that.

I told Marta, "Please, see what you need to feed the children. Send someone with Marcos to a store and I will pay for what you buy."

"Oh, no! I cannot accept anything unless the mayor or the

secretary of education allows it."

I guess I needed to hear that, to begin understanding the local rules before making a plan for spending Elena's money. I really wanted the villagers to recognize and appreciate her, even though it was too late for them to thank her in person.

Unexpectedly the next day I learned that news from my first visit to the village school had spread. Everyone was talking about the American woman with money who was staying at Maria Angela's hotel. Soon, many locals were dropping by in the evenings, and having conversations about the United States. The hotel's living room became a "hot spot" in town. Listening to the talk, I surmised that many of the youths wanted to learn English.

The first few weeks, I emailed Grace almost daily. While the geographical distance was great, we became closer friends. At the same time, I frequently thought about Brendon. But I never asked Grace about him, nor about Cindy and Abby.

I was relieved that, for now, I was fairly unknown to the Brazilians around me. Not knowing anything, they could not judge my actions. It felt like I was born again, and as long as I stayed in the present, I would be fine.

With Maria's help, I asked for a meeting with the mayor of Terra-do-Mato, Pedro Jacinto. He was the administrator of the town and its villages, and everyone advised me that his support would be essential for my research. He was a popular man and the people clearly depended on him although at the same time they distrusted the government.

My appointment was for eleven at town hall. Arriving with Marcos on time, there were already about fifty lined up to see him. I asked Marcos about the crowd. "This is a daily routine," he said, "and typically many people try for days to see him about their matters. Some ask for money for groceries and medicine, or to pay their electric bills. Others need transportation. There are many reasons."

"Does the mayor give them money and other things?"

"Most the time he does. That's how he and his friends get re-elected. The people feel that they owe him a favor so they vote for him and for anyone else he tells them to vote for."

"Are all these people from town?"

"They are from everywhere: town, villages, farms." He winked at me, "Do you think this is a lot of people? You haven't seen the line in the months after the *moagem* when the sugar-cane is harvested and processed. A lot more people show up."

We managed to pass through the crowd, mostly women with young children. I tried to not look directly at them but there were so many that it was impossible. The adults all wore expressions of profound sadness, yet many were talkative and the children seemed cheerful enough. When we reached the mayor's secretary, Marcos introduced me to her. The secretary's name was "Clara" and she contrasted greatly with the other women in the room. Clara was well dressed, wore makeup and perfume, and seemed too young for the job. She asked me to wait and then she went through a door behind the desk. A couple a minutes later, the door opened and Clara asked me to follow her inside.

There was a man sitting behind a desk. He stood and shook my hand. "Hi Cecilia, it is a pleasure to meet you."

"Nice to meet you, too, sir."

"Can I offer you anything?"

"Coffee would be fine, thanks."

The secretary nodded and went for coffee.

"So, Cecilia, I heard you are a nurse from the United States. Is it true?

"Yes sir, it is."

"Please, call me Pedro. Do you have family here?"

"No."

"That's interesting. So what are you doing in such small town?" He did not allow me to answer, but continued. "I heard you are doing some research, but it seems that no one in the local health clinic knows about your visit." He paused and looked me in the eye, "So, what are you really doing here?"

"I am really interested in the health of the population in the villages. So, it is true that I am doing a kind of research. But I am also representing someone who wants to finance projects here."

"What projects, and where?"

"We are interested in helping Village Aveverde."

"Cecilia, I am going to be as direct as I can possibly be. Some of my supporters are suggesting that you are working for someone who will run against me for mayor of this town in the next election."

The receptionist knocked on the door, entered the room, served coffee, and left again. Then, he continued:

"That is the thing. If you came to do politics against the people who represent this town, then I cannot welcome you. We all live here in harmony, working together, and I don't want you to interfere in their lives."

"Sir, I am not interested in politics. My interest instead is in helping the people."

"So, you would not care if one of my assessors helps you in your projects."

"Yes, I would care. I have enough people to help me right now."

"Okay. Then, who are you representing? I would like to meet them."

"The ones I represent want to stay anonymous for now; and you would not be able to reach them."

"I see."

"But if you feel that there is a problem, you can talk to me anytime."

"Another thing—the next time you feel the need to interfere in the school affairs, please see me first. Too many people are talking about it."

"I'm sorry, sir. Now I know it's your responsibility to provide for the children."

"I'm glad you understand. I just don't want people to start to talk about these things. Now, how much you are thinking about investing here?"

"We don't know yet."

"From what I gather, the investors are gringos. What do they want in return?"

"Nothing."

"I hope you agree with me, this is very strange. You come from nowhere, work for no one knows who, with the best of humanitarian intentions. Cecilia, from my own experience, no one does anything wanting nothing in return."

"Sir, what I can say is that we do not care for your politics. We just want to help the people."

"But why?"

"Why not? Maybe the people I represent have too much money and they want to give some away. This is a poor area. Why not do it here?"

"Interesting. Okay, you are welcome to stay and visit any municipal place in this town and its villages but I want to know your plans step by step."

As if it was one of his political strategies, he asked me many questions about the United States, debated about its illegal immigration, closed off his office for the rest of the day, and invited me to have lunch with his family. We left the room through a back door that led to an exit behind the building. His driver was waiting. We left the town hall and all the people waiting in line and went to his house—or should I say, his mansion.

The mayor's property occupied two streets. It was like an oasis in that Brazilian desert. Surrounding his mansion was rock wall about fifteen feet high, with a security system on top and a guard at each entrance. Each of the mayors' two sons and two daughters had their own private dwellings separate from the main house but surrounded by the same wall. In the back, there was a gigantic swimming pool that could refresh a whole village in those hot days, yet it's blue, clean, quiet water was empty of people. The property also had an outdoor kitchen that could easily feed dozens of families. It, too, was empty. There was a garage for about ten cars, full of shiny vehicles. All of this was surrounded by well-tended gardens.

Everything was so perfect that it made me uncomfortable. I wished I could have said that I didn't speak Portuguese so I could have left the place as quickly as possible.

The mayor's wife, Regina Jacinto, received us as if she was already expecting visitors. She seemed to be uncomfortably nice, polite, and sophisticated. She introduced me to their older son, Jorge, an attorney who was ready to run in the following elections to replace his father, and said there were a younger son and daughter studying in Maceió. Then she introduced me to a sister, Tania, a social worker who ran the local health care system. The mayor's wife did not bother to introduce me to the rest of the household, but there were many more employees than family members.

To freshen up for lunch, Regina herself directed me to the bathroom, a room so large and impressive that I had to douse my face in cold water to come back to reality. When I was ready, a servant led me to the dining room.

Marcos chose not to accompany me, saying he wanted to have lunch with his family and that I could call him for a ride after lunch. Clearly, the mayor's house was not his favorite place in town.

Although there were only five for lunch, the table had a dozen seats, and if every one was filled, there would still be enough to feed twelve with the food that was served for just us five. Having earlier seen the line of poor people waiting at town hall, my stomach began to reject the lunch before me. The family, however, had no trouble digging in, and between mouthfuls, they questioned me. The mayor's son, Jorge, began, "Your Portuguese is perfect for an American, Cecilia."

"I was born in Brazil and went to the U.S. when I was almost eight. But I always spoke Portuguese at home."

Tania followed up, "Where are you from here in Brazil?"

"A small village in Minas," I answered, hoping that would satisfy her. "How many villages are in this town?"

Tania answered, "Twenty-one villages and seven farms. It used to be more farms. But most farmers decided it was more profitable to turn the homesteads into sugarcane fields."

"And where do the workers live now?"

"Many moved to the villages but most moved to town. Unfortunately, the violence has increased drastically with so many more living here." She paused and then said, "And they keep having children they can't afford."

"And for jobs, are there enough for everyone?"

Jorge rapidly answered, "Not really. But we have many ideas to bring more jobs. We have been talking to business people from the south and we are hoping to bring jobs here."

The mayor joined in, "Jorge has many ideas for this town. He is going to be an excellent mayor."

"Too good ideas," said the mayor's wife, as the others ate hungrily. "You see Cecilia, when I was growing up, this town was quiet. People respected authority. There weren't so many sleeping in the streets. It's a shame that we can't even go from home to church without being stopped by beggars and everything else. I prefer to spend most of my time in Maceió or even in São Paulo where they don't know who we are. If it weren't for my husband's and son's political work," she continued, "I would only come here occasionally. But they have too much feeling for this place and don't want others to destroy it."

"Please, Mom! Forgive my mother, Cecilia. She doesn't like the elections," apologized Jorge.

"I understand."

The mayor said, "My wife highly dislikes all the gossip we have to deal with. But it's part of the job.

"I'm already curious about the elections," I confessed.

"Luiz and Maria Angela at the hotel can tell you a lot about them. They are nice people... and long-time supporters," said the

Mayor.

"Yes, they are nice. I will stay there until I find a place to rent or buy."

"It must be hard for you here, having lived in the U.S. The village may seem like a little bit of hell to you," commented the mayor's wife as full platters of food kept passing by.

"Well, things are still new and exciting to me but there really are some lifestyle differences I've noticed."

"If you need anything, please let me know," offered Jorge.

After lunch, I stayed for about an hour. We all had coffee, talked more about the locals, and the mayor's wife showed me the rest of their mansion. Jorge offered to bring me back to the hotel but I thanked him and called Marcos for a ride.

The next day, while we were driving around, Marcos gave me more information about the Jacintos. "Pedro Jacinto was just a normal local friendly guy before winning his first election. His godfather, an alderman, manipulated the mayor at the time to give Jacinto a job at town hall. Later, Jacinto became secretary of finance and then, the mayor invited him to become vice-mayor. Halfway into his term, the seventy-five year old mayor died and Jacinto succeeded him. Since then, he has controlled the town. My grandfather used to say that Jacinto was a lucky man."

"But his family was already wealthy, right?"

"They had less than my family does now. My grandfather helped the Jacintos through many hard times."

"How did that happen?"

"The mayor's wife, Dona Regina, was from a wealthy family that suddenly became poor when her father lost his farm after years of gambling, drinking, and prostitutes. Jacinto was already mayor when he married her. People say she was the most beautiful woman in town. Then from nothing, they began to buy farms and houses everywhere and became the wealthiest family around, just "working" as a mayor. And now they live like royalty, while most of Terra-do-Mato is unemployed and can barely put food on the table.

"But why do they still elect him?"

"Wait until you see an election. It's ridiculous. People sell their votes. They actually do... for anything from a trip to the doctor, to a denture, a day's work, to everything in between."

"I don't understand. How is the school involved in this? I mean, the schools debate about the legitimacy of the elections and people's rights."

"You're in another world. The teachers have their own problems to worry about. Besides, they are appointed by the mayor and aldermen. So they are afraid to lose their jobs if they complain or protest. Teachers have families to feed, too."

"Do you think teachers encourage the people not to use their voting power?"

"I don't say they encourage it. But I think when the students see their parents and teachers giving as much power to politics, they will grow up to do the same.

He continued, "I love this place. I was born here, but I can't understand the people. I'd like to go somewhere else. My brother said he will only support the alderman who guarantees me a job in a local school. But I find this very humiliating.

"As a child, I always dreamed of learning about the land, you know? Being an agronomist. I always had the best grades of my class. But when you are in public schools, your efforts mean nothing. Next year, I'm going to college to become a mathematics teacher because that is as far as I can get from where I am now. I've seen many teachers lose their jobs as punishment just because they wouldn't agree with the mayor's and his families' ideas. It's their way to keep people in check. And the others, who can already support their families, they don't care for the ones who are going through hard times. I don't like politicians. But I also blame the people. We are afraid to think, to speak our minds, and we are so afraid of changes."

I listened to Marcos quietly as we drove through the villages. Poverty was everywhere. I wondered what, if anything, I could fix. Elena's money was a relative fortune here, yet the necessity appeared to be deeper and greater than any one person's generous and wishful bequest.

I discussed everything long distance with Grace. We agreed that I should settle in Aveverde as it was a much quieter place than Terra-do-Mato, and I required more time to develop the plan. Besides, I wanted to avoid the mayor and his family for now.

With some of the money, I bought a vacant lot in Aveverde, and for the next two months while my house was being built, I got acquainted with the people of the village. Without specifically mentioning Elena, I asked many of the residents for the best way to spend her money. I knew I could not simply give them a bank check; that would be a waste.

After a month, I got to know many of the locals. They were genuine and welcoming, maybe even innocent. It was easy to develop relationships with them, especially with the always-curious children. Life there was basic, but dynamic, and the days seemed longer, as if the passage of time had slowed.

I moved into my house when it was mostly complete but still under construction. And, I employed Lia, a local young woman, to keep house and live with me. But in reality, Lia was a "do-all" like all the other women: She cleaned the house, did laundry, cooked meals, watered the plants, shopped for groceries, listened to my troubles. In the beginning, I was a little uncomfortable having someone so close all the time. But, after a while, she became essential. I gave her Sundays off, but she almost never took them as she was living in my house. Lia was always there.

My first Sunday in Aveverde, a woman's scream woke me up very early. I ran outside to see what was happening. Lia was already on the porch. José and Marilda, my neighbors, were having a loud argument. Soon, everyone in the village was awake and gathered in the street, watching the couple's argument turn into a violent fight.

José hit his wife in the face with his open right hand and knocked her to the ground. Then he got down and kept slapping her while she tried to protect her face with one arm, and her breasts and belly with the other. Their three-year old son, Pedrinho, and seven-year old, Juju, were crying desperately nearby.

I could not be angrier. Impulsively, I looked around and found a thick, long piece of metal. Running towards José, I attacked him with it. I was like a monster out of control and wanted him dead. José was bleeding badly when finally a few guys took the weapon from my hands. Then they took him to the clinic. Marilda got the children and went back in the house. Lia and I went back to my porch where I collapsed into a *priguiçosa* [a kind of chair made of cloth and wood].

Many thoughts flew through my mind: legal charges, failing to accomplish Elena's wishes, my uncontrollable reactions, my reputation in the community. While we were all waiting to hear about José and if he needed a hospital, Vitor Valério stopped by on horseback. Vitor was Julio's younger grandson. That was enough for me to dislike him, if it wasn't for the fact that Vitor was actually a nice man.

"How are you?" asked Vitor.

"I'm fine, thanks. But I'm worrying about José. I don't know how he is doing."

"Don't worry. I am sure he will be fine."

"What do you think it will happen now?"

"What do you mean?"

"I attacked him. Will someone call the police or something like that?"

"No. Nobody will call anybody. Don't worry. I will talk to him. He deserved what he got. He needs to learn to be a man. And Marilda should not allow him to treat her like that. The problem is that she always forgives him. Just two or three months ago, I interfered in a fight between them and I thought that was the last of it. It's a habit and they are not the only ones.

You will get used to it."

"I don't think so.

"Don't let it bother you so much."

"I'll try."

"I'm going to see how he is doing."

"Please, let me know if there is anything I can do to help."

Vitor went to see José. About half hour later Vitor, José, and Lourdes, a nurse's assistant, emerged from the building. José was crying and being supported by the other two. They came to me and he asked me to forgive him. The drama suddenly became a comic problem. How was I supposed to forgive José if I was the one who attacked him? I looked at Vitor and saw the humor in his eyes.

Vitor gave José a week's vacation to recuperate. As expected, Marilda cared for his wounds. The matter was soon forgotten as there were other exciting attention-grabbers to come—love affairs, gossip and family fights were all part of the local entertainment.

That Sunday morning was the first time Vitor and I formally met. Even though we heard of each other, we had never been properly introduced. His name would always manage to find its way among gatherings. He was an independent, attractive man and appeared to be older than his age. People said he shared a small house in town with a woman for about two years, but no one ever saw her. The girls seemed to know everything about him. I learnt some things Elena never knew.

When Julio died, he left his wife Luiza with their son Vitorio and their daughters Lucia and Rita, Vitor's mother. Luiza and the girls went back to Maceió while Vitorio stayed with the grandparents in the village. Luiza remarried to a businessman, had another boy, and did not want anything to do with the village and the farm. Lucia became a nun, while Rita went back to the village.

By then, Vitorio was managing the farm with his aunt Maria who had never married. The other aunt, Amelia, had been disinherited by the father, Mr. Valério, because she secretly married one of his farm workers. They had to leave the village and no one knew what happened to them.

When Mr. Valério died, and then his wife three years later, Maria, Vitorio, and Rita inherited all the family properties. Vitorio never married. Rita married the village school teacher, José Francisco, and gave birth to Analia, Maria, and Vitor. Analia moved to São Paulo after marrying a college teacher and there she had two girls. Maria became a social worker in a town close to Maceió, married a policeman and had a son and daughter. Vitor studied agronomy and with his uncle Vitorio managed their properties.

Vitorio demolished several old farmhouses and covered the area with sugar cane. But unlike most farmers, he built homes in the village for his permanent workers. He was respected in the village and was politically powerful even though he was not directly involved in politics. Residents would ask Vitorio and Vitor who they should vote for. When I first arrived in the village, Vitorio was in São Paulo with Rita and Francisco for health checkups and Vitor was busy with all the preparations for the harvest.

Vitor was charming, and we became friends. We bumped into each other almost every day. He was still living with his parents even though he had his own home. But he was independent, strong, and dependable. I tried to compare him to Brendon but they were so different.

After the incident with José, Victor started to visit me frequently. We had some long conversations in the dark nights as the stars seemed to exponentially increase after the Moon set.

"How long do you think this harvest will last?" I asked him once.

"Maybe we'll go through mid-March but no longer than that. Why?"

"Some of the women are already worrying about the winter."

"They always do. It's tough. I wish I could keep everybody

working, but there's not enough. Believe me, my parents do what they can to help everyone. During the winter, Mom works harder to make sure there are lunches at school, and then she makes weekly food distributions to the families. At the farm, we set aside a large area for the village to grow beans and other crops. Unfortunately, none of it seems to help in the long run."

"What do you think should be done?" "I don't know. The worst problem is the number of people. It is still increasing even though many youths move away to São Paulo, Parana, Mato Grosso, and Minas Gerais for better lives."

"Why are you still here?"

"This is my home; the place I was born and where I want to die. When I was living in Maceió, I only wanted to return home. I went to many states in Brazil and visited many places, but here is the only one I can call home. Here is where I want to raise a family someday."

"I hear you look just like your grandfather. Do you know anything about him?"

"Not much. He had a terrible death. He was caught in a sugar-cane fire and had burns all over his body. That happened years before I was born. Uncle Vitorio remembers the episode very well, though. He can tell you about it. Even better is Dona Josefina. She is like a book about this village. She knows everything about everyone. But she doesn't know her real age. In her birth certificate, she is now eighty-one years old but that was just one she got when she married. She came here from the north with her aunt's family when she was a child and had no documents with her. This is what she says, but no one knows for sure."

"It seems that happened very often at back then."

"It did. Most children were born at home with no one who could document the births. Dona Josefina can definitely tell you some stories and she would be glad to have someone to talk to."

"Good, I'll visit her," I said, then asked, "Whom do you think will win the next election?"

"It's getting tougher every year, but Jorge will win this one."

"Do you support him?"

"I support the people in this village. The other candidate has the same principles as the Mayor. There is basically no difference between them. But at least we know what the Jacintos are up to. If it was only for myself and my family, we would not support anyone, even though by law everyone must vote. But if life is tough now when we support the Mayor, imagine how it would be if we didn't."

"At the same time, though," he continued, "there are villages that have nothing. The mayor closes his eyes to them. So, each election, he is losing support. The day a decent candidate appears, the Jacintos will be out."

"I find it strange that people still vote for this mayor and his family even though they don't really care for the people."

"No one will fix all the problems. There are just too many problems, and the people don't seem to want to take responsibility either. Here's an example: As I told you, every year, we set aside some land for people to farm during the winter months. The land is free and we also give the seeds. But many don't accept the gift because they think it is too much work and responsibility. This is just one example. I sometimes get frustrated with them."

"We have a school here but it is still difficult to convince parents to send their kids. And this is only one village. The town has over twenty villages with similar problems. While most people want a better life, they seem to want it all to be given to them. I have worked with them. Many times I have sent them home because they simply don't want to work."

He paused, then continued, "Do you think it is easy to manage a farm? When the weather is against us, we lose. When the price of sugar drops, we lose. When people don't want to work, we lose. When we have to borrow money from the banks, we lose because the interest is too high. I usually wake up 4:00 in the morning, and I have no time to sleep. The *usina* [sugar mill] didn't even pay us all the money for last year's *moagem*. So we had to borrow money for this year."

Vitor took a deep breath. "Most people do not understand what it takes to work for a better life. I know that corruption is bad, and it delays development, but even the most honest politician will not be able to fix the problems here. And I know it is even more difficult for the women. They are the ones who have to worry about how to feed their families day after day, and the kind of work we offer is harder on them than on the men."

"Do women work for you?" I asked.

He looked at me for a second, "Can I kiss you?" It was a strange answer to my question. I laughed, "What?"

He continued, "Normally, we kiss first and look for a response. But somehow, for the first time, I cannot tell what a woman is thinking. May I kiss you?" "No, you can't kiss me!"

"Just for the sake of putting it in the right box, is this *no* for now, or for always?"

"Do you put feelings in boxes?" I was laughing.

"Yes, I do. It's a system I have with everyone, even my family. It helps me determine how much I can trust someone. For example, Mom and Dad, I put them in a box, and Uncle Vitorio. I trust them the most. Then I put everyone else in a separate box. So, is this *no kiss* for now or for always?"

"I don't know yet…" But I knew that even though I was happy to be close to him, I did not want to be added to his ex-love collection box.

"I just open a new category: *Unidentified*. You are there alone…" He smiled. "And, yes, we do have a few women working in the fields and they are good workers."

"Do you have children working, too?"

"We used to let children go with their parents but it is illegal now. The parents liked the way it was before, so they could make a little more money, and the children liked because they would have some, too. Anyway, I approve of the law because children should really be at school, not in the field. And I like the idea of avoiding accidents with children. But you still see children in the fields because some farmers continue to allow it. It is cheaper labor and the kids keep out of trouble."

"What else women could do here?"

"I don't know. But whatever you plan to do, you need to respect them."

"What do you mean? Am I disrespecting them?"

"I know it's not your intention, but I think they don't like the way you talk to them."

"What do you mean?"

"Cecilia, you tend to make them feel that you are better than they are, smarter than them, and that you know better than they do. If you are here to help like you said, you can't impose your beliefs to them and you can't interfere in their lives. If you want to stay here, you need to accept their culture."

"I just don't know what to do. Everything seems wrong."

"If you want to give them hope, it has to be based on their reality, not on yours."

Vitor understood the villagers. He knew them and was part of their lives. Despite all the problems, there was a kind of unity. Despite the violence, there was also a measure of security. Despite all the disappointments, there was still a sense of hope.

CHAPTER 11

Christmas season arrived, my first in Brazil since I was a small child. Vitor invited me to spend Christmas Eve with his family, and he had invited many other villagers, too. Earlier in the day, I overheard some children in my front yard discussing Santa Claus.

Isa said, "My mom said that Santa isn't real.".

"But I saw him in the movie on Dona Josa's television," said Ciça. "He left presents in the kid's homes."

Then Zé said, "Television isn't real Ciça. It's all made up to keep people watching and to make rich people buy things."

"But I saw. The girl wanted a doll and Santa brought her one," replied Ciça.

"Even if Santa is real, Ciça, he isn't from Brazil. He lives far-away like Dona Cecilia. Santa doesn't know where we live," said Isa.

"The place he lives has snow, nice homes, fireplaces. We have none of that. And it is too hot here for him with all his puffy red clothes. And we don't have food for him," said Zé.

"I wish we had cookies, milk and snow just for tonight," said Ciça.

"And just Dona Rita has Christmas tree in her house," said Isa. If Santa goes somewhere around here, it will be there."

"If Santa could listen to us, what you two would ask him for Christmas?" asked Ciça.

"Ciça, he can't listen to us. He doesn't know us. Why would he care?" asked Zé.

"Just *if* he was real and could listen to us," insisted Ciça.

"*If* he could listen to us, I would ask him to give me a nice soccer ball, like the ones on television," said Zé.

"I would ask for a box of chocolates. They look really good on television," said Isa. "What you want, Ciça?"

"I want two pairs of sandals; one for me and one for Zinho. This one is broken. Mom put a nail on the bottom to fix it, but it's almost broken again."

"Your mom can't buy you another one? My mom bought mine two Sundays ago," said Isa pointing to her new blue flip-flops.

"Mom said she will buy sandals when she pays your dad the money he lent her for our food," said Ciça.

"I'd like Santa to listen to us. But he won't. He never has and he never will. He just doesn't exist," Zé said.

"Will Dona Rita's grandkids come this year?" asked Isa. They always show their Christmas presents to everybody. Maybe they'll let us play with them."

"Hey!!" screamed Juninho from far away. "I found an old tire on the road. If you guys help me to make a swing, we can play." And all the kids left.

Later, Marcos, Lia and I went to the general store in Terra-do-Mato. It was closed but the owner didn't mind opening it for us. I bought everything that could fit in Marcos' car: toys, candies, Christmas tree decorations and the children's three special wishes. At the last minute, we set up a tree. I was full of joy to be able to offer the children something special on Christmas morning.

Around eight that night, Lia and I went to the Valérios. There were Rita, Zé Francisco, Vitor, Vitorio, a few employees and their families. The house was beautifully decorated and everyone seemed to be happy. Lia, however, was quiet. She seemed to be the stranger of the night.

"Lia, are you okay?" I asked.

"Yes."

"What's the problem?"

"Mazé is looking me and it's making me nervous."

"Why is she looking at you?"

"I used to work in the sugarcane before you came here, and her husband was my supervisor. He checks the work of the field hands. People started to say that he was giving me easier jobs and paying me too much attention. So Mazé went to my mom and said that I was not allowed to work in the fields anymore and that she didn't want to see me around."

"Did you have anything with him?"

"No, Cecilia. But I think he tried." She paused. "I swear to you that I never allowed him, and I never will."

"So, don't worry about her." I said. "She won't do anything."

"I don't know. These women are crazy."

Victor approached and asked, "Hi. Do you want a drink?"

"No, thanks," I said. "It's a beautiful party, Vitor. Thanks for inviting us. Where is your mom? I haven't seen her yet."

"She's in the kitchen. She'll be here soon," he answered. "Where were you two this afternoon? I went to your house, Cecilia, but you weren't there."

"We went to town. I needed some stuff."

"Today? Weren't the stores closed?"

"We went to the general store. You know, they will open any time if there's a customer."

Vitorio approached. "Here you are, Cecilia, my favorite foreigner!" he said. "You know, I was looking forward to having you with us this evening."

I stood up and kissed him respectfully. "You are always a gentleman Vitorio. How are you?"

"Better now."

"Uncle, sit," Vitor moved Vitorio's favorite chair closer to us.

"Thank you, son. Nana!" Vitorio called for one of the house-keepers.

"Yes, sir" answered Nana.

"Bring one of the bottles that came yesterday from the mill," Vitorio ordered.

"Uncle, Cecilia is not used to it," said Vitor.

"She can at least try it," Vitorio replied. "You will like it, Cecilia."

Nana placed the bottle and some whiskey glasses on the table. "Thank you Nana," said Vitorio while serving us.

"Cecilia, I usually don't open up to people until I know them well. Vitor knows that, and can tell you about it. But when I first saw you, I knew you were a good person."

Vitor laughed and leaned over to me. "I guess miracles really happen. I never saw Uncle like this."

"Because there was nothing to be nice about," replied Vitorio.

"Usually you are grouchy with newcomers."

"Just with those who aren't interesting. Not many neighbors would attack one of my employees to defend a woman."

"Please, Vitorio don't remind me. I still feel ashamed."

"Don't be. More women here should stand up for themselves the same way you stood up for Marilda."

"Uncle, please, don't give her any ideas."

"Hey," I said, laughing. "I am behaving well today."

"I know, and I want you to stay out of trouble..." said Vitor.

"Vitor you are worrying too much," said Vitorio.

"I think I came just in time to try the first bottle," said Zè Francisco, Vitor's father. "Vitorio, your sister wants me to make sure you don't drink too much."

"And she told me not to let you drink at all," said Vitorio to Zè.

We all laughed.

"It's better we do this before she comes," said Vitorio serving Zè with a shot. "Merry Christmas for you all."

"Merry Christmas!" said everyone.

"This one is very good," said Zè.

Everyone was looking at me waiting for a reaction. The drink was strong, powerful enough to wake every cell in my body. I coughed a little, trying to clear my throat.

"It's really not bad," I said. But my voice seemed to come out of a horror movie.

"Just two people got this cachaça [*a type of tequila made from sugar-cane in the local mills*]: the owner of the mill and me."

"Mom is coming," said Vitor.

Zé hid the bottle under the table.

"Hello, Cecilia," Rita said. "Thank you for coming. It's nice to have you with us today."

"Thank you Rita. I'm happy to be here."

"Where is the bottle?" she said.

"Which bottle?" asked Zé.

"The one with the cachaça that filled those glasses," she said.

"Son, you could at least hide the glasses," said Zé.

"And miss this moment?" Said Vitor laughing.

"Rita, we are just having fun. It is Christmas!" Vitorio insisted.

"I know Vitorio. But you and Zé need to slow down. Remember what the doctor said."

"If I listen to that doctor, I will not even get out of bed," said Vitorio. "I'm fine."

"Dinner will be served in about fifteen minutes," said Rita. "Where is Lia?"

I thought it strange she'd ask about her. I looked around. Lia was gone.

"I don't know," I said. "She was just here."

"Mazé is very upset because Lia is here," said Rita.

"Why is she upset?" asked Vitorio.

"Remember the episode between them? Mazé thought João was having an affair with Lia?"

"Oh, that. Stupid Mazé. João goes after every woman in the field. If I receive one more complaint, I will fire him from the job," said Vitorio.

"I told him already," said Vitor.

"You should tell Mazé, too. She is saying that if she sees Lia near João, she will show her what a woman can do."

"What? I want to see what she can do in this house," said Vitorio. "Rita, I know you like her and that's the only reason I tolerate her in the house, but she better respect this place."

"I told her I didn't want a scene today,"

"If Lia's presence is causing problems, we can leave," I said.

"Absolutely not. You and Lia stay," said Vitorio. "You two are my guests. Rita, Mazé was supposed to be a help to you today, not look for trouble."

Then, Nana came with more news, "Dona Rita. Mazé is arguing with Lia in the front yard!"

Vitor, Rita, and I ran out to see. There was Mazé shouting at Lia like an angry dog barking. João had a tight grip on his wife, preventing her from taking a swing at Lia.

Vitor yelled, "Shut up Mazé!! What is the matter with you?"

"I saw, Vitor!" Mazé screamed. "João sent a drink to this prostitute!"

Lia looked at me. "It's not true, Cecilia. Mano sent me that drink."

"Liar!" Mazé yelled. "You want to take my husband from me!"

"That is easy to discover. Mano, did you send the drink to Lia?" asked Vitor.

"Yes, I did. I didn't know it would create problems."

"Thank you, Mano. There's no problem."

"João and Mazé, I want to talk with you both inside," said Vitor. "You all please forget about this incident."

Lia came and said, "I am sorry, Cecilia. I came to see Mano."

"Don't worry about it. You two stay here. I will check on it."

I went back to the house. Vitor seemed upset.

"Uncle Vitorio wants me to fire you, João. He is very upset that you are not respecting the women in the field. And Mazé, you should be angry at him, not with the girls. Do you think a beauty like Lia would want someone like João?"

"Vitor, everyone knows I don't like that girl." "Mazé, that's your problem. I don't want to know about it. What we all want is for you to respect this house. You are a good woman, Mazé; but you're letting João play with you."

"Hey Vitor, don't say that. I'm not playing with anyone!" said João.

"I'll talk to you tomorrow. Mazé, go back to help my Mom and leave Lia alone. As you see, Lia is interested in Mano, someone who's young and responsible."

Mazé flopped on the sofa and started to cry into a pillow. When Vitor and João left, I stayed with her.

"Mazé, can I get you anything?" I asked.

She took the pillow away from her face and looked at me, "I don't need your pity. Just because you have money and Vitor likes you, you think you are better than everybody else. You came from a perfect world. You don't know me. You don't know what it is to be a woman in a place like this. You don't know what it is to love and not be loved back. You don't know what it is to be abandoned with your children by your own husband. You don't know what it is to be a single mother. You don't know what it is to look around and have nothing to feed your hungry children. Don't judge me, girl; you don't know where I come from. You don't know what I have been through."

"I am not judging you, Mazé. But you are judging me wrongly."

Rita entered and took us by surprise, "Mazé, I need your help in the kitchen. Dinner still needs to be served."

"Sure, Dona Rita. I will be right there. I am sorry for your pillow. I will wash it tomorrow."

"Don't worry about it, Mazé. I'm waiting for those beautiful pillow cases you are making."

Mazé went to the kitchen.

"I hope you can forgive Mazé," Rita said to me. "She is a good woman, but life has not been easy for her."

"I understand."

"Some years ago her husband left her and her three children and went to live with someone else. Every once in a while, Mazé sees him but he never helps with the kids."

"I thought João was her husband," I said.

"No, he isn't. They only live together. She felt lucky to find someone like João to look after her and her children. But it seems like he doesn't want the situation any more, and she doesn't want to let him go. I understand her. Maybe only a mother can understand another mother. And, be careful about what you hear from the people in the village. Chances are that they instigated the situation with Mazé this evening."

"Did she make these pillow cases?" I asked.

"Yes. She is very talented. She makes beautiful pieces by hand. Too bad people don't pay enough for her work. She makes tablecloths, too. I'll show you. They are works of art."

Dinner was served in two locations, the dining room and the front yard. Vitório, Zé, Rita, Vitor, João Mario (the farm manager) and his wife Maria Cicera, and I had dinner inside the house. The others seemed to be outside by choice. I asked Lia to stay and eat with me, but she said, "I'd really prefer to stay outside, Cecilia. It's better."

We ate turkey, the traditional Christmas meat of Brazil. For dessert, the incredibly delectable Brazilian pudding [condensed milk and caramel flan] was served. By the time dinner was over, the party outside had become four times larger and was still growing. To feed them, workers had slaughtered a steer. As more beer bottles were emptied, the diners became happier and louder. At midnight, fireworks announced that Christmas had arrived. A sense of contentment took over the place. Vitório's "special bottles" tasted a lot better after midnight.

Among us that night, there seemed no difference between rich and poor. Brazilians were just celebrating the holiday. And I was not an outsider anymore. I was just Cecilia, someone without a past or a future, only a present. I also felt secure that Vitor was always there, protecting me. The Cecilia that was there was happy to hold Vitor's hand every now and then and dance with him to the sound of our own music. That Cecilia was delighted to say, "You can take me out of the 'undecided' box and place me in the 'kissed' one." He kissed me while we were dancing. That Cecilia was happy. I liked her and I did not want her to ever go away.

But slowly the sunrise gave us the sign of a new day.

After sleeping awhile, I awoke with the worst headache ever. I could not even move from bed. Interestingly, Lia, who seemed to have partied even more than I, was already working as usual and looking after me. That morning, I really appreciated the fast relief of modern medicine. Meanwhile, the village and the people seemed to have retreated a bit, at least until Lia reminded me that we still had the children's gifts under our Christmas tree.

I asked Lia to tell Isa, Zé, and Ciça that we had things for them. I also asked her to distribute the rest of the gifts to other village children. Lia went to the square and gave my message to the three children, who rapidly multiplied to about twenty in minutes. They were soon on my doorstep, with more on the way. When I saw them, I prepared for another headache.

"Lia, what is this?" I asked with surprise.

"Cecilia, I only told the kids in the square. They must have told others."

"That's okay. Now, please tell Isa, Zé, and Ciça to come and find their gifts."

The three were fascinated with the tree. The lights reflected in their eyes. It did not matter how soon they would have to grow up, today they were still children with all their innocence and dreams. For the other children, Lia suggested that we have a lottery to award toys and chocolates. Everyone would have a numbered ticket. The grand prize would be the Christmas tree. Lia and the children's parents took everything to the square, and I stayed behind. I really didn't want to be part of it, and I wished I had purchased more gifts.

When the lottery began, things were fine until two children from the same family had lucky numbers. By coincidence, their mother, Josita, was helping pick the winning tickets. Suddenly I heard some agitation and naming-calling. I tried to ignore it. It was Christmas after all and that kind of behavior was totally unacceptable despite their culture or desperation. And it was only chocolates and kids' toys. Nonetheless, Lia came running back to me to ask my advice.

"Lia," I said, "I think only one gift per family would be better. Maybe Josita's children should keep only prize. And from now on, after someone wins, no other child in the same household is eligible."

"But Cecilia, Josita refuses to return the second. She said no one told her that only one child per family could win."

I mumbled to myself, "I think these people never heard the word 'share' before."

There was a knock on my opened door. "Come on in," I said without looking.

"What's happening in the square?" asked Zé Francisco.

"Yesterday I had the stupid idea of buying gifts for a few village children but there weren't enough for everyone. Our little lottery isn't working. Zé, why do people have to act this way?"

"Cecilia, I guarantee they would behave much worse for even less. But they still respect you, so what would you like to do?"

"I'd like them to finish distributing the gifts and then forget about the lottery."

"How do you want to distribute them?"

"Lia was there doing it. Lia, tell Zé how you were doing it," I said.

Zé went to the square with Lia and in seconds he calmed the crowd, distributed the gifts, and soon the kids were having fun and the adults were peacefully talking. I wasn't sure if I failed to show authority by staying behind, or if these people only obeyed someone in Valério's family.

Zé returned later. He came more as a teacher than a friend. By then, my headache had subsided and I could think a little more clearly.

"Thank you Zé, for your help today. I really didn't know what to do," I said.

"I understand how you feel. Many times, I feel the same. When I first arrived, I was just out of high school. Teaching was the only work available. I was frustrated and unhappy. At first,

I hated these people. I thought their children were impossible to teach because they were just little animals in human skins. I had grown up in a civilized town and, for me, these were more like hungry primitives.

"But," he continued, "I met Rita and learned to see the village through her eyes. These are forgotten people. They have little to no education and no chance for political discourse. The village school is just a disguise. The teachers pretend they are working for the community so they can keep their jobs, and the central government is seldom seen. In fact, the government pretends this part of the country is making progress. Meanwhile, the clerics brainwash everyone to believe in Paradise after death. In this way, everyone is resigned to suffering. In this way, the whole system - government, education, religion, everything - works against them, generation after generation. Do you know that this school actually carries the name of the worst dictator in the history of Brazil?"

"Really?"

Zé continued, "That tyrant and his generals led us into the worst of political times. They jailed, tortured and killed so many Brazilians; it was a terrible period. But today, our little village school bears his name, and the teachers tell the students to be proud of him because he was a president. The parents don't even know what that man did to their country.

"Today," he said, "you did exactly what every foreigner does - sends old clothes and toys just to make themselves feel better about helping others."

"What?" I exclaimed. "Zé, you are insulting me. I thought it would be nice for the children to have gifts at Christmas time."

"Today, it would have been better if you had told them why you didn't have enough for everyone, and the reason they had to share. Many of the children were crying because they were not lucky enough to win a toy. You don't know this because you were not there to see their faces."

"Zé, it was not my intention—"

"Cecilia, you have to stop acting as a foreigner or a tourist," he said. "You can be anywhere you choose, not just in a backwater village in northeast Brazil. So, why are you here? What do you want? For months, we have watched you building your house, being interested in the school, talking to everyone. If you came to help them, do it, but be sure they trust you enough to tell you what they need. If not, don't give them hope and don't manipulate them. Enough others do it already, with very little success."

He seemed angry now, and continued, "When I was teaching, a child came to me during break time and asked if I could let him out for a second so he could give his food to his mother who was outside. I asked if he wasn't hungry. He said, 'My sister and I will share our food with Mother. Please teacher, open the door. Mother hasn't eaten since yesterday."

"Cecilia, I cried over that. But even my cry was selfish. It was not just because of the child's situation, I also cried because of my misery as a human being. I used to think that some children had no brains, so couldn't learn. After awhile, I began to think he may be a better human being than I."

"There are countless heartbreaking real stories here. Rita can tell you even more than I can. She loves them and she doesn't judge them. In our home, Vitorio, Vitor, and I just pretend that we wear the pants. With Rita's love, she controls everyone." We both laughed then, though uneasily.

"Most of the time, Rita has the last word. If you follow her one day, you will see that she dedicates most of her time to the villagers. Because of that, we decided she could never manage the farm or in less than a year we would lose everything!" He smiled. "Vitor loves this place as much as his mother does, and the people admire and respect him too."

"I know Zé. Vitor is a good man. Zé, I am here to help. I just don't know how to do it."

"Maybe Rita can give you some ideas," he said.

"I'm sorry for what happened today. I should have talked to

someone. It won't happen again, I promise."

"Don't make promises, Cecilia. It seems that in this place, people are never able to keep them." Then he looked around. "I like your house. It's nice; very well done."

When Zé left, I went out to try to look at the village with new eyes. It all seemed ancient and alien. I wondered where everyone came from? What had happened to them? What were their secrets? How did they feel? What did they want? I thought I already knew most of them well, but I really didn't. I only knew what they allowed me to know. Although I did not feel a complete outsider anymore, I was still a foreigner to them.

Through the road dust and the bright Christmas sunlight, I saw a group on Josefina's porch. I joined them. Josefina was telling stories of the village's old times when she was a child. She was the best storyteller I ever met. To many, her stories might sound make-believe; but if so, she had an extraordinary imagination. Nonetheless, Josefina swore they were true. That day, I recognized one of them.

"The last time I saw as many people in this square as today," she said, "was when Elena's father beat her almost to death. It all happened here, many, many years ago."

"Dona Josefina, we all know this story isn't true," said Maria Cicera.

"Seu Vitorio already told us isn't true," said Rosa Maria.

Josefina said, "That's because Vitorio wants to preserve a fantasy. He doesn't want to accept that his father could behave that badly."

"But Dona Josefina, where is she and her family?" Tonha asked.

"Oh! No one knows."

"People think you invented this story, Dona Josefina," said little Zé João.

"Why I would do that, boy?"

"Because you want us to come to listen to you."

"There's no need for that."

I took a breath and then began, "So, no one believes that Elena was real?" Suddenly, everyone looked at me. "If I say that I met her, would you believe?" Nobody answered. "Elena died a few months ago in her beautiful home in the United States." The silence became even greater. "I worked for her the last year of her life."

Sitting among the group, I calmly and precisely told them what I knew about Elena and Julio and her life in the United States. I ended the story with, "She never forgot about her village even though she was forced to leave."

"Why did she send you?" someone asked.

"I have some work to do here before I can answer."

It was getting dark. The group drifted away from the porch, leaving me with Josefina. "I wonder if Elena told you the whole story," said Josefina.

"I don't understand. Elena wrote everything in her journal and I translated it to English. At least, I think she wrote everything."

"Possibly she didn't know what really happened here. Now that everybody is dead, I guess it doesn't matter."

"It matters to me, Josefina. What actually happened? What didn't Elena know?"

"It was so long ago," said Josefina. "If people were right about my age, I was about ten years old at the time. I was always so curious. I used to play near the grown-ups just to hear what was going on, and I always knew before everyone else.

"Elena was about four or five years older than me. All the girls were jealous of her relationship with Julio. They all wanted to marry him. Not because they loved or admired him but because of what marrying him meant. As his wife, she would be an important person, just like Julio's mother.

"No other girl was as close to Julio as Elena. She was a pretty girl. But what made her different was that she was a wonderful girl too, a good soul. She was not a complainer like the others. She was always happy. She attracted the eye of many men, even from other villages.

"One wealthy widower, an ugly old man, offered Elena's father a house and a lot of money to marry Elena. The widower was Julio's father's friend. They used to play cards on that porch"—she pointed to Vitorio's house across the street—"Eventually, everyone including Julio learned about the offer, that Elena was supposed to marry that pig of a man. But I don't know if Elena knew what was in store for her. Some thought she knew because Julio knew. They were very close.

"At first, people saw Julio and Elena more like brother and sister; not as lovers. Then, there was the business with Julio marrying Luiza. Mazé's grandmother, Rita Lucia, and another girl knew where Elena and Julio used to meet every few days in the afternoon. One day, they took Maria, Julio's sister, to spy on Julio and Elena. That did it. Elena's father lost his business and Julio's father lost his wealthy friend. But Elena got the worse right here in this square."

"Elena was betrayed?"

"Yes, she was."

"I don't think she knew about it."

"Maybe she really never knew. Her father was obsessed by the loss of his business. You see, the other girls did not want to marry the widower, but they also did not want Elena to become wealthy. So they made sure Elena would not marry either Julio or the widower."

"And Elena's mother?" I asked. "Did she know?"

"No. She was told the day Elena was gone. Poor woman, she screamed aloud that everyone would pay for what happened to her daughter. At the time, the villagers thought she had cursed them. You know that Julio's death was horrible."

"How was Julio?"

"He wasn't bad. Sometimes, when I see Vitor, it is just like seeing Julio. But they are different, too. Vitor is not afraid of anything. Julio was weak. He was more afraid of his father than of the Devil. His father was not a good man, he was rude, a bully.

Julio would never do anything to upset him. Julio was not so bad. After Elena fled, he was eaten up with guilt. Elena became a dirty name. No one wanted to talk about her. Others left the village and life kept going on. But I always thought I would see Elena again."

"What happened to Elena's family?"

"One of the brothers died, I don't remember how. The others married and moved to other plantations. After her mother died, her father moved and we never heard of him again."

"Did Julio ever see Elena again?"

"I heard something but I was never sure it was true. Lucrecio told me that once he and Julio went to a bordel and saw Elena there. I did not really believe it because Julio never mentioned it. There are also stories that Elena wrote letters to her mother. But her mother never said it. I am not sure what's true. People talk too much in these villages."

"Why do you think Vitorio doesn't want people to believe Elena was real?"

"Vitorio knows what I say is true. He wants to preserve the image of his father as respectable. Vitorio has a strong sense of justice. It would be too much for him to believe that his father let a best friend and lover almost die in front of everybody. Vitorio would have to hate his coward of a father, and he can't do that.

"Julio was an important figure for Vitorio. He followed Julio everywhere. You would never see one without the other. The day Julio died, Vitorio was there. He was there when the fields burned and heard the men say Julio was caught in the fire. They had to restrain Vitorio from plunging into it. Now that you are here, it is going to be very difficult for Vitorio to face the facts, even after so many years."

"I understand," I said. There was a long pause.

"I'm glad to know Elena had a good life," Josefina said.

"She did," I replied. "She had a beautiful family and a loving and dedicated husband. But it seemed the memories of this place never left her. Her childhood and Julio's friendship were still very much alive."

"And you, girl? From what I hear, you and Vitor are becoming more than friends."

"I don't know. It is complicated."

"What's complicated?" she asked. "You young people want to make everything complicated. Let me see. Are you married?"

"No."

"Are you sick or dying?"

"No."

"Are you in love with another man?"

That took me few seconds to answer. I didn't know for sure. I was changing, and my feelings were changing, too. I admitted I liked Brendon. But I was not sure if he would ever be the one, even if I had that choice. "I don't know. But there is that woman that everyone talks about."

"Which woman?" She seemed confused.

"Vitor's girlfriend." "That is an old, new, old, new, and then again, old story," she replied.

"What?" I asked.

She explained, "Vitor has a house in town, and every once in a while we hear there is a woman there. But the girls here don't really know anything. They make up most of these stories because of Vitor's silence. I don't know much either, but I know Vitor does not have a girlfriend."

"He might not want one either," I said sadly.

Josefina consoled me with, "Just don't listen to these girls. They don't like to see other people happy. The times may be different, but the people are the same."

Walking home later, I saw Vitor in front of my house. I didn't remember exactly what happened the night before and I was embarrassed that I probably made a fool of myself. Vitor was on the front porch when he saw me.

"Hi. How is Josefina?" he asked.

"Telling all, just like always."

"How are you?" he asked, kissing me on my forehead.

"Good."

We sat together on the porch. A few silent seconds made me feel awkward.

"I'm sorry for last night," I began.

"Sorry for what?"

"I don't know. I drank too much, and I'm not used to it. I don't remember exactly what happened."

"Nothing happened. We just danced and kissed and you had a few shots and some beers. Then I brought Lia and you home, and I left. I didn't even go inside. I waited until you were both inside with the doors locked. Then, I left."

"Thank you."

"You don't have to thank me. I like you. And I like to be with you."

"I like you too. I never lost control over myself like that."

"Don't worry. It wasn't that bad."

"You have been a gentleman and a very good friend. I am just very confused today."

"I came because Mom wants to know if you'll come for dinner."

"Oh! Please, thank her for me. She is very kind. But I don't feel well."

"She will understand."

"Please, tell her that tomorrow morning I will go over to talk to her."

"Sure. I hope you feel better."

"I will."

He left.

I was really confused, trying to read between the lines. I did not know exactly what "I like you" meant. And I was afraid to become just one of his girls.

The next day, I woke early. The birds were singing loudly on my windowsill. There was the smell of fresh cut *jaca* [a big fruit with pointy skin, a strong smell, and a sweet taste] that left me with no reason to stay in bed. I got up and went to the kitchen.

"Bom dia, Lia. Why are you cutting jaca so early?

"So you can eat it cold, the way you like. I will put it in the refrigerator for later."

"Where did you get it?"

"Mano brought it."

"This early? I bet he really wanted to see you."

"They already went to work. I saw when Vitor left."

"Lia, what did I do at the Valério's house?"

"Nothing. Just drank a little."

"I know that. Did I say or do anything strange?"

"Not really. Why?"

"I just don't remember. Do you know if Vitor and I where alone at any time?"

"Vitor was always with you, and you both were with us. And, when the party was over, he brought us home and left. The only strange thing was that Vitor didn't drink at all. He normally drinks with the guys."

"I am going to get ready. I will visit Rita."

"Cecilia, is it true that you know the women who was Seu Vitorio's father's lover?"

"Yes, I knew Elena. How do you know this already?"

"Many people said they heard you saying it. Does Vitor know?"

"I don't know. I never told him. But now you know it. I wonder who else?"

"How was she?" Lia asked.

"Who?"

"Elena. What did she look like? I heard many of Dona Josefina's stories, but this one was my favorite because of Elena. I always imagined her beauty and wondered what happened to her. Sometimes, I didn't know if she was real or just a story."

"She was really a beautiful woman in every way you can imagine. If I hadn't met her, I would never believe she was real, either."

"Did Seu Vitorio's father love her?"

"I don't know, Lia. I don't know. But I know he was always in her heart."

"I wish I had known her," said Lia, looking at the container full of jaca pieces.

Later that morning, I walked to Rita's. By then, everyone knew about my connection to Elena. But Rita did not seem as interested.

"They are all dead," she said. "Let's leave the dead alone." Then, we went on to talk about her work in the village and how I could support it.

Rita told me that for years she and a few women had been already talking about ways to make money. Most of the women were talented embroiderers. All the women knew the art and some could even teach it. To give them incentive, Rita bought some of their work to resell, decorate her home, and give to friends. She even tried to sell it at the weekly *feira* [fair] in town. But, there weren't enough buyers. The women were just 'breaking even.' For Rita, however, the activity kept the women together as they sought company or solace during the hard times.

I was persuaded that the best way to help the village families was through the women. But I still did not know how I could use Elena's money in a way to do this. Walking back home, I was halfway between the Valério's and my house when I heard someone calling me. It was one of the Valério maids, saying that Vitorio wanted to see me. I went over. He was sitting in the shade of the porch, protected from the hot sun, and a slight breeze was blowing through.

"Bom dia, Vitorio!" I said.

"Dia, Cecilia"

"How are you this morning?"

"Good. Good. Please, sit." I took a seat in front of him. "I heard you are here because of someone my father knew,"

"And, I know you met her, too, once," I replied.

"How do you know that?" he asked.

"Elena wrote a journal and she let me read it. And, there was one encounter she gave special mention. It told how she met you at a wedding reception."

"I didn't know who she was until much later when my father told me their story and how much he loved her."

"Did he love her?"

"Oh, Cecilia, my father was a tormented soul and my grandfather was the devil. My father and my aunts were beaten to unconsciousness all the time when they were children. My grandfather thought beatings would educate them. But he truly was more a devil than a man. He did not have a loving cell in his body. He was so cold-hearted that he would wait until the night when his kids were in bed, and then suddenly wake them to punish them for something they did during the day. He would go in their bedrooms with a wide leather belt and tell them whatever he was angry about. Then he would whip them loudly for the whole house to hear."

Vitorio continued, "The kids would never know when to expect it. And it was a rule that whatever happened in his house stayed in his house. No one was allowed to talk about it outside. They were trapped, like slaves. But my father loved that woman, more than he ever loved anyone else. Cecilia, what I will tell you now must stay with us at least until I am dead. Can you give me your word?"

"Yes."

"I know my father killed himself. He could not live with guilt anymore. As I told you, he was a tormented soul."

"So," I asked, "why do you tell everyone that Elena is not real?"

"I never said she was not real, I just never confirmed Josefina's story. I don't like to talk about it with these people. They didn't know my father, they would never understand what happened, and it doesn't concern them. Anyway, I don't know if everything she says is true."

"Elena never forgot your father. And she never forgot this

village."

"When we finally brought him out of the fire, he kept calling for that woman until her mother came. I am an old man, Cecilia, I am an old man; but that final image of my father is still in my head as if it had just happened."

"Your mother, how was she?"

"She was forced to marry a man who loved another woman to death. That's what she had to live with for the rest of her life. Josefina is right when she says that the woman's mother cursed everyone in this village. There is no happiness here. Not even the sugarcane grows as it used to."

"Is it true that Elena was supposed to marry your grandfather's friend?"

"The first time I heard about it, my father, grandfather and grandmother were already dead and almost everyone who they knew were gone. Josefina was the only one who had the story. So, I don't know if it's true. She told many stories, some true from beginning to end were correct and some not so true. For Josefina, that is the only explanation for what Elena's father did. But knowing the devil, the only option for her father was to make her leave the village."

"Why did your grandfather go to such extremes?"

"He was awful. He helped many families by giving them work and places to live. In return, he wanted them to work hard and recognize his family as superior. He was still living in the past, the time of slavery, and did not know how to live in a new world."

"Elena was different," I said. "She did not belong in this world of Brazilian villages."

"People will talk more about her now. I want to ask you to avoid talking about all this with Rita. It's even harder for her. She knows how difficult this was for our mother. You do whatever you came to do, but don't create problems. My sister has been working to help these people long enough to be respected by everyone. I'm sure she'll do whatever she can to help you but if you are determined to bring back such a painful story, leave Rita and the rest of the family out of it. There is no point to keep digging. They are all dead."

I felt sorry for Vitorio. He was trying to convince himself that it was time to forget. It is never time to forget.

At home again, I began to collect as much information as possible for a business plan the women could use. But part of my mind was on Vitor. I did not want to admit he had become important to me, and I was worried that he would think I lied to him for not telling about Elena. I was nervous and afraid that he would stay away.

When I first arrived, I thought that I could just create a new me and start from scratch. Then, as I was worried about Vitor, I realized I was not able to erase who I was. I acted and felt just like the Cecilia I knew from before. Elena's words came to mind, *"Your past travels with you wherever you go."* All my life until that point, I had been trying to let it go and forget the past. I really did not want to be attached to anyone. I just knew how to let it go. I did not know how to stay and fight. I felt like a bundle of loose ends.

It would have been easy for me to just pack my stuff and leave again. All that day after Christmas, I thought about doing it. But Elena held me there. I had a responsibility to her and, by extension, to all the women in the village. It was a new thought for that Cecilia.

By evening, I nervously expected to see Vitor. I was already used to the idea that he would show up. After dinner, I went to the porch and waited. He did not come. I wanted to ask Lia to go after him, but that would show weakness—I did not want to show such weakness.

Next day, life was a frustrating business. I spent most of it trying to e-mail Grace and waiting for chance to talk to Vitor. Neither seemed possible. Vitor wasn't around and internet wasn't working. Time seemed to be in abundance.

After lunch, I sat on my porch to relax, but couldn't calm

down. It was hot. Besides, about every twenty minutes, a truck full of sugarcane passed by, stirring a cloud of fine brown road dust, blurring things for a minute or two. This dust was Lia's biggest complaint; it kept her busy cleaning.

The villagers were starting to gather on their porches, mostly women, working on their crafts. Their mouths worked as quickly as their hands. They were *fofoqueiras,* [gossips]. They knew all about everyone's affairs and what they didn't know they would assume or invent. Generally, the porch across the road and two houses to the right of mine was a popular spot. Seven women were talking, gesticulating, and laughing. To them, the heat and dust did not seem a burden.

Another truck full of cut cane passed.

I waited until the air cleared then crossed the street and approached them. The women suddenly fell silent, watching me. Even the air, leaves in the trees, and clouds were still as I approached.

"Good afternoon, ladies!" I greeted them.

"Afternoon!" They all said in a lower voice.

For a couple of seconds, there was this eerie silence as they stared. I expected the lady of the house, Vanda, to invite me to sit, but she didn't. So I continued approaching and asked, "Do any of you have something ready to sell?" I wasn't sure I actually wanted to see what they had because the cloths in their hands were yellowish and somewhat dirty.

"Sure, we do," Vanda answer. She pointed to a very large piece on which two women were working.

"What is this one?" I asked.

"A bed sheet," Nana answered in a low voice, without raising her eyes. Nana was young and brown. Her blouse was finely embroidered. At the time, I did not know her name, and I thought she'd be too young for such a group.

"How did you learn to do it?"

"Mama taught me," she answered, not looking at me.

"Are you in school?" Another woman answered, "School is

over, now. It's vacation. School ended last week."

Again, to Nana, I asked, "Which grade do you attend?"

Another woman whom I later learned was Nana's mother, answered, "Oh, this poor girl, she is not very good at school. Her head can't hold a thing. She is thirteen, but she only knows how to write her name and a few other words. I took her out of school months ago. Most of her friends know much more than she does. At least she's learning to take care of a house and to cook, and she's good at it. She doesn't have the head to learn anything in school." The mother seemed proud of her decision.

I felt sorry for Nana. There she was, listening to all this talk without contesting. Likely, she'd heard it all before. I looked at her and said, "This is a beautiful piece. You are very talented." I wanted to give her many more compliments and tell her that only a smart girl could do that kind of work.

"I want to send gifts to the United States," I said.

"What kind do you want?" Vanda asked. "We have curtains, tablecloths, pillow cases, bed sheets and we can make whatever you want. We can show you designs and you can tell what you like."

"Can I see what you have ready?" I asked.

"Nana, go in and bring the box on my bed," Vanda said, and Nana immediately obeyed.

"I've some ready too," another woman, Lourdes, said. I felt she needed to show me, but I wasn't sure if she wanted attention or just money.

"Can you bring it here? No, even better, let's all go over to my house, eat bread pudding and drink coffee. You all bring can whatever you have ready." They all just looked at me, so I assumed they agreed. "I am going back to tell Lia and will see you all there."

I crossed the road before the next sugarcane truck passed.

About twenty minutes later, there were not only the seven women from the porch group, but there were five more, altogether in my front room. For a second, I recalled the crowd of children on my doorstep the day before, and resolved that this encounter would turn out better.

Each of the women had brought some of their handiwork to show me. I was surprised at how clean and neat the pieces were, every one washed, carefully folded and boxed. As we looked over them, the women became talkative. They told me where they were born, how they came to live in the village, and a little about their families. I began learning their names. On the surface, there was nothing special about their Brazilian lives. None of them had a Cinderella story. Instead, they had common tales of sorrowful poverty, with few rewards for their bravery.

As a group, they seemed to have come from the same past and were heading toward the same future—poor, bored and unappreciated Brazilian girls, wives and grandmothers. Their eyes shared the same expression. If they sat side-by-side, you could look into their eyes and not be able to tell one woman from another. I wondered if they wanted to make me feel guilty for being different from them. I had come from a different past and probably would have a different future. But I didn't feel different except for being blessed to see what they could not.

I asked if any of them had gone to school. I learned that half had finished fourth grade and the other half had not even gotten that far. A few thought they'd like to attend the local adult literacy program, evenings Monday through Friday, but none had enrolled. I thought it was strange that they did not take advantage of it. Some said their husbands prohibited them, and others just did not feel the need to learn anything new.

After an hour of looking at their pieces, I bought two of the best from each woman, twenty-four pieces of handiwork in all.

I was on my front porch thanking the women when Vitor passed on horseback, came close to me and leaned from his saddle. "What happened?" he asked.

"Nothing happened. Why?"

"You all together in front of your house. Something must have happened." "It was nothing. They were just showing me some of the stuff they made."

Vanda was standing beside me. "Vitor," she asked, "Who you will bring to Minas Gerais?"

"I don't know yet. But when I decide, I will let them know," he answered. I could see he was a little annoyed. With that, the women almost rushed back across the street to their activities. Vitor and I were left alone.

"Are you going to Minas?" I asked.

"Yes. Uncle has land there and he used to attend every year. But he's not well, so I have to do it now."

"Why didn't you tell me?"

"I came to tell you but you did not want to talk."

"Can we talk tonight?" I asked.

"Sure. What time?"

"Whenever you are available."

"I will have to pay the workers tonight. I can come after that?"

I nodded.

I knew it was too early for him to be back from work. Then I noticed that his left hand was bandaged and he was not moving it.

"What's wrong with your hand?" I asked.

"Nothing, really," he said.

"Can I see it?"

He unwrapped the bandage and showed me. There was a long, open cut on his palm.

"You have to go to the hospital. You will need stitches."

"I will go home now and Dad will take me."

"Can I go with you?"

"No, I'd prefer not. I don't want you to see me crying." We laughed.

"Go at once and take care of it."

"I will see you later on."

He pulled the reins, tapped the horse with his spurs, and started again at a natural pace as if everything were fine.

During the afternoon, I packed a carton full of the women's handiwork to mail to Grace.

Before night fell, news about an incident in the sugar-cane field had already spread through the village. Two workers had started a fight over how much land was theirs to work. It became violent when one of them cursed the other's mother. They threatened to kill each other and started to attack when Vitor intervened. One man cut Vitor's hand with a machete. Vitor then pulled his gun and ordered them both off the land.

After dinner, Lia and I sat on the porch while she waited for her favorite television soap opera to come on. The reception seemed better at night, and I was glad the electricity was reliable. Then Mano joined us. He was always looking for a chance to see Lia.

"Do you know whether Vitor's home?" I asked Mano.

"Yes, he is," he answered. "He went to town earlier, but now he's at home paying the workers. I was just there."

"Did you see the fight?"

"Yeah. We're all working when we heard the screaming and we all ran to see. Zé Pedo and Toinho were yelling at each other and showing their machetes. They were out for blood. Vitor happened to ride up. He jumped off his horse and told them to leave. Toinho was really angry. He started swinging his machete and almost cut Zé Pedo's head off. Vitor tried to grab Toinho's hand and the machete cut him. Then Vitor pulled his gun out and I thought he would kill them both. He ordered them off the field. Zé Pedo and Toinho are cousins. I don't know, but people say that their wives are at fault."

"Why?" I asked.

"'Cause they don't like each other and they're both jealous of what the other has. People are saying that Zé Pedo's woman was angry that Toinho had more land to work than Zé Pedo. I don't know. That's what they are saying."

"Where are they now?"

"Gone. We won't see them again. They're afraid of Vitor.

People are saying they both ran away. It's sad for the kids."

"They have kids?"

"Toinho has a boy and Zé Pedo a boy and a girl. They are at home with their mothers."

I knew Mano and Lia wanted to be alone, so I went inside and left the porch for them. I didn't expect to see Vitor that night.

Finally, the internet came back on—the signal was only strong at night. I looked over the e-mail I'd begun to Grace earlier in the day, then added a few things and sent it off. My message was about the embroiderers, their work, and my intention to help them sell their pieces. I attached a snapshot and mentioned I was mailing her some samples. I asked if she'd evaluate their quality and thing about who would buy their work "up north."

I sat thinking about the village embroiderers when Lia came in and with a low voice, as if telling a secret, said, "Vitor is here."

"Is he? Tell him to come in."

"Do you want Mano and me to leave so you two can have the porch?"

"No, you two stay there. Ask Vitor into the living room."

She went outside again and after a moment, Victor entered.

"Hi," he greeted.

"Hi," I greeted back. "How's your hand?"

"Not bad. It'll be fine."

"After that wound and all, I thought you might not come."

"It's not the first time I've been hurt in the field, and won't be the last."

"Do you think they'll return?"

"No. They won't. There's no work for them here or in any farm in the region. And if I see them again, I will make sure they stay in jail for a few days."

"I feel sorry for their kids."

"Their mothers will have to take care of them. Maybe now they will worry about their children and let me run my farm. I heard you talked to Mom. Was she any help?"

"Yes! She was very helpful. I'd like to bring these women together and sell what they make."

"Why don't you create a _cooperativa_?"

"What's that?"

"It's like a company but owned and maintained by the group, like an association. Everyone can sell their products through it."

"And how are the profits divided?"

"The members own their products, and receive the money for what they sell minus a fee to maintain the _cooperativa_. There are few successful ones in Alagoas."

"I am sending some of their work to a friend in the States." I didn't say it was Elena's step-daughter. "I hope she likes them and has ideas for selling more." I paused. "You probably know by now why I am here."

"I know two things. For some reason, you want to help the village. And a woman sent you. My field hands have plenty of time to wag their tongues while working."

"I am sorry for not telling you about Elena. I did not know how you would feel about this whole thing."

"I don't care for that story, so it doesn't affect me at all. To me, it's just old people's stories."

"Elena's story is not just old people's stories. She was real, and I see how even the mention of her name affects people in your own family."

"They are all gone. My grandfather made mistakes, my uncle and my father made mistakes, my mom made mistakes, I made mistakes, you made mistakes: We all made mistakes. We are not perfect and we have to live with it. I got upset with you because you doubted me. Cecilia, I am a man. If I tell you that nothing happened during or after the party, it is because nothing happened. My word should be enough. Asking others shows that you don't trust me...yet. But I will tell you, I am capable of getting drunk and having sex with a drunk woman. It's happened before. But I am not a liar. If something had happened between us, I would have told you. Don't doubt my word."

"Lia! That girl! I am going to choke her," I said.

"No, you won't," said Vitor. "This is between you and me. Lia trusted Mano and he trusted me. They knew me before they knew you. All this is to stay between you and me."

"I was just confused and embarrassed," I said.

"Cecilia, I like you. I understand that there are things I don't know about you. There are things you don't know about me, too. Three years ago, I went to Carnaval in Recife with some friends. There, I fell in love with a girl from Maceió. It was just *amor de carnaval…*"

"What is *amor de carnaval?*"

He laughed.

"Love that starts and ends with the carnival; from Friday night to Wednesday morning."

"What happened?"

"It was a big party and I was irresponsible. We had sex without protection. She became pregnant and I have a son. Only my uncle knows it."

"Oh my gosh! Your parents don't know you have a son?"

"They don't. For a while, I doubted he was my son, but we did a DNA test and he is mine. If you see him, you would know he is my son."

"You have a son." That affirmation would be enough for me to stay away from Vitor, but his honesty made me admire him instead. "What's his name?

"Gabriel. I try to see him once or twice a month and I pay all his expenses. His mom teaches part-time in a private school. She is a good mother and a good woman. First, I thought she just wanted to mess up my life and, you know, 'What kind of woman would degrade herself to that point? Not a mother of my son, for sure.' But the truth is, she has been a good woman, and I have been a jerk. Someday, I will tell my family about Gabriel. I want to be part of his life."

"Would you marry his mother?"

"Yes. But she doesn't want to. If I marry her, it will be just to make things right for both of them. She doesn't want that."

"Is she the one who stays in your house in town?"

"How do you know about the house in town?"

I laughed. "People talk," I said.

"I would never bring her and my son there. I bought the house a few years ago just as an investment. Now it is a kind of community property. Every time a friend needs a place for their 'other woman,' that's where they bring them.

"I brought women there a few times. But too many people know me and it was, like, people always know my business. I wish I had bought a house farther from the village. Anyway, there is a woman living there now, the mistress of one of my friends."

"People think she is your girlfriend."

"I know. I don't care what they think. Actually, my friend is buying the house from me. We will complete the sale soon. Then I want to bring my son here. I don't want to confuse my family or have to explain my friend's business."

"All this just doesn't seem like you."

"I am not perfect. But I am taking responsibility for my mistakes."

"It's just difficult for me to understand how people can go on making mistakes that affect others."

He smiled. "You probably will understand when you become a parent because, as a human, you will go on and on making mistakes that affect others. You just have to take responsibility for them and fix them the best you can. That is, if you care for anyone."

"Today you are a philosopher!"

"I'm just tired. I had to get another big loan from the bank to keep the farm going. The *usina* didn't pay us yet but I still have to pay my workers. I went to the bank and got the loan. I want to treat our workers better than the *usinas* treat us. Unfortunately, the first thing most of these guys do after I pay them is go to a bar and drink away their wages. Now, when winter comes, I will be the one hearing my mother preach about helping the poor. Couldn't they just put their money away and care for their own families?"

"My father did the same thing," I said. "He drank us away from him." That statement was an open door into my life, and that evening in the living room, I told Vitor everything I could remember about my childhood. I trusted him in a way that I never thought I would trust a man. I even told him that I compared every man in my life to my image or preconception of Brendon, even though I really didn't know him, either.

Our night passed in conversation. Mano went home and Lia went to bed. She missed her favorite soap opera that night but didn't seem upset.

"Are you really going to Minas?" I asked Vitor.

"Yes. I will have to stay there for a month or so. Do you want to come with me?"

I didn't answer. Something was blocking me. Going back to Brazil was like going back to the language, the culture, and to people like me. Going to Minas was like going back to an eight-year old girl with a drunken father. It would be like facing the monster in the closet.

"Maybe your grandmother is still alive," Vitor said. "You never know."

"It would be cruel to look for my grandmother just to tell her that her daughter is dead. I couldn't do that."

Before he left for home, we kissed awhile and he said, "There is an old tradition here that I will use to make sure we know what is going on."

"Okay," I said. I was excited, confused, anxious, and afraid all at the same time.

"Cecilia, would you be my girlfriend?"

We burst out laughing.

"Tradition says the woman has to answer," he continued.

"Yes. I will be your girlfriend."

Then, he asked, "Do you want to spend New Year's Eve in town? Normally we all go."

"Yes. I would love that."

He left. I couldn't sleep that night. I was beyond happiness but also could not stop wondering about the old people of Minas.

CHAPTER 12

January was a busy month for those in the village who liked to wag their tongues. During the first week, a wing of the school collapsed during a storm. But the public workers were on vacation, so no one noticed and the damage was ignored. A few days later, after Vitor sold his "secret" house, he told his parents about his son, Gabriel. The news was less painful to them than he expected. They were upset about his behavior but delighted about the boy's existence. That weekend, Rita organized a lunch for the child and his mother. Rita invited me but I felt a little uncomfortable with the whole thing and decided against it. Instead, I sent Lia to say that something had come up and I had to make some phone calls to the States. I hoped she'd explain to Vitor. I was happy for Vitor and Gabriel but was not sure I fitted into such a family reunion.

The internet was working that afternoon, so I was in my bedroom reading the news on an American website. I heard Vitor on the porch asking Lia if I was home. She knocked excitedly on my door. I didn't answer so she knocked again. "Come in," I said.

She opened the door slowly, "Vitor is here with Gabriel. He is so cute, and has beautiful eyes. You have to see him."

"I'll be right out." I wasn't ready but I knew this time would come. As I opened the door and stepped out, I saw a small boy trying to sit on the couch. Vitor helped him up and I came forward.

"Hi," I said.

Vitor grabbed the boy on his arms and said, "Cecilia, this is Gabriel."

I smiled and looked into his eyes. They were green, the kind I could look at for the rest of my life.

"Hi, Gabriel. I'm pleased to meet you," I said, hugging him.

He fell easily into my arms.

"We came to get you for lunch," Vitor said.

"I sent Rita a message. She didn't tell you?"

"No. What was the message?"

"Oh, nothing important, I guess. Just give me a second and I will go with you guys."

"Cecilia, what was the message?"

"Nothing important. Just saying that I would be late. I had some phone calls to make."

I gave Gabriel back to Vitor, went to the kitchen, and asked Lia, "Did you give my message to Rita?"

"Yes," she answered, somewhat confused.

"What did you say?"

"That you may not be able to go because... I told her what you told me, Cecilia."

"Okay," I said. But I wasn't convinced. I went to my bedroom and quickly changed out of my shirt and jeans into a colorful dress.

We walked to the Valério's, Gabriel between us, with me holding his hand. As we approached the house, a woman came out and waved to us from the porch.

"Mamma, Mamma!" Gabriel screamed, leaving my hand and running towards her.

'That must be what love looks like,' I thought.

The woman caught the boy and held him tight, and waited for us with a smile.

Vitor said, "Ana, this is Cecilia. Cecilia, this is Ana, Gabriel's mother." He made the introduction as we stepped onto their porch.

"It is nice to finally meet you, Cecilia. I feel I've known you for a long time. Probably it's because Vitor, Rita, and everyone else talks a lot about you."

"Hi, Ana. It is nice to meet you too. Welcome to Aveverde."

"I was afraid Gabriel would be trouble for you. He is not very well-behaved when he's hungry."

"He is adorable," I said. "We are happy he is here."

"Thank you. I think he is happy too," she said.

Vitor interjected, "If I know my mother, she is starting to get upset. It's after noon and we are still not eating." He guided us into the house.

I was glad the focus was not on me. This time, Ana was the stranger.

During lunch, Rita was unusually talkative and Vitorio oddly quiet. Rita and Ana kept the conversation going, while the rest of us listened and ate.

Ana wore a constant smile even while talking. I was not sure what that meant. Maybe she was just excited, or maybe nervous. At any rate, she was friendly and kept us entertained with stories about Gabriel, and about her family. When lunch was over, Vitorio went to the porch as the party dispersed. I followed him. "How are you, Vitorio? You're awfully quiet today."

"It's a nice breezy day," he answered. "Do you know, people change faster than places? For over fifty years, I've come out on this porch and I have seen almost the same view over and over." He paused to look out at the dusty road, the cane fields in the distance, the yellow-brown hills beyond. "Not too long ago," he continued, "we had values everyone respected. But today at lunch, I saw Vitor, his son, his son's mother, and you, all sitting at the same table and eating the same food. Vitor and Ana are not married, Gabriel is illegitimate, and all that has become normal and accepted. And, you are now Vitor's girlfriend. This is a family? I never thought I would live to see it."

"Vitorio—"

"No, Cecilia. That is how I feel and I know I can tell you, because you are as straightforward as I am."

"It's just a different time. You will get used to it."

"Oh, no! This is not my time. My time passed."

"Vitorio, did you ever love?"

"Yes, once. But it wasn't right. And I won't tell you about it. It is not worth it."

"I would love to hear it."

"You just want me to assure you that love is real. I will tell you that love might be real, but a happy ending is just a wish. I will tell you, if my father had married that woman—"

"Elena. Her name was Elena, Vitorio. Stop calling her 'that woman!'"

"if— my father had married that woman and they had a family, my father would soon have wished to escape with someone else. It would not have been a happy marriage. It is just the way we are. We want what is out of reach."

Zé appeared from inside the house. "What are you two doing here alone?"

"Talking about your son and your new grandson," Vitorio answered.

"Cecilia, don't listen to this old man. The older he gets, the grouchier he becomes," Zé said.

"Take your future daughter-in-law to join the rest of the party. I already did my duty. Now I just want to have a nap right here on the porch where things always stay the same."

"What?" Zé asked, confused.

"Come on Zé," I said. "Vitorio's just tired. He needs a nap." I held Zé's arm and we both walked back inside. In the living room, Rita and Ana were looking at a set of pillowcases Mazé had made. Rita could see how much Ana liked them, so she gave them to her. Ana was all smiles.

"Where's Vitor?" I asked.

"Gabriel fell asleep, so Vitor is putting him on my bed," Rita answered.

"I will let you ladies talk and will do the same as Gabriel and Vitorio," Zé said, walking away from us.

Then Vitor came in. "I am going to check the fields. We are preparing to burn cane today."

"But today is Saturday," Ana said. "You should have time off."

"During the harvest, I don't have a day off." Vitor replied.

Looking at me he asked, "Are you going to stay here until I come back?"

"No. I have to be home soon. I am waiting for a phone call."

"Did they install your phone already?" Rita asked

"Oh yeah, I forgot to tell you. I have a phone at home now. Vitor knows it. He didn't tell you?"

"Vitor only comes home to eat, shower and sleep. Sometimes he even eats at your house. He likes Lia's cooking."

"She is good," I confirmed, and looking at Vitor I said, "We need to change that bandage today."

"I'll see you tonight," he said giving me a kiss. "Ana, João will be here around four to take you two home." With that he left, as though he needed to get away rather than because he needed to go somewhere.

"And I will see what is going on in that kitchen," said Rita, leaving.

It was just Ana and me. She kept admiring the pillowcases and I knew she was trying to think of something to say. She did not know how to fake it. I didn't speak. Instead, I waited for her to break the uncomfortable silence.

"How's it like to live in the United States?" she asked.

"It's nice. There's a lot more convenience and infrastructure. It's easier and safer to drive, and the local governments are more organized and less intrusive than in Brazil. But here, I feel we have more time to interact. And, working mothers have four months' paid leave. I even heard lawmakers want to make it six months. That would be great. In the States, most women have six weeks but they are unpaid. I like Brazil and I like the United States both. In soccer, I am Brazilian all the way, but in basketball, 'Go, 'Magic Team!'" We laughed.

Ana said, "I have a friend in Boston and one in London. They are working on their Master's and doctoral degrees. They are both teachers. I always wanted to teach and travel. Besides the experience, teaching boosts your chance of working in a university. But after 9/11 it became very difficult and more expensive to get visas to the States." She continued, "Mom says that I destroyed my life even though she loves Gabriel. I don't feel like I destroyed it. I just know I will not be able to do some of the things I dreamed of. But Gabriel's smile makes up for it all."

"He is really cute."

"Cecilia, I have been dating someone for about two months. Vitor doesn't know anything about it and I am afraid this will complicate everything."

"Why would you think that? Do you think Vitor would not want you to be with someone else?"

"No Cecilia, that's not it. Vitor is a good father. Most don't even pay child support, they don't care. But Vitor pays for everything. We live in an apartment he bought for us. If it weren't for him, I would be living with my parents and that would be hell. Vitor visits Gabriel all the time. He worries and cares about us. But he doesn't love me. What we had was crazy, emotional and meaningless. If it were not for Gabriel, we would probably not even remember each other. Still, I am afraid that having someone else in our lives would change what we are lucky to have now. If Vitor doesn't like the situation, I am not sure what he would do. Or what I would do."

"I am sure Vitor would understand it. Does your boyfriend know Gabriel?"

"No. Not yet. And he has not yet been to our home."

"So, unless you plan to introduce him to Gabriel or bring him to your home, I don't think you should worry about anything. I don't think you should tell Vitor either. What you do with your life, if it doesn't involve Gabriel, is not Vitor's business."

"I am glad you will be Gabriel's step-mother."

"We are not planning to marry."

"Vitor loves you."

"He never said it."

"He won't, unless you say it first. But what he does is more important than what he says," Anna said, looking the pillowcases. "I heard you are creating a *cooperativa* with the local women."

"Yes, we are working on it."

"Do you want some pudding for dessert?" asked Rita, coming back into the room.

"I would love some," said Ana smiling. I realized she had stopped smiling while talking with me.

"Rita," I said, "thank you very much but I have to go. Grace is supposed to call me today. Ana, it was nice to meet you and I hope to see you again soon."

"It was nice to meet you," Ana said. She walked towards me, and gave me a hug.

Despite paying extra fees, it was the end of January before Grace received my package. She loved everything and within a week had sold it all to her friends.

With Rita's help, we created the *Cooperativa Bordado de Mãe*. We brought an attorney from the city to explain to the women what a cooperative was and how it would help them sell their work. All the women became members. By the end of March, we shipped our first batch. We sent pillowcases, table clothes, bed covers, towels, handbags, baby clothes and curtains, all in many shapes and colors.

The goal was for Grace to place everything in stores around the Massachusetts, New Hampshire and Maine seacoast. She was also considering inviting all her friends to dinner every month so she could sell some more. Grace was an enthusiastic sales agent. I think she was also happy to be part of something that would be important to Elena. I knew that with Grace on board, the *cooperativa* would succeed.

Then Grace found problems with what we sent. She reported that half the pieces were unsuitable to sell. There were too many flaws. In response, we created a committee to examine each piece before accepting and shipping them. And we voted

Mazé into the supervising position because her work was always perfect.

Vitor donated an old house to the *cooperativa*. The yard had weeds all over and for many years the house had been home to rats, frogs, snakes and all sorts of bugs. It took two men three days to clean up everything, and about a month for another two men to do repairs. Josefina said that Julio had built the house for his wife but they never lived there because she did not like its simplicity. Vitorio never confirmed the story, but in front of the house there was a century-old tree that had a square carved in the bark with the words "JE Para Sempre" [JE Forever]. But J and E were very common first letters for names. Some villagers even thought the letters meant "JESUS Forever." I just preferred to believe Julio's wife never wanted to live there because Julio would never cut that tree.

After the house's restoration, it became our cooperative's headquarters. I knew Elena and my Mother would be proud to know their lives and sacrifices had resulted in this accomplishment.

In mid-March, Vitor went to Minas and took some workers with him. They took trucks and other machines from the farm. Without him, we felt unprotected. Vitorio put a man to guard both our houses at night. Vitor never did that before. Just his presence was enough to make us feel safe.

A week after Vitor left, he sent me an e-mail with the directions and map with his location, and also the location of the town where I used to live. It was a three-hour drive through villages, mountains and historical places. At first, I was angry. I thought he had no right to invade my life like that. But then I realized that it meant he cared enough to put it all together.

I was overwhelmed and frightened. I wished they were all dead: My father, my grandmother, everyone. If they were all dead, I would not have to face them. I built a scenario in my mind: I would go to Minas and discover that my father and grandmother had passed away and I would simply visit their gravesites. I would go on with my life. It all made perfect sense to me. After all, people die. I could not bear the idea of facing my father, the drunkard who used to beat my mother. I felt safe with the idea that they were dead. I also missed Vitor. I decided to meet him a couple of days before he was to leave Minas.

Meanwhile, the village children returned to school in March, a month late. Part of the school—a classroom and the teacher's room—was still damaged from the storm. I heard this meant that there were fifty-seven first graders crowding into a single room.

I did what everyone else did: talked. Everyone complained but no one had the nerve to do anything. It seemed they wanted me to talk to the mayor. But the Valérios stayed away from it and I stayed away, too. I did not have children in school, therefore it was not my problem. However, I did tell some parents that if I had a schoolchild, I would have a protest in the front of the mayor's office, I would call all the news channels, and let everyone in Brazil know what kind government we had. The parents said that was an American way of doing things, not theirs. So I washed my hands of it and put it out of my mind.

To make the situation worse, the new school bus that took the kids to middle and high schools in town seemed to have been put together in a junkyard and most of its glass windows were missing. But all we did was talk about it.

Mid-April, I flew to Belo Horizonte in Minas Gerais where Vitor was waiting for me. I was numb to the place. The last time I was in that airport there was with my Mother. She held my hand tightly. Suddenly, I felt my heart beat again. I held his arm just before we left the airport and said, "Vitor, I can't go."

"We are here already," he said.

"I can't go looking for my grandmother or for my father. I don't want to see them. I will take the next flight back to Maceió."

"Cecilia, that's crazy. You are here already."

"I know, but I can't do it. I am done with them. I am done with everything. I just want to go home."

"What do you mean?"

"I don't know. I just want to go away from here."

"Okay, we don't have to go anywhere. We can just go to the farm. I'll show you around and we'll go home the day after tomorrow. What do you think?"

"Okay," I agreed, but I wasn't convinced. We drove for two hours and then passed an entrance to a farm.

"This farm belongs to Pedro Jacinto, our mayor," Vitor said.

"He sure knows how to expand," I observed.

Another hour later, we arrived at a big old farmhouse with large wood-frame windows and a lot of metal and wood artifacts all around. There were a lot of trees and a pond with domestic ducks. It was a peaceful place. There was also a building about fifty yards from the house.

"What's that?" I asked Vitor pointing to the old structure.

"It used to be a *senzala* [slaves' quarters] in the old days. Now, we use it for the animals."

"You should just destroy it."

"It is a piece of history," he replied.

"Who wants to remember that?" He did not comment.

When we were ready to enter the house, he said, "There is a woman there, Nega Benta. She takes care of the house. Sometimes, she is not nice but she is a very good cook and she manages the house well. Just don't mind her."

"I won't."

"Are you hungry?"

"No. Just tired."

"Let's go in."

He got my luggage and we went up eleven steps before reaching the front porch. He opened the door and it made a loud, aggressive noise. The floor inside seemed a little wet. As soon as Vitor got inside, a woman started to scream, *"Mas será o ben-*

edito! Ess piso num pára limp!" The first part was an expression that defies translation. The second part indicated she was angry about the floor not staying clean. Her voice and dialect instantly connected me with the past.

The woman came into the living room with the warmest of manners. But at first sight of me, she cooled off, *"E quem essa?"* [Who is this?]

"Nega Benta, this is Cecilia," Vitor explained.

"Oxe, come in girl, come in. Don't stay by the door," Benta said warmly.

I walked in and she said, "Come, come to the kitchen. I have fresh coffee and *pão de quejo quentinho.*" [Warm cheesy bread]

Vitor thought Benta had already forgotten about him until she said, "And, you Vitor. I work here by myself, no help. You and your men should feel sorry for a poor old lady like me. I cleaned this floor twice today. You and your men keep coming in with your dirty boots. One day I will do nothing and then we'll see how you like it."

"Nega Benta, I will tell them to stay out of the house," Vitor said.

"Remember that yourself, too, boy…" Benta said.

Vitor looked at me and at my shoes and he had a funny expression on his face.

Benta did not mind him. "Come in girl, sit here," she said as she showed me a chair. "They don't care for nobody but themselves." I wanted to laugh but was afraid to do it.

"I will check the workers. Cecilia, I will be back soon and will show you around," Vitor said and left.

"Girl, you look sad. Eat something," said Benta.

"Thank you, Benta."

"What you doing here? Your parents let you come by yourself? Vitor is a good man. But he is a man. You are not his wife," said Benta.

There, in that old style, warm, aromatic kitchen, I told my story to Benta. The story that I did not want to share with anyone, the story I was so embarrassed to share until recently when I told it to Vitor. But I told it to Benta as if she were an old friend.

After I told her my story and explained my fears, she said, "Girl, you *have* to look for your Grandma. She's waiting, hoping to one day see her grand-daughter again! Look at me. My husband left me with five kids - two girls and three boys. One day he grabbed a bag full of stuff and left. And I have not seen him again in twenty-five years. Now, what can a woman without any school do with five kids? *Five!* Every time I thought about giving them away, my heart would squeeze, and I'd say, 'Poor kids, their father already abandoned them and they are about to lose their mother,' and I didn't do it. I couldn't live without my kids. We were hungry together, we slept on the floor, sometimes we were homeless together. And, I would do it all over again.

"My kids are worth it," she continued. "Today, they are all grown, all married, and they all have children. The girls are in Belorizonti. They are all rich and everything. Their husbands have cars, and they have telephones, and their kids go to school. They want me to live with them, but I can't leave my boys. They have their wives and kids and they are good, hard workers. But I can't live in the city. Too noisy, too noisy. And, who would take care of this house? Who would help this boy, Vitor. His uncle is too old and sick to work anymore—"

"Do you know Vitorio well?"

"Oh, yeah, yeah. He helped me and my kids. He gave us a roof over our heads and gave us work."

"How long have you live here?" I asked. By then I was more interested in Benta's sad story than in crying about my own misfortune.

"When my husband left, we were living at another farm nearby, just a few kilometers. When that farm sold, the new owner told us to leave. They drove their tractors into the houses, smashed everything, and today it's all sugarcane. There was nowhere to move. We stumbled over here, looking for work and food. Valério wasn't at home but the administrator had pity and allowed me and my kids to stay in an old place over on the hillside. It isn't there anymore.

"I helped in the big house even though they didn't pay me. I walked around the farm looking for things to do. Then one day Vitorio arrived from the north. I was so afraid that he would make us leave that when I saw him, I fell on my knees and asked him to let me and my kids stay 'For the Love of God.' I cried. I didn't know what to do. He let us stay and put me to work in the house. So I raised my kids here. When they were all grown and out on their own, he told me to stay here in the big house and when I moved in, they drove the tractor into the old place on the hillside. But this time I didn't care.

"Vitor thinks I need help to take care of this house. Sometimes, they bring twenty, thirty men to eat here and I feed them all. This time, only eight men came from the north with Vitor. It's a lot work but I like it. Vitorio is a good man.

"Go see your Grandmother, girl. She deserves to know what happened to her granddaughter. If she is alive, she is waiting."

"Are you still waiting for your husband?"

"Well, no and yes. We were married in the church and he'll always be my husband and my kids' father. Sure, I want to know what happened to him."

"I'm going to look for her. If she is in the same house, I will find her," I said.

We spent the rest of the morning talking while Benta did housework. I was amazed to see how rapidly and precisely she worked in the kitchen. All in the space of a couple hours, she slaughtered, plucked, cleaned, cut up, tempered and cooked three chickens. She cooked beans, rice, and pasta. Fixed a salad. Baked a cake. Made orange juice. I offered to help but she rejected it and I was afraid to stand up and get in her away. She had speed and I didn't want to break her rhythm.

Lunch was ready and on the table by the time Vitor came back with the workers, fifteen men in all that day. The men filled their plates and scattered into small groups throughout the porch and under the trees. Vitor and I ate in the kitchen. Benta accompanied us but didn't eat. She had the habit of waiting until everyone else was finished.

"I decided I want to look for my grandmother," I told Vitor while we were eating.

He took a long breath and said, "Okay. Sure. Changed your mind again?"

"You don't have to go with me. I can rent a vehicle and go by myself."

Benta said, "I tell you, men are good for nothing. This girl, she don't see her family for almost twenty years, and that's how you answer her when she says she wants to see them. Go girl, go see your family."

"Nega Benta, I'm not letting Cecilia go alone. We'll go early in the morning. It's too late now," Vitor said in a more serious tone than usual, as if he were showing us that he was in authority.

Vitor and I spent the rest of the day together. He showed me the farm and told me some old stories about it. We sat on the bench by the pond while the ducks peacefully cruised the waters.

"This feels like Heaven on Earth," I said.

"It's nice," he said. "I like to work here. Normally, there's no drama."

"How long has your family owned it?"

"It belongs to Uncle Vitorio alone. He bought it about thirty years ago with his own money. He used to live six months there and six months here."

"Why didn't I hear about Benta before?"

"Because my mother doesn't like Benta or this farm."

"Benta seems nice and Rita is nice. What's the problem?"

"About twenty ago there was a severe drought in Alagoas. We were about to lose the farm up north. Mom asked Uncle to sell this one and loan the money to the family. Uncle refused to do it and Mom blamed Nega Benta. They got a loan from a bank instead and this farm paid for it. But Mom thinks that Nega Benta used magic to convince Uncle to let her stay and keep the farm. I know it sounds stupid—"

"Of course it does."

"Cecilia, just don't interfere in this situation. And when we go back home, don't mention Nega Benta or this farm to my mother. This is between Mom and my uncle. The Valérios have their own ways to deal with their problems. Last year I brought Vanda's son to work with me. When we got back home, he spent his time off gossiping about this place and about Nega Benta. Vanda wanted me to bring him here again, but that's out of the question. When we get home, Vanda will probably ask you why I did not give the job to her son. Just tell her you don't know and send her to talk to me. I heard her husband already talked to Father. I want them to ask Uncle. He knows how to put these people in their place."

"You seem to really like Benta. The way she talks to you..."

"I do. She's a hard working woman. We say that she has the strength of a horse. Without her, we would not be here today. Uncle considers her half-owner of the farm, because of all the work she's done. And, this place has saved our farm up north many times. It is much more productive and less expensive to maintain. You know, Mom has three girls working in our home and we spend a lot on the villagers. Nega Benta works by herself and feeds more people because we always bring men from the village. She gets up at three, four in the morning and goes to bed nine, ten o'clock at night. She doesn't stop. I told her to find someone to help but she said she would let me know when she is ready to retire. I hope that never happens. I don't know what we will do without her."

"If this farm is more productive and already helped your family's business, then why is Rita still upset?"

"Mom is a little too proud sometimes. She also thinks that Nega Benta doesn't respect us as much as she should. You know how Nega Benta is. And, Mom still feels that our family needs to be respected for our past. That's something I'll never understand. My mother is a good person and she loves to help people, but she also likes to be noticed and respected for it. And, she didn't like Uncle spending so much time here. Growing up, though, I thought Uncle had the greatest life ever and I wanted to be just like him."

"It's hard to believe that Rita would work so hard to hate a total stranger," I said.

Vitor replied, "You should know she doesn't love your Elena, either."

"So she relates Nega Benta to Elena. How's that even possible?"

"I didn't say that. Mom doesn't like to talk about either one of them." He paused, then asked, "Did they repair the school yet?"

"No. They didn't even remove the debris."

"Uncle said they were planning to rebuild the old classroom and change the name of the school."

"To whose?"

"The villagers will need to decide, but right now they want to name it after my great-grandfather's father. His family was the first in the village."

This made me upset. "That is not going to happen. If it does, I will go back to the United States and give Elena's money to some others who deserve it," I said.

"What do you want?" Vitor asked. "Put her name there instead?"

"If they plan to change the school's name, I think Elena deserves the honor more than anyone else. She was a teacher. Did you know that?"

"No. What I know is that some villagers say she had been in some places not so respectable, like bordels."

"I doubt she had been in less respectable places than your grandfather."

A pause. Then Victor said, "Anyway, I doubt you can convince anyone to name a school after her."

"I bet I can. And, I also bet that the mayor himself will help me."

"I can win this bet without lifting a finger. The mayor would never go against my Uncle."

"We'll see. I think the name needs to change but to reflect real change, it cannot be your family's name."

"Okay," said Vitor. Then he changed the subject. "Are you ready to meet your father tomorrow?"

"Yes, I am. But I know that if he kept drinking as much as he did, he is no longer among the living..."

"I don't know. I heard stories of drunkies who lived longer than expected."

Now I changed the subject. "Vitor, Ana is a young woman. Did she ever appear to be interested in somebody else?"

"No. Of course, not. She has a son."

"Yeah. But she is a woman and she is young. Don't you think that sooner or later there will be someone?"

"No. Gabriel should be her only concern. At least until he is old enough to be on his own. If she decides to be with a man, I will bring my son to live with me. Why are you asking me this?"

"Are you jealous of her?"

"No. I'm not. But I will protect my son and he will not be around people that I don't know."

"It's not fair to Ana."

"Do you know anything?"

"No. I was just thinking about her." I was disappointed that Vitor, who most of the time was so understanding, was also much like the men in his family.

That evening Vitor's workers made a campfire in front of the house, and a local musician came over with a guitar. He played, and we all sang old songs.

'Luar do Sertão'
"Não há, ó gente, ó não
Luar como esse do sertão
Não há, ó gente, ó não
Luar como esse do sertão"

Oh! que saudade do luar da minha terra
Lá na serra braqueando folhas secas pelo chão
Este luar cá da cidade tão escuro
Não tem aquela saudade do luar lá do sertão

Não há, ó gente, ó não
Luar como esse do sertão
Não há, ó gente, ó não
Luar como esse do sertão

Se a lua nasce por detrás da verde mata
Mais parece um sol de prata prateando a solidão
E a gente pega na viola que ponteia
E a canção é a Lua Cheia a nos nascer do coração

Não há, ó gente, ó não
Luar como esse do sertão
Não há, ó gente, ó não
Luar como esse do sertão

Mas como é lindo ver depois pro entre o mato
Deslizar calmo regato transparente como um véu
No leito azul das suas águas murmurando
E por sua vez roubando as estrelas lá do céu

Não há, ó gente, ó não
Luar como esse do sertão
Não há, ó gente, ó não
Luar como esse do sertão"

(Catulo da Paixão Cearense / João Pernambuco)

The next morning, we headed to where my grandmother used to live. I was anxious. When we arrived, I was surprised to see the town had not changed much. The houses looked older and smaller and the streets, narrower. But I recognized Grandma's house right away. My fears were that she had moved away.

We drove up to the house. I hesitated for some time before knocking on the door. I knocked one, twice. No one answered. When I was about to knock again, Vitor held my hand still and nodded to the woman standing in the side yard. She looked me for a long time. Then, crying, she asked, "Cecilia, my girl, is it really you?"

"Yes, it's me."

"Oh my God! Thank you God!

"Grandma!"

I hugged her. She was much older now, and looked tired.

"Where is your mother?"

I was well prepared for the question, but when it was time to answer, I didn't know what to say. My heart was breaking.

"Let's go inside, Grandma," I said. I noticed some curious people nearby and I did not want to have a public event.

"Yes. But I don't live in this house anymore. I live in that one," she said pointing to the one next door.

"Vitor, this is my grandma. Grandma, this is Vitor, my boy-friend."

He offered his hand, she held it, pulled him towards her, and kissed his face.

"Thank you for bringing my girl," she said.

"Are you coming inside with us?" I asked Vitor.

"No. I will drive around for awhile."

"Just come in when you return," I told him.

I took her inside. She had two wooden chairs in the living room, a very old television on the top of an old student desk, and a statuette of Brazil's principal patroness, *Nossa Senhora Aparecida*, on one corner of a smaller wooden desk – there were white candles, wild flowers, and the rosary around it. We sat on the chairs and when we were ready to talk, I could only cry. My words did not come out. I remembered the last time Mother and Grandma saw each other. She was the only one who loved my mother more than I did.

"Mom died a couple of years ago..."

I'm sure she could understand my pain because hers was greater still. My mother was her only child.

This was like going back to the day we left home and then suddenly fast-forwarding to the instant of Mother's death. Everything in between faded. Grandma stood and walked over to the statue. She knelt and cried.

After a while, I helped her back to the chair and slowly told her what happened. It helped calm us down to face the newer reality.

"Grandma, I was afraid you didn't live here anymore and I'd never be able to find you again."

"I couldn't move too far. I always wondered if you and your mother would one day return. I knew if I moved, you'd never find me. I have spent most of my days praying for you two."

"Grandma, what happened to Father?"

As if it were yesterday, she began to explain. "He came here two days after you and your Mom left. He was furious, drunk as always. I told him I did not know where you were. He went to the police, but no one did anything. He came to me a few more times. The teachers from your school came too, because they were concerned. They even thought your father had done something to you. After a while, people stopped talking. Your father had a few girlfriends and had three more children with them, but he never remarried because he and your mother were still married. So now he is a widower and can marry again. But he may be too sick to do it."

"What's wrong?"

"Everything. He is in and out of the hospital. His drunkenness and guilt have caught up with him."

"Is he still living in the same house?"

"Yes. They say he hallucinates. They heard him screaming at you and your mother a few times. Do you really want to see him?"

"Yes, Grandma, I do. I don't want to talk to him, just see him. Who is living with him now?"

"His girlfriend and their sixteen year old daughter."

"Where are the other two children?"

"I don't know, Cecilia. They might be anywhere. The girl who's living with him now is the one who first lived with your father after your mother left. After a while, she became pregnant and left for São Paulo. Then your father lived with three or four other women, and a couple of them had children. Three years ago the old girlfriend returned with her daughter and they have lived with him ever since."

"Where are his relatives?"

"I don't know much about his family. Your mother met him at a dance club. He said he was from Maranhão, but it might not be true. He said his mother died when he was five, and when his father married again, the stepmother constantly beat him. He said when he was ten years old, he left home and never returned. He was always looking for jobs here and there. That's when he met your mother."

"Grandma, what happened to Grandpa?"

"He died when your mother was nine. He was forty years older than me. My father arranged the wedding and I went along with it. At that time, we didn't have much of a choice. But I resented my parents for doing that to me."

"But you never remarried."

"No, Cecilia. I was better off alone."

Grandma, do you want to come and live with me in Alagoas?"

"Are you sure you want me with you?"

"Yes, Grandma, I am sure."

"Then I am going with you. I have nothing left here."

"Do you have anybody to take care of your house?"

"This is not my house. I had to sell it to pay for you and your mother to leave." Pointing across the street, she said, "They were the only people I told about you and your mother, the ones who originally bought my old house years ago. I had to tell them in case you looked for me there. Since then, the house sold two more times. Five years ago, this one became available for rent and I moved here."

"Who owns it?"

"Mariano Batalha. He lives in the main street."

"Did you sign a contract to live here?"

"No. But we have an agreement: As long as I live here, I pay a hundred *reais* a month. Just yesterday I paid for this month."

"That's good. What do you need to take with you?"

"Nothing. Just some clothes and *Nossa Senhora Aparecida* and some pictures that I have. Everything that I need will fit in my old suitcase."

"I will let you pack while I go home... to Father's house. And, when I return, we will give the key back to Mariano Batalha and then we'll leave."

I looked outside. Vitor was already there. We drove down the road to my old village. I remember walking with my mother on that same dirt road and it seemed a long way. Surprisingly now, it was only a five-minute drive.

Soon, I was there again, in front of the house Mom and I ran away from. It looked ancient. It did not have my mother's beautiful flowers around it. It looked dark and dirty, weedy and unkempt. It was not the house I remembered.

An old man was sleeping on a chair in the shadows of the side porch. I supposed it was my father, but it didn't resemble him. This was not the strong, angry man I knew.

A woman appeared from inside and stared at us. I got out of the truck and approached her. There were still woods on both sides of the property. I changed direction and went towards the trees. There were birds there; I could hear them. I closed my eyes and I could also hear Mother laughing while we played together. She was happy. I had never seen her so happy again. I opened my eyes and she was gone. Vitor, behind me, gave me a hug.

"Hey, are you okay?" he asked.

"Mother and I used to play here together. She was happy."

"That crazy looking woman wants to know what we are doing here," he informed me. We walked to the house. Father was now awake. He kept looking at me, confused. When I was close enough for him to recognize me, he said loudly, "Maria! Maria! You came back. I knew you would come back. I wanted to clean the house for you but I don't have the strength. They don't know how to clean and cook like you do. Maria! You came back. Where is the girl, Cecilia? Where is our girl?"

The woman started to say something to him but he pushed her away, "Get out! Out! She came back! This is her house. Out!" He screamed. And then he cried.

I looked at Vitor, "He thinks I am my mother."

The woman signed for us to move away from him. We went to the other side of the house. When we were far enough away not to be heard, the woman came over.

"Are you his daughter?" she asked.

"Yes, I am Cecilia."

"He always talks about you and your mother. Where is she?" She was looking round, over my shoulder as though expecting to see someone.

"She is not here."

"He is sick and can't work anymore. He needs a lot medication and it's all expensive. I need money to take care of him. I'm alone here and no one pays me anything."

"Where is your daughter?"

"I don't know. That girl is good for nothing. She goes from house to house all day. She doesn't help. We need help."

I went back to the truck, wrote a check and gave it to the woman. I did not love my father but could not hate him any longer. The man I needed to hate was not there.

Vitor, Grandma, and I went back to Vitorio's farm. As we expected, Grandma and Benta treated each other as if they were old friends. Two days later, we drove back to Village Aveverde, as we could not convince Grandma to take an airplane.

CHAPTER 13

During my first winter in Aveverde, we bought all the embroidered products the women made, even though we would not be
able to sell everything because some were flawed, damaged or
unsatisfactory. But if we were to keep the women busy, we had
to pay for their work. That was the only way to help the families without giving them unearned money or food. We used the
imperfect pieces to explain how they could improve them. Mazé
was our manager-trainer. She supervised the work and made
sure every piece was perfect. Rita was our general manager. I fo-
cused on making it financially sustainable. Vitor and his father
helped us find attorneys and financial advisors.

As Grace deposited the money from sales, we would pay the
members according to the quality of their work. In many cases,
the women were teaching the men how to be in business, and
supplementing the household income.

Soon, our supply exceeded demand, so we opened a store in
town as an additional outlet. There were many levels of final
products and Grace only wanted the perfect ones. We sold the
remainders locally for a fraction of the export price. That winter,
the cooperative was so successful that some woman became the
breadwinners in their families. It created change.

By August, the election campaign season was taking shape.
Jorge, the mayor's son and would-be successor, was going from
village to village seeking support. I was invited to a meeting
with the candidate at the Valério's house. It was a learning experience about people, politics, and corruption.

When I arrived at the meeting, there were about a hundred
people in front of the house. Vitorio, Jorge, Zé, and Vitor were
talking privately. Rita was supervising ten women in the kitch-
en, preparing refreshments for the crowd and dinner for the private party.

"When is the meeting supposed to begin?" I asked Rita.

"I'm sure, soon," she said. "They've been talking for a long time. I would think that by now they have reached an agreement," she said in a lower voice.

"What kind of agreement?"

She just signed to me that we would talk later and changed the subject, "How's your grandmother?"

"Good. Lia and Grandma can't come. They have important things to do, you know. This coming Friday will be the last episode of the eight o'clock soap opera." All the women in the kitchen started to talk about the characters in the soaps as if they were gossiping about real people.

Around seven, the private meeting ended and the general one started. Jorge was polite, and the people seemed to like him. He gave a five-minute speech that did not say much. Actually, it didn't say anything. He just thanked everyone for their support. He assumed that the deal they reached in private was by extension everyone's deal. Then he walked around, shaking hands, while the women served refreshments.

"So you made a deal with him?" I asked Vitor.

"No. I don't make deals. They did. I don't even know why I was there. I thought you should have been there representing the *cooperativa*. The farm was already well represented. But I am sure Uncle will talk with you soon."

"Is Vitorio the new candidate?" I asked sarcastically.

"No. But he is used to represent the people here."

"You two!" Rita called. "Dinner is served!"

"This is the dinner for the leaders. I don't think I am supposed to be there," I said.

"Stop it. Just sit there as my girlfriend," he said. I smiled, and shook my head.

We all took our seats at the table and Jorge started, "Cecilia, where have you been? Father was complaining you did not come back to visit us."

"Give my compliments to your family. They are nice people.

We have been working hard here."

"I heard the *cooperativa* has been a success. Thank you for your work and for supporting our campaign. We need more women like you."

I was putting rice on my plate but I stopped. It was one of those moments. "Jorge, thank you for such a nice compliment. But I am not supporting you." Everyone stopped eating and looked at me. I continued, "At least, not yet."

"Jorge," said Vitorio, "I did not have a chance to talk to Cecilia yet."

"Vitorio," I said, "We don't need to talk about it. You made your deal already. Now, I am going to make mine and it does not need to be private. Jorge," I continued, "You are the candidate. What kind of support do you need?"

He hesitated for a moment. "I will need your vote and the votes of those in the *cooperativa*."

"Okay. I can guarantee you my vote and the vote of every member of the *cooperativa*. But I want something in return."

As I had everyone's attention, I went on, "I want a new school to be built—"

"Yes, we have been talking about it," Zé interrupted.

I just ignored him, "—I want a new school to be built in this village. And the deal is, you give me the land and all the permissions, and I will build the school with the best that is available and you will inaugurate it as a local public school after I have named it. And you will sign a law so that the name can never be changed, or else the property will return to the original owner."

"Cecilia, I already talked to Vitorio about it. And, the school will be named after the first Valério that came to Aveverde."

"Jorge, I will build the school and it will be named 'Escola Elena Maria Santos Woodard' after the woman who will finance it."

"Cecilia, are you crazy. You want to name a school after a prostitute?" Vitorio shouted.

"No, Vitorio. I just don't want it to be named after the family of a coward like your father, or of an unscrupulous man like your grandfather!" I shouted back. "Unless you accept this deal, I am not going to support you. Instead, your adversary will get my vote and those of the families in the *cooperativa*. And if you still win, I will leave and the *cooperativa* and a new school will be no more."

With that, I threw my napkin on the table and stood up. "I'm going home now. Let me know if you accept it or not. I may not prevent you from winning this election but I will make you spend more money than your family has available." I said good night to everyone and left. Then, I remembered something else, so I turned to Jorge again. "Two more things: I want you to promise to give Marcos, Luiz' brother, a job in the town hall and fix that road, I am sure you can see how bad it is."

Jorge bowed. Then I left.

Power can corrupt a soul.

I felt powerful but ashamed and ungrateful. Vitor and his family had helped me. I just would never have forgiven myself if I had let the Valério's walk over Elena again.

Vitor did not visit me that evening. I worried I had gone too far. But I fell asleep knowing that I did what I had to do and would deal with the consequences of it. The next morning, at breakfast with Grandma and Lia, someone screamed, *"Boa de casa! Boa de casa!"* [It is an expression without real translation; it means the same as a knock on the door]. Lia went to open the door and then quickly returned to the kitchen.

"Seu Vitorio!" she screamed. "It's Seu Vitorio."

"Alone?" I asked.

"Yeah!"

"Is he inside?"

"Oh! I forgot to let him in," she said, confused.

"Lia!" I said walking quickly to the door. Vitorio was standing there, leaning on a cane. It was the first time he had been to the house.

"Good morning, Vitorio. Please come in and have breakfast

with us," I said. I took his left arm and we walked to the kitchen. He sat with us while Lia set a place for him.

"Vitorio," I said, "even though I appreciate your visit, you did not have to walk here."

"Oh you know... Nobody is ready when you need them," he said, catching his breath.

"Vitorio, I was about to pay you a visit. I have beautiful tomatoes from our backyard," said Grandma.

"How come you plant tomatoes and they grow beautifully, and I plant them and they don't even grow?" asked Vitorio, still breathing hard. Grandma and Lia finished eating and they both went to work in the garden, leaving us free to talk.

"Yesterday, we were not fair with you. You should have been invited to that meeting," he said. I did not comment. I remembered someone saying, 'The wise talk when needed, but the fool can't keep his mouth shut.' That moment, I wanted to be wise.

"Before our meeting with Jorge, Vitor, Rita, Zé and I talked about what we needed in order to support him. You should have been in that meeting, too. We appreciate your work and your presence, but it's difficult to share our community with you and to respect you as the strong young woman you are." He took a deep breath and then continued, "If Vitor and you were not dating, if your grandma were not such a nice lady, and if I did not like you so much, I would see you as an enemy and would do everything in my power to throw you, your *cooperativa* and your school out of my village.

"But I can't do that anymore," he continued. "You are as much part of our family as that little boy Gabriel. And, I can't suppress that woman"—he stopped for a second—"Elena, anymore. I remember the day I met her. I was about five or six years old but I remember her face. And, I remember thinking that she was beautiful and kind. That day, I just wanted to stay with her. When I was older and learned who she was, I felt as if I had betrayed my mother. But now, I want you to build the school and name it after her. She deserves it. After all, she cared enough to send you to us." He paused and looked through the window.

I was amazed that I had kept silent. He probably was surprised too, but he kept talking. "But there is something you need to learn. The people in this village do not need to know everything we do. You tend to make our business known to the public and it is not necessary. There were quite a few women in the house last night and this morning your deal is everyone's business.

"My family has been in this village for over a hundred and fifty years. We have been keeping this place safe because the people here respect us. If everything happens the way you want, they may lose respect, we lose control, and it will be up to you to set the rules and keep them safe. Vitor is going to be the head of this family. The people respect him. You respect him as well or you will have to take his place in this village. Are you ready for that kind of responsibility?" I was not ready and I didn't want to do it. I did not answer.

"We have a plan and you can accept it or you can just go on with your plot. You can build the new school, we are going to give you land as our gift to the community. You can name it as you wish. The old school will became a health center after the town makes the renovation and it will be named after my great grandfather, the first Valério who settled in this land. The mayor promised that a physician will come once a week. The people will know that we came to terms. And Jorge will know that we are a strong community that he needs to respect." He paused again.

I took a deep breath and gave him my answer, "Okay. It's okay. It's a good plan. Does everyone agree with it?"

"Yes. Even those who do not agree, support it. Now, Vitor is upset with both of us. I apologized to him for treating you the way I did. I suggest you apologize for talking about his grandfather the way you did."

"I will apologize, Vitorio. But I did not mean to hurt him, I meant to hurt you."

There was a moment's silence; then we both laughed.

"You are quite a young woman. I do not have children. But I would have been proud to have a daughter just like you."

"Thank you."

"And, I would be happy to see a daughter marrying a man like my nephew."

"Oh, Vitorio. Your nephew likes his bachelor's life. He just wants to be free like you. I don't think he wants the responsibility of married life."

"Vitor and you have more responsibilities than any person in this village. I always had more responsibility than any married man I knew. We are not afraid of responsibilities. We might be afraid to commit our lives to one person. We might be afraid to trust and to change."

"I met Benta."

"I know. She is a good woman and a hard worker. But Rita doesn't like her."

"I'm sure Rita would like Benta if she got to know her."

"No. That is not necessary anymore. Some things are better left untouched," he said.

lessons of philanthropy

Jorge, as expected, won the elections in November and became a celebrity. He was young, wealthy, single, and mayor. That was a perfect combination to drive some women crazy. In January, he took charge of the office but he did not care for his job as much as he cared for his social life. Also in January we began to build the school on some acres given by the Valério's. It was designed as a construction that would never collapse, that would last as long as the village lasted. It had a library, science and computer laboratories, a gymnasium, a soccer field, and everything that a school in the developed world would have.

At the same time, the cooperative was succeeding. We opened a store in Maceió and Ana's mother was managing it. Grace put up a website for us and it became a home-based business for her. As the *cooperativa* was supporting itself, I had more money to spend on the school. And, as the school was being built, old homes nearby were also rebuilt. These were signs of a stronger, wealthier community.

First was Mazé's house. When she heard that her live-in boyfriend was having another affair with a woman who just moved in the village, I thought Mazé would fight her like she did Lia. Instead, she packed his clothes in a sugar sack and threw it out her front door. The next day, she and her three kids moved into one of Vitorio's homes for about three months. During that time, she tore down her old house and built a nicer one with three bedrooms. When the boyfriend tried to return, she set her dog on him. She became a proud woman.

Following Mazé's steps, many other families began to rebuild their homes; Aveverde became a village under construction.

"I never thought I would live to see so many changes in this place," said Rita one night as I had dinner with them.

"I guess it's what progress feels like," said Vitorio.

"Yesterday, I was counting the number of families rebuilding their homes: It is about twenty. Now instead of debating who will go hungry this winter, they are debating whose house has the best color paint," said Zé laughing. "Cecilia, today Zezinho asked me if you or Vitor will be the next mayor."

"Please Zé, I'm having a good time. Don't spoil my evening," I said with a smile. "But, I agree we need to decide what to do in the next election."

"What do you think we should do?" asked Rita.

"I already told Vitor. For me, we should find someone who can win against Jorge," I said.

"You know, it will be very difficult to win an election against him. His father still has strong support in town," said Rita.

"There are other ways to win," said Vitor, and everyone looked at him. "It is too early to do anything, but we can start to plan. We may not be able to elect another mayor but we can replace a few aldermen. There are nine. I know we can replace at least two in the next election - one from town and one from a village. And, there are already three against Jorge. With the majority of the alderman against him. By the middle of his next term, we would have a name to replace him."

"Son, you would be a perfect mayor," said Zé laughing.

"I am a farmer, Dad, not a stupid politician," said Vitor. Everyone laughed.

"Vitor, we also need an alderman to represent this village. It is time for us to have our first direct representative," I said.

"I think the *cooperativa* should propose someone. There are more women coming to this village than men. The *cooperativa* is now politically stronger than the farm; and it has the store in town," said Vitorio. I was surprised to hear him saying it.

"I can only think of one person; but I don't want to lose her in the cooperative," I said. "She is our best."

"Mazé!" Zé and Rita said at same time.

"I think Mazé would be good but I think the cooperative can propose someone who doesn't work there," said Vitor.

"Vitor, if the cooperative will put money to elect someone, it will only happen if it is someone we can trust. And, we also have Marcos in the town hall. I am sure we can help him become more influential there." I said.

By the end of September, the school was completed and ready to be furnished. We agreed to inaugurate it in January for the beginning of the following school year.

Time had served its purpose. I had lived in Aveverde for two years and the *cooperativa* was making a difference. But, I did not know if, as a result of local prosperity or a consequence of Brazil's governmental crisis, we began to have a new problem. The homeless and the landless from outside the region were moving to our village at a rapid rate and bringing poverty with them.

One rainy morning by the end of November, I heard the trash cans rattling. At first, I thought it was a dog. They used to make a lot of mess when they were searching for food. But it was not a dog; it was a child, a young boy about seven years old.

"Hi," I said. When he heard me, he tried to run but I grabbed him by his arms. He screamed.

"Hey, listen to me. Stop screaming. Listen. Are you hungry?"

When Lia came to see what was going on, the boy ran to her.

"Lia, who is this boy?" I asked.

"His name is Chapa. He and his parents live with the homeless people at the edge of the village," she said.

"How do you know him?"

"I went there yesterday with Mom and some other girls," Lia said.

"Lia, take him inside and feed him. Then give him a shower and see if Marilda's kids' clothes fit him."

I drove to the edge of the village. The homeless and landless were packed into a small space there, living in small, black, thin tents, one per family. They were worse off than the villagers had ever been. I had been frustrated many times before, yet never like this. I resented people bringing more problems than we could solve.

I learned that this group was in a legal dispute with the government for part of the sugar factory's land. They believed the factory was holding that land illegally and that the people had the right to it. While there were other contested properties, they had chosen the one closest to Aveverde.

The process of removing them from the land or granting them legal ownership could take years. How would they survive until then? Looking around, there were more children than I could count. Outside the tents, there were wood-burning stoves made of mud. Only two were lit.

I went back to Aveverde and, instead of going home, I went to the *cooperativa*. I needed to tell Rita what I had seen Mazé was there as well.

"Cecilia," Rita said, "we can't tell people where or how they should live. We can't stop them from coming. There is nothing we can do about it. And it is not what we are here for. The best we can do is support them with food and clothes or whatever they need according to our possibilities."

"I know Rita. But I had so much hope for this place."

"Did you really believe you would solve all the problems?" asked Rita.

"I don't know. I thought we could work for this one place only, without having to deal with the problems out there. I thought we could make this place an example so other villages and towns would see and do the same."

"How would they do the same, Cecilia? To do the same they would need to have an Elena and a Cecilia." "How would you expect them to stay away from green grass when they can't grow any of their own? And that land should have been given to them long time ago. The *usina* is not paying the taxes required to keep it. That land belongs to the government and should go to the ones who need it," Mazé added.

"Why hasn't the government done anything?" I asked.

"Because nobody cares. You should know this by now. Have you seen all the people looking for work? Our training classes are full. Soon we will have more products than we will be able to sell, and we will be forced to lower our prices. Or we can just accept new members as we need them. People are coming from everywhere," Mazé said. Listening to her, I thought she'd be perfect for politics.

"It's just sad that so many babies are born every day without the least chance of a good life," I said.

"Cecilia, Naiara came earlier to show us her new baby. She is the cutest little girl."

"Oh! I went yesterday to visit them but they weren't home," I said.

"Her sister told her you went there."

"She didn't need to come here," I said.

"She came to tell you she named the baby "Elena" because if it was not for Elena she would never be able to support a child as a single mother. You see Cecilia, there are also children born with more opportunities because people like Elena keep supporting life even after their death."

I was still not used to hearing Rita talking about Elena.

Someone knocked on the door; it was already half-open. It was Vanda.

"Hi, Vanda," said Mazé. "I thought you were supposed to go to the store today."

"I was on my way to town but the road is blocked."

"Why?" Rita asked.

"They found a burned body on the side of the road. It smells horrible, and there is a crowd."

"Who's there?" I asked.

"The police and a lot people are watching."

"At least the police came this time. Anybody know who it is?" I asked.

"I doubt it." said Mazé.

"Hopefully, it is not from Aveverde. No one had been killed in Aveverde for over four years. I don't even remember who was the last person," said Rita, looking at me.

"It was Manuel, Zé Borge's son. The whole family left about a year after he got killed, remember?" said Vanda. They all nodded.

"Manuel liked to fight," added Mazé.

"Who killed him?" I asked.

"He got in a fight and a man stabbed him," Vanda said.

"Is the killer in jail?"

"No. He ran away and no one ever found him."

"I am sure nobody ever looked for him either," I said.

"But everyone knew Manuel would not last. He just got into too many fights. I just hope this time it's not someone from Aveverde," Rita said.

"Rita, did you place the new order for all the material we need," I asked

"Yes, it is costing a lot more. Every time we place a new order, it costs more than the last one. It's ridiculous. It takes so much of the profit."

"I know. I wish we could produce the fabric ourselves… I can't take those people out of my mind," I said.

Vitor came to visit me that evening. I was still frustrated as I could not see a future for Aveverde with so many homeless there.

"You don't have to solve their problems. There isn't much we can do," Vitor told me.

"But how can we live knowing they are there and we are not doing nothing about it? They are people. Do you know how it feels to live knowing that no one cares to what happens to you? Do you know what it feels like for a mother to know that she can't protect her child? Or, for a child to see her mother in distress and have no way to help? Vitor, do you know how it feels to be an outcast? Tomorrow feels like a scary place when you have nothing left."

"Sometimes we have to let people find solutions for their needs."

"This is not an individual problem. There is a whole group of people out there. We can't ignore them. I can't sleep comfortably in my bed knowing that right now those children are sleeping on the ground."

"I am afraid to ask—but, what do you want to do?"

"I don't know. Do you know the process for that land?"

"The uisina didn't pay the loan. The government can take it and distribute it."

"Is it big enough for all those people to produce a living?"

"No. But it is enough to build a home grow food."

"And then what? Sell it off and go to starve in a city?"

"I don't know. If that's what they want to do it, they will do it."

"It is an old cycle: getting something for free to later on give it up and ask for something else."

"It is how it is. We all know that."

"It doesn't have to be that way."

"Cecilia, what do you have in mind?"

"The land could go to the town and we could manage it."

"And, do what?"

"We could build houses and an industry. More work available for every one. And, the school could offer courses for the youth like computer and software. They don't have to go anywhere. We can bring teachers."

"You are dreaming too far ahead. What is your idea for that land?"

"Build an industry that can offer jobs and build houses around it. The first group that helps build the houses can keep the house as long as they live in it. If they leave, it goes back to the town."

"What kind of industry do you possibly have in mind?"

"I don't know. We buy so many things. Think about it, we grow mangos, oranges, caju, passion fruit but we buy fruit juice that comes from the south. Why not make juice? We pay high price for the fabrics we use in the cooperative, why not make it and sell to the whole country? Why can't be more than one industry? There is so much land unused."

"You know, even if all this was possible, we would have to keep worrying about creating more jobs because people would keep coming."

"That is a challenge I want to face. We can't ignore the fact that half of the adult population in this town has no jobs. They don't have the education or resources to produce their own income. We do. The cooperative is an example that we can do it."

"How would we finance all this?"

"The town seems to have enough money to support the Jacinto's lifestyle. There must be federal incentives for new companies."

"So what now, you are going to tell the Jacinto's to stop stealing and start financing industries?"

"That is exactly what I am going to do. I will call the mayor tomorrow and will invite him to come for dinner. And, I will tell him as it is. You will see. Tomorrow I will bring food and supplies to them and toys so the children entertain themselves while this is going on."

"I'll take you there."

I didn't know what I was doing, but I knew something had to be done. Vitor delivered the supplies with me and he talked to the men while I was dividing the food. They were part of a national movement for redistribution of land. I knew that kind of idea wouldn't work on the long run. The women cooked a meal and we all shared it.

About two days later, the mayor came to have dinner in my house. I really didn't know him well. So I started telling him about the new people in the village. Vitor helped me by explaining what happened to the land. They both knew the situation well. I then told him my idea for the land.

"Cecilia, it is a great concept but one that takes time and a lot effort," the Mayor commented.

"This town has been exploited by political corruption for so long—"

"Cecilia, do you think I don't know that. Do you think I don't know my father's business? I know it well. I have to live with it. But believe it or not, I am taking control of the politics in this town. Things will change. I cannot do my job when I have thirty, forty people everyday asking me to provide food, money, favors. Do you think I want this? I wish I could simply say no to everyone and go on to do my job. I would never be elected again if I did that and I cannot do everything in four years. It is more complicated than you know. And, I wish there was an easy way to solve all the problems."

"I don't expect to be easy, Jorge. But I expect to be done. It is easy for you to go along when you don't have to face the consequences. These people don't have a choice and they don't know what they did wrong to deserve their life. They were born into poverty and that's all they know. Do you think you are in a difficult situation? Try to feed a child out of thin air. Try to think about a mother waking up in the morning and know that her child will wake up any time hungry and she has nothing to offer. Try that. There are no jobs, no money around. How are they supposed to live? You want to take your time in respect for your father but these people have no time to give to you or your father. You want to put fault on them but you are the one who knows better. Tell them 'no' if you have to. Tell your father 'no' if you have to. You are a leader now. Lead. Care. Fight. Bring change. These people need change," I said.

"Jorge, I thought Cecilia was going crazy with her ideas until I visited them with her. I just went because I was concern about her safety. But I will tell you, after you meet them, it is impossible not to care," Vitor said.

"Don't you two think I see it every day. They have already been in my office. Just yesterday I sent a truck load of food to them. I know them well."

"If they get that land for free, it will be a waste, you know it. If the usina keep, it will be a disgrace. But if the town develop it, we might be able to turn it into a source of income to anyone who needs work," I said.

"There is a lot more involved than just the land. There are the federal and state laws to overcome. They do not make easy for businesses of any kind. We are over loaded with bureaucracies. I am just being realistic. But I will promise you that I will look into it. And, if there is any chance we can do it, we will do it."

"You are making me a promise. And I will make you one. I will curse you, if you don't keep your promise," I said.

We laughed.

"Cecilia, I am already cursed."

We talked for a long while. It was like meeting the mayor for the first time. He talked about his political challenges, his family, his goals, his trips to the U.S. and Europe years earlier. They talked about the farms in Minas. We promised to meet again soon and he left.

"What do you think?" I asked Vitor as we watched the mayor driving away.

"He is more of a man than I thought. Let's see if he can keep his promises."

"The roads are much better now. He kept that promise."

"Cursing him? I thought you didn't believe in it."

"I don't, but he might."

January 22, 2006. This date is in the town files.

Earlier that morning, I emailed pictures of the new school to Grace, Michael, and Brendon along with Elena's journal. I had a sense of accomplishment. But my heart was with Brendon as I imagined him reading it.

Grace emailed me that Brendon was engaged to be married - to a lawyer he had worked with. When I read the words I felt - I don't have the words, somehow – grief, longing, saudade. There were so many unspoken words between Brendon and me. Saudade of a dream that couldn't be mine. Yet, there was an undercurrent of release and freedom.

Later I was there when about five hundred people gathered in front of our newly-completed school, curious to see what was so special about the building. Some were parents from town and other villages who wanted to enroll their children there. Vitor and I gave the key of the school to the mayor, and we presented Mazé as the person representing the woman in the cooperativa and the parents in the village. Even though five aldermen attended, we did not allow any to speak, as it was not supposed to be a political event. As usual, the mayor spoke a few words. After he concluded, the only words that stayed in my mind were,

"Now I give you Escola Municipal Elena Maria Santos Woodard."

And then he cut the ribbon hanging across the front door. I looked up into the sky and hoped Elena saw it.

I looked around and did not see Vitorio. But I saw a gentle, emotional, old lady sitting on a wooden chair and I walked up to her. Josefina looked at the big lettering on the wall of the school entrance, "I saw all of it, girl, I saw everything. I was there, and I am still here. I saw people throwing that woman out of this village, and today she's back with honor."

I hugged Josefina. She seemed to feel the importance of the event as much as I did. I walked into the school, following the crowd. And another lady caught my attention, I greeted her. "Hi Grandma. Are you okay?"

"Yes. I just wish your mother were here to see what a strong woman you became," she tearfully whispered in my ear. "I know she must be so proud of you. Go on, girl. Vitor and the mayor are looking for you. I will be fine with Lia."

I found Vitor and the mayor and together we walked through the building. Everything was new, clean, made with the best that Brazil had to offer.

Elena e minha mãe influentiaram minha vida. Quando comecei a entendê-las e apreciá-las, elas faleceram. Elas nunca se conheceram. Mas é como se elas tivessem conspirado, como anjos, para me ajudar a crescer. Estes são os seus contos. E Aveverde? Não é o fim; é o começo.

[Elena and my mother shaped my life. Just as I began to know and appreciate them, they died. And they never met. But it was as if they conspired like angels to help me grow. These are their tales. And Aveverde? This is not the end; it is a beginning.]

About The Author

Cristiane has been writing fiction since she discovered it as a way to explore real life through fiction when she was 15 years old. *The Language of Belonging* is her second novel. Her first book, *Todos os Rios se Dirigem Para o Mar*, was published in Portuguese only.

Cristiane was born in the northeast of Brazil. At 13, she started to work as a pre-school teacher in her village's public school. The experiences she had with her students and their families during the following 13 years inspired her to create characters such as "Elena" and "Cecilia's Mother." At 18, she was accepted at the Universidade Estadual de Alagoas as a Portuguese, Literature, and English. At 26, she went to the United States with intent to improve her English. She met her husband and almost a year later they married. They have one daughter. She resides in New England with her family.

Life continues to inspire her to write.

Acknowledgments:

I want to thank my Brazilian-American family and friends for their support and inspiration which influenced the writing of this book; and Holland House Books' editors, artists, and collaborators, especially Robert Peett, the editor who guided me through the publishing process of this book. Finally, to all of you who read and review it; thank you for your time and kindness.

compelling story
immigration in NE - timely
even in rural areas

2 Brazilian Q's stories
and a book
female empowerment as form
of community empowerment
to bring even
generosity - giving after death
telling/sharing stories, even
those that carry shame

too much dialogue
could be edited way down
proofreading

about working to solve systemic
problems - corruption, poverty,
abuse - through individual
efforts w/out treading in cultural
or walking that fine line differences

CPSIA information can be obtained at www.ICGtesting.com
Printed in the USA
BVOW05s0022111115

426527BV00001B/1/P